*Feather on the Moon*

*Books by Phyllis A. Whitney*

FEATHER ON THE MOON
SILVERSWORD ·
FLAMING TREE
DREAM OF ORCHIDS ·
RAINSONG
EMERALD ·
VERMILION
POINCIANA
DOMINO ·
THE GLASS FLAME
THE STONE BULL
THE GOLDEN UNICORN ·
SPINDRIFT
THE TURQUOISE MASK
SNOWFIRE
LISTEN FOR THE WHISPERER
LOST ISLAND
THE WINTER PEOPLE
HUNTER'S GREEN ·
SILVERHILL
COLUMBELLA
SEA JADE
BLACK AMBER
SEVEN TEARS FOR APOLLO ·
WINDOW ON THE SQUARE
BLUE FIRE
THUNDER HEIGHTS
THE MOONFLOWER ·
SKYE CAMERON
THE TREMBLING HILLS
THE QUICKSILVER POOL
THE RED CARNELIAN

# PHYLLIS A. WHITNEY

# *Feather on the Moon*

**Doubleday**
NEW YORK
1988

Library of Congress Cataloging in Publication Data

Whitney, Phyllis A., 1903–
Feather on the moon.

I. Title.
PS3545.H8363F4   1988      813'.54      87-6692
ISBN 0-385-24286-7

For Sara Courant
Director of Patchogue-Medford Library

Affectionately, and with my thanks for wise advice
and tireless help in my research—all given generously over many years.

I want to thank Madeleine Aalto, Chief Librarian of Greater Victoria Public Library, for her hospitality and generous assistance in my research. My thanks as well to Carol Martin, in reference service for the library, who drove me where I needed to go, answered endless questions after I returned home, and sent helpful materials from the library.

I am indebted to Virginia Tibbs, author (under the name of Virginia M. Scott) of *Belonging,* the story of a deaf teenager, for opening to me a greater understanding of the world of the deaf; and to my friend Harold Lawlor, who has faced the barrier of deafness courageously for most of his life.

My special gratitude to Princess Abkhazi, whose enchanting Victoria garden I have borrowed for a setting in my novel.

"Radburn House" was inspired by Victoria's Regent's Park House. I am grateful to Carl Rudolph for his interest and for showing me through Regent's Park, the house that he has restored so magnificently and opened to the public.

My thanks for the hospitality of Mary Elizabeth Bayer and Anne Du Moulan, whose attractive apartment I have borrowed for "Dr. Joel" in my story.

*Feather on the Moon*

# 1

I held the telephone tensely as I listened. The woman from the Center sounded compassionate, kind, considerate—all those good things that I'd needed so desperately in the past. Only now I dreaded the opening of old wounds. Seven years had gone by since Debbie was three, and the chances of finding my lost daughter grew slimmer all the time.

"It's a very long shot, Mrs. Blake," the voice said, "but I know you want to follow up on the slightest lead, so perhaps you would talk to this woman in British Columbia. It isn't a matter for the police yet, and she seems a responsible person with good credentials."

Clear across the continent in Canada! But then, Debbie could be anywhere.

"Have you a pencil?" the voice on the phone asked.

I always had pencil and paper ready by this telephone in my bedroom, and I wrote down the name, Mrs. Corinthea Arles (it had to be spelled) and the phone number in Victoria. When I hung up, the shaking started, just as it used to do. I longed futilely for Larry to hold and comfort me. But Debbie's father had died more than a year before our daughter was lost. I lived with my parents now, and in a few moments I would go to where they sat in the living room watching the closed-captioned television program they couldn't hear. For a few moments, however, I stayed quietly where I was, remembering seven years ago—a scene I'd lived over again and again. Too many times.

That Saturday morning I'd driven to a supermarket a few miles beyond the Connecticut town where we lived. Debbie was with me—a bright, happy little girl, with deeply blue eyes and long straight hair just a little darker than blond, caught back in a bouncy pony tail and tied with a green plaid ribbon. I remembered so many details—but never enough of the right ones.

The usual weekend shoppers crowded the aisles and the store seemed as usual—a safe and friendly place. Debbie loved to ride in the grocery cart, often instructing me what to buy, and smiling at everyone. I'd finished my shopping and was pushing the loaded cart toward checkout when I remembered the cans of pineapple I'd overlooked on my list.

Strange that I could still recall the item I'd missed that morning, and had gone back for in so happenstance a manner.

"Deb honey," I said, "stay right here in the cart and watch our groceries. Don't get out. I'll be back in a minute."

She hadn't minded. "I can watch the cart, Mommy," she'd assured me. The independent threes!

I hurried several aisles over and was reaching for two cans of pineapple when the woman in dark glasses spoke to me. Later the police said she was probably part of a team, her purpose to delay me. She must have been deliberately nondescript, with a faded scarf tied over her hair, so I couldn't see its color, or the color of her eyes behind the glasses. She wore slacks—I recalled that—but not their color, or anything else she wore. I noticed that she had seemed timid and uncertain as she spoke to me—the sort of person one wanted to help.

"Please, ma'am, I'm new around here. Can you tell me where I'll find the mustard?" Her voice was so low and hesitant that I could hardly hear her, and there seemed no special accent. The "ma'am" could be Southern or Western —anything.

I pointed the direction for her four aisles away and took down my cans of pineapple. She stayed where she was, blocking my path, apparently bewildered by the big, unfamiliar store. I felt sorry for her. Sorry for *her!*

"Come along and I'll show you," I said.

She tagged after me, and I left her staring at jars of mustard while I hurried back to Debbie. The cart was there with its load of groceries, but my small daughter was gone. That was the last time I had seen her.

The rest was a miserable blur. I'd rushed about frantically, asking questions of strangers, looking down every aisle. I didn't see the woman in dark glasses, or even think about her until later. The manager instituted a search and eventually called the police. No one remembered the woman who had spoken to me, and no one had seen Debbie lifted from the cart. Small children were going through the checkout stations with their mothers all the time, and no one had noticed Debbie.

By the time the police arrived the Saturday throngs in the store had already changed. We found no one then or later who knew anything. Debbie might have called out or, in spite of the way I'd warned her not to talk to strangers, she might not have remembered. She'd been such a loving, trusting little girl. The only clue we ever had was when a woman brought the police a trampled green plaid ribbon she had found in the parking lot. But no one had seen that particular little girl carried away. This was Saturday and a small crying child wouldn't be all that unusual.

No ransom note ever came, no phone call. Debbie's great-grandmother on my mother's side was still alive and well to do, but she lived in Florida and the family name was no household word. All of which left me with the other, even more terrible reasons for child-snatching. The very fact that

3

there seemed to have been a plan of sorts—with more than one person involved—was frightening. It was as though *my* child had been a special target, and these two had been watching us for an opportunity to take her. But *why?*

For years I played the useless "if only" game that never changes anything, and my sense of guilt was part of what I had to endure. You think you can't bear any more pain or loss. But you do. Time passes and the unbearable becomes something you can carry, after all. At least, my work helped.

Because my parents were totally deaf, I'd always been interested in the problems of the hearing impaired, and since I was proficient in signing, I turned to the teaching of such children when I got out of college. I still taught in a private school for the deaf, giving affection to children who weren't mine but who needed me.

Sometimes I fantasized about marrying again, about having a home, a husband, and more children of my own. The longing was there—the hunger. But it was as though something in me had died with Debbie's disappearance—something that men shied away from uneasily. So I'd formed no new close attachments. Perhaps my sense of a terrible, unfinished business still haunted me and blocked me from life.

Now, without warning, had come this phone call that opened all the doors to hope once more, and all those doors to despair that might follow. I wasn't sure I could go through that yo-yo course again.

I turned off the bedroom lights and went into the living room to explain to my parents about the woman in Victoria who had called the National Center for Missing and Exploited Children. These days their telephone number appeared everywhere, as hadn't been the case when Debbie was taken. There had even been a recent magazine piece that surveyed the types of places from which children had been kidnapped over the last ten years. I had been called by the writer, and Debbie's picture had been used for the article. Perhaps the woman in British Columbia had seen this piece.

In the living room my father sat on the sofa—a big man, tanned from his outdoor work, his hands idle in his lap for the moment, his eyes on the color TV picture. My mother sat in her small rocker with her usual book, glancing from its pages to the screen now and then. She always claimed that she could read and watch television at the same time and understand both—with no sounds to distract her.

I stood in the doorway for a moment, regarding them with love, remembering how much they cared about Debbie, how much they'd suffered with me. They'd been so proud of the way she began to "chatter" to them with her hands almost as soon as she learned to talk. Sometimes I wasn't sure whether Ameslan, the American sign language, was her first or second language.

Dad saw my face and nudged Mother. I sat down and began to speak to them with my hands, my face, my shoulders. As soon as I'd explained, Dad indicated that I must call Victoria right away, and Mother nodded and agreed. I understood very well the loving dynamics between these two, though sometimes when I was younger I'd resented the way my mother always allowed my father to make the decisions. It had taken years of growing up for me to understand how much he had needed the confidence she'd managed to instill in him. My mother had the advantage of having lived in a hearing world until she was seventeen, when a severe illness had deafened her. My father had been born that way, and he'd had no chance to form a normal English-language base, as young hearing children do by listening and imitating. Consequently he was still uncomfortable in a room full of hearing people.

Mother spoke to me gently in her voice that wasn't quite like other voices in my world, because she'd lost the sound of her own speech long ago. At the same time she moved her

5

hands in her animated way, so that Dad would understand what she was saying and not feel shut out.

"Yes, Jennifer. Your father is right. You must make the call. Then come and tell us, so we can consult about what should be done."

British Columbia time was three hours earlier than ours, so perhaps I could reach Mrs. Arles right away. I returned to my room and dialed the number.

A man's voice answered the ring, his words formal and courteous: "Mrs. Arles's residence." I asked to speak with her and said I was Jennifer Blake, calling from Connecticut. He said, "Please hold the line, madam. I will see if Mrs. Arles is in."

So it was like that—a butler, money?

In a moment or two Corinthea Arles came on the phone, and I heard her firm, rather aristocratic tones for the first time. Her voice carried a no-nonsense authority that was reassuring, and it was not a young voice. The words were carefully, precisely spoken.

"I told the people at the Center that this was only a slight chance," she informed me. "But I insisted that I must talk with you as soon as possible. I came upon an article in an American magazine a few days ago, and the photograph of your daughter seemed to resemble a little girl of ten who is staying in my home at present. Of course the years from three to ten make for a great many changes, yet I had a curious flash of recognition when I first saw the picture. It was so strong an impression that I felt I must get in touch with you. I am sorry you live so far away."

I made up my mind instantly—something Larry, had always cautioned me against. "I'll come out there," I said. "I don't want to miss the slightest chance. I've always thought that I'd know Debbie immediately if I saw her again—no matter how many years have passed, or how much she may have changed."

"Wait a moment, Mrs. Blake." Corinthea Arles's voice was

dry, faintly disapproving. "Don't decide too quickly. You know nothing about me. I will have my attorney send you information, and it will be mailed at once if you'll give me your address. Then you can take time to consider what you want to do. If you wish to come, you can let me know."

Her sensible approach was reassuring and made me all the more anxious to see this child. I suspected that Mrs. Arles wouldn't move impulsively into anything, and I agreed to wait. "Can you tell me more about the little girl?" I asked. "Why do you have doubts about her?"

"I'm afraid that's impossible to explain on the telephone," Mrs. Arles told me. "The situation is too complex, and you will have to meet the persons involved before you can even begin to figure this out."

That sounded mysterious, but before I could say anything more she went on.

"I must warn you that I *hope* this child will not prove to be yours. It is to my interest, Mrs. Blake, that she not be. But I must be sure, if that's at all possible. Should you decide to fly out here, I will be grateful if you can stay for a few days' visit in my home. I will say nothing about your purpose in coming —at least not at first. You will simply be the daughter of an old friend. I don't want to get the wind up, as my grandson used to say. We must play it by ear. I hope everything may be decided quickly, but I'm not sure that your coming will make any difference. Could you get away conveniently?"

The private school where I taught would give me leave, I was sure. I had an excellent rapport with the director, and she had always been understanding and sympathetic. At least the chance to take some decisive action had stopped my shaking. I gave Mrs. Arles my address, said good-bye, and hung up. Her words about "getting the wind up" had an ominous ring, but I could only put them aside until I reached Victoria.

In the top drawer of my desk was a photograph—the last one taken of Debbie at her third birthday party. This was the picture that had been used in the magazine and that had caught Mrs. Arles's attention. At first I used to look at Debbie's smiling face every day, trying to bring her close to me, trying to project her safety, wherever she was. Praying a lot. Sometimes I talked to the photo, telling her about me, and willing her not to forget me. The plaid ribbon was in the drawer too, frayed from much handling, and I held it as I'd avoided doing in the last few years, not wanting to torment myself. Now the pain was there again, the wound open and aching.

In the photograph Debbie wore a pony tail on each side, and bangs across her forehead. Unfortunately, she had no particularly distinctive characteristics, no identifiable marks. She resembled too many other small girls her age, and she didn't look much like me, or anyone else in the family. Nevertheless, Mrs. Arles had experienced that "flash"—which might mean anything.

When I returned to the living room my father held out a hand to me, and I went to sit beside him, aware of how solid and dependable he was. My mother seemed in contrast slight and delicate, though always filled with light and hope, no matter what happened. I'd been told that I looked like her, but if I'd ever had her radiance I'd lost it years ago. Each of my parents was strong in a different way.

I watched their faces as I signed what had happened. When they understood they sat quietly for a time. My mother reached over to take my father's hand, cupping it around hers as her fingers spoke to him, spelling out private words I couldn't watch. I remembered that she'd told me once how she could lie beside my father in the dark and they could "whisper" to each other, with no need to see or hear.

I sat waiting, checking my impatience, my need for action, thinking about them both and of the marvel of how they came to be together.

When Martin Thorne was twenty-two, he'd gone to work as gardener for my mother's parents. Betty, at nineteen, was struggling with her own recent loss of hearing, and she found comfort in the presence of this strong, handsome young man who seemed so assured in the outdoors and so uncertain inside a house. She was learning to speechread— which was easier for her than for those born deaf, because she knew the form spoken words took. But she was also learning to sign, since she was eager for all forms of communication.

Though Martin had been born deaf, as an orphan he'd gone very young to a children's home, where his disability hadn't been recognized at once. There had been a year of primitive communication, during which he was thought retarded. Finally, after a perceptive aide realized that he couldn't hear, he was sent to a state school for the deaf. There he had been taught to sign. My mother persuaded him to help her learn Ameslan, and for the first time he had something *he* could give to another human being.

When she discovered his wizardry with plants, she encouraged him to develop the magic his hands knew so well. He possessed the talent of a sculptor when it came to hedges and topiary, and my mother must have been a mind-expanding and totally loving experience for him. Perhaps the first he'd ever known.

They had run off to be married, escaping the disapproval and shock of her parents, and it was my mother who had helped to turn Dad into the well-paid landscape artist he became. Words had little to do with those marvels he created. Plants and flowers seemed to thrive at his touch, and all the frustrations of being deaf disappeared while he worked in a garden. She had made herself a partner in the business end, able to speak for him, and by this time well able to read lips—which was a skill not every deaf person is able to achieve.

My grandparents, after their first distress, had the heart and courage to learn understanding, and they came to love Martin as a son. We didn't see them often now but kept in touch through letters and the telephone, on which *I* could reach them.

My parents had no other children, and I was thankful over and over again that my mother had lived in the world of speech and books and writing, so that she could understand the subtleties that words could convey. Ameslan isn't really English in its form. It is a beautiful, graceful, visual language, as difficult to learn as any other foreign language, and graphically expressive in its own right. I learned from both my parents and became a better teacher with the children in my charge as a result.

Nevertheless, by the time I was eighteen I'd wanted to be more a part of the outside world where all my friends lived. My parents had never held me back, remembering their own escape, and I rushed headlong into love.

What a chance I'd taken in marrying a man to whom mountain climbing was the most powerful passion in his life. Heights terrified me. Yet we'd had those few good years together, and Larry had loved me in his own way, and he'd adored Debbie. Until he fell down a mountain in Vermont that wasn't all that high! The thought wasn't as flip as it sounded. For a long time there was a deep anger in me because Larry had thrown his life away so senselessly. His was an obsession I'd never understood, and perhaps it was anger itself that helped to keep me going until the pain of his loss faded to some extent.

Debbie had been the great reward of my marriage, and by this time it was as though Larry belonged to a more remote past than she did. *She* might be alive somewhere, and one of the hardest things for me to control had been my imaginings of a child molested, tortured, hurt psychologically and physically. Such thoughts were terrible to live with, and I'd needed counseling for a time to get by.

With Larry dead, and Debbie gone, I'd moved into my parents' home. They needed me and I needed them as I tried to pick up the pieces of my life. I joined groups of other parents like me—it seemed terrible that there were enough of us to form "groups." Part of our work was to educate parents who still had their children—to teach others to guard and protect, yet without instilling destructive fear.

In the living room we'd all been still for a while. Silence was normal in this house, when it came to a lack of speech, though my father could sometimes be noisy without realizing it. My mother had the memory of sound that she would never lose, and she was careful of pot-banging in the kitchen, careful not to turn up the television, lest it be too loud without her knowing it.

In the silence my father had been thinking. Now he signed, asking a question: "Where place you go?"

I got out the atlas and we looked for Canada's British Columbia—for Vancouver Island, which is separate from the city of Vancouver across the water. Victoria, the capital of British Columbia, clings to the lower tip of the island, close to the United States, with the Strait of Juan de Fuca between. Vancouver Island is the largest island on the Pacific coast, stretching north for two hundred and eighty-five miles along the coast of mainland Canada.

Mother had read about Victoria. "Very beautiful. British influence. Many flowers and gardens," she told me, interpreting for my father.

Dad flung signs at me in warning. "Planes. Dangerous. Go train."

I smiled at him and nodded. It was better to agree and not upset him. Mother would bring him around. All I wanted was for the days to pass until mail came from that far island and I could be on my way.

I didn't tell them the strange thing Mrs. Corinthea Arles had said—that she didn't want the little girl in Victoria to be mine. That was something I could only deal with when circumstances had been explained to me and I had seen the child.

11

## 2

In my anxious state of mind, the flight from Kennedy Airport seemed endless. All I could do while the plane ate up the miles was read and nap a little, and try not to think of what might lie ahead.

I'd had an exchange of letters and phone calls with Mrs. Arles and was now familiar with her expensive stationery that bore the name RADBURN HOUSE at the top. Her "references" were of course superior. I'd learned that she was a widow, and that her husband's family had once owned an important printing house in Vancouver. Radburn was her maiden name, so the house where she lived belonged to her side of the family.

There was no question about her background of wealth and respectability. All this reassured me, in spite of her continued warning that the child in question was unlikely to be mine. So far, I knew no more about the little girl than I had in the beginning—not even the name by which she was called. Mrs. Arles would discuss nothing until she could talk with me face to face, though she'd made one troubling request.

"It's best if you don't use your own name when you come, Mrs. Blake. Perhaps your maiden name would serve?"

I was Jennifer Blake, but my friends called me Jenny, so I told her I would be Jenny Thorne.

By the time we landed in Seattle it was late afternoon, and I had just enough time to board a small plane for the half-hour flight to Victoria. We flew over water dotted with wooded islands that would have been interesting to see, if only I could have kept my mind quiet and my heart from thudding.

Mrs. Arles had told me on the phone that her car would meet me, and as I waited in the small airport building a dark-haired, muscular man, probably in his late thirties, approached to ask if I was Mrs. Thorne. An impressive pirate's mustache drooped on each side of his mouth, but I couldn't see his eyes because of smoky dark glasses. He wore a gray uniform and chauffeur's cap, and while his manner was courteous, there seemed a slight flourish to his movements. I had the curious sense that he might be *performing* the role of chauffeur. He touched his cap, told me his name was Kirk, and took over capably with my bags as he led the way outdoors.

The air of mid-September seemed wonderfully clean and fresh, and the grounds about the airport displayed colorful plantings and emerald spreads of lawn. Mountains on Vancouver Island were visible to the west; the Gulf Islands to the east.

"This way, Mrs. Thorne." Kirk gestured toward an elderly gray Mercedes that was probably a valuable antique. Once or twice he had given me a direct look that was out of character for this "role" he played, and I began to be curious about him.

"Have you been with Mrs. Arles for long?" I asked as he opened the door of the car for me.

He answered cryptically, "Long enough," and I must have looked surprised, for he grinned and touched his cap again in an apology that wasn't entirely genuine.

"Sorry, madam. I haven't really been on this job for all that long. Only about six weeks, so I'm still learning."

His manner might be just short of impertinent, yet it was

somehow engaging. As though he played a good-natured joke.

"An actor out of work?" I guessed.

He started to laugh and then restrained himself. "You're way off, Mrs. Thorne. But I'm an expert driver, and that's all Mr. Dillow has required."

He waited for me to get into the back seat, and I settled into leather luxury while he went around to store my bags in the trunk.

The well-paved highway to Victoria cut inland, with traffic coming toward us from the city, heading out to suburban homes after work. At times, tall stands of fir or cedar followed the road, so that I had the sense of a north country. The airport was surrounded by farms—market gardens for the city.

Perhaps Kirk could be a source of information about the house I was to visit, and I tried a question.

"This is my first visit to Victoria, and I'm not acquainted with Radburn House. Who is Mr. Dillow?"

The chauffeur answered readily. "He manages the house, and I guess he's been in the service of the family for years. He's more than a butler. He's secretary, housekeeper, sometimes nurse—name it, and that's what Elbert Dillow does. Since Mrs. Arles had her stroke, he runs everything."

I hadn't known she'd had a stroke. On the telephone Corinthea Arles had sounded vigorous and very much in charge.

"She's recovered, hasn't she?"

"Some, I suppose. I don't see much of her, except to take her for a drive once in a while, but she seems to be a pretty powerful lady, even in a wheelchair."

"Who else makes up the family?" I asked.

He didn't seem to mind my questions, and as he answered he kept his attention properly on the road. "There's just the old man left, it seems. Mrs. Arles's younger brother. Which doesn't make him very young. Mr. Dillow claims he's a little daft and they hide him away up on the third floor."

"And there's no one else in the house?"

"You said *family.*" His tone changed and I sensed hesitation. "Right now there's a visiting magician and his wife and child."

"Visiting *magician?*"

Kirk, whose last name I had yet to learn, experienced a sudden attack of propriety. "Mr. Dillow and Mrs. Arles had better answer your questions. I'm too new on the job, madam."

Thus reproved, I kept still for a time, though propriety was not my governing virtue. I didn't need to ask whether the child was a boy or a girl, or how old she was. I knew. But that her "father" was a magician sounded somehow both ominous and promising. The word had an itinerant, circusy ring—people who might easily snatch a child and disappear.

After a time Kirk spoke again. "We're in Victoria now, Mrs. Thorne, and since the sun's going down the lights will be on. We'll drive along Government Street, so you'll catch the nighttime view. There—look ahead—you can see the Parliament Buildings."

The sight was dramatic. A wide spread of stone buildings, all etched in light, stood against the darkening sky. The tall central dome, and every smaller dome, column, window, all glowed with dots of gold—like a stage set.

Kirk took on the role of guide. "The Victorian architect who designed those buildings—Francis Rattenbury—was mixed up in a sex and drug scandal and went off to England, where he was murdered by his wife's lover. Pretty colorful stuff! Look over there across the corner of the Inner Harbor, Mrs. Thorne—that's another grandiose Rattenbury creation. The Empress Hotel."

These tidbits were delivered in what managed to be a mock-respectful tone. As though Kirk knew himself out-of-order, and enjoyed stepping over lines.

15

The hotel, set at a right angle to the Parliament Buildings, was immensely impressive—massive, sturdy, foursquare, its front covered with ivy.

"The Empress dates back to early in the century. When you go sightseeing, you'll visit it and catch a glimpse of the way things used to be in the days when retired British colonists came here from India."

Sections of slate rose steeply, with rows of peaked windows, and corner towers with their own vertical roofs. All the front of the hotel shone in the glow of spotlights, and the central facade gleamed a warm amber. Tall letters above the door spelled EMPRESS in white lights that were large enough to read as we drove along.

The lights of all the buildings were reflected in harbor waters, multiplying the effect.

My interest was passing, only momentary. I wasn't here for sightseeing, and what lay outside this car couldn't matter to me for long. In a little while we would arrive at Radburn House, and after that there could be a meeting at any time with the child who might be my daughter. But I mustn't anticipate and make up imaginary scripts. It was better, for now, to talk to the man who was driving me.

"Are you from Victoria?"

"I'm from all over," he told me lightly.

Obviously, he wasn't going to talk about himself. I was silent again as we left the central buildings of the city behind, following a long street where rows of lighted houses stood side by side, fronted and separated by gardens. The street climbed and the car wound its way toward the top of a hill that must command a splendid view in the daytime. Houses and streets were left behind as the car's headlights picked out a winding drive that climbed toward a structure commanding the hilltop.

"Here we are," Kirk said, and I looked out to see the house that was to figure in my life for a longer period than I expected.

16

The front grounds were lighted, and there were lights in several tall windows. At first the house seemed narrow and cramped, but as I left the car and Kirk brought my bags around to steps that mounted from the side, I saw that it widened and ran back a considerable distance. There were two main stories, and a smaller addition that added a third floor at the top.

"Do you like gardens, Mrs. Thorne?" Kirk asked as we mounted the steps. "I expect you know that Victoria's a city of gardens, but Mrs. Arles's private garden is something special. It drops down a level or so at the back, and runs along the hill. Mr. Dillow says her parents planted it early in the century."

I did indeed like gardens, thanks to my father, but now the front door of the house had opened upon the entry porch, and my attention was held.

A man who could only be Elbert Dillow stood in the lighted doorway—a small man, dressed in black, probably in his late fifties, with a straggle of graying hair around his otherwise bald head. His bright dark eyes examined me sharply, and I had an immediate sense of dignity, as well as an air of competence and authority that would compensate for his slight size.

"Good evening, Mrs. Thorne," he said. "Please come in. I am Dillow." Apparently I was to dispense with the "mister." He nodded to Kirk. "Just take Mrs. Thorne's bags up to her room. You know which one?"

The chauffeur's manner was properly restrained again as he picked up my bags and went into the house.

"Perhaps you would like to go to your room first, Mrs. Thorne?" Dillow asked. "Then Mrs. Arles wishes to greet you. She would like you to dine with her tonight."

This seemed fine, and I stepped into a lighted foyer, where a lower hall reached back behind the stairs, with doors opening down its length. Ahead, a staircase, carpeted in dark red, rose to a landing. Polished golden oak banisters

17

ran upward, wide to my hand, with wings curving right and left. When I took the right-hand stairs at Dillow's direction, I could look down toward the entryway to see two long stained glass windows on either side of the front door, gleaming blue and ruby red under electric lights.

"Your room is at the front, Mrs. Thorne," Dillow said behind me.

The upper hallway was dimly lighted, but a door stood open and lamplight welcomed me. Kirk placed my largest bag on a luggage rack at the foot of a double bed and bowed slightly as he passed me and went quickly away. At another time I would have been very curious about that young man.

The butler cast a critical eye about the room and seemed to find everything in order. The bathroom across the hall would be mine, he said, and moved toward the door.

"I won't be long," I told him. "Where will I find Mrs. Arles?"

"Just come down the stairs, Mrs. Thorne. Since Mrs. Arles's illness she prefers to stay in a first-floor room that overlooks the garden at the rear and is more convenient. The door will be open."

When he'd gone I stood staring around the spacious, turn-of-the-century room. The walls, which had probably been papered when the house was built, were painted a pleasing blue-gray that reached to an oak picture rail. Above that, the strip of wall blended into the ceiling—a pale fawn color.

Patterned red Turkestan rugs lay scattered upon the dark parquet floor, at the foot of the bed and at the sides. A fireplace with an oak mantel, again dark and golden, had been set with wood, though no fire was needed as yet. Long windows on each side of a french door were framed with flowered blue draperies. I opened the door to step outside, where carved wooden railings enclosed the small private porch. Beyond, the view was tremendous. I could look toward city lights and follow the shining, spangled water of

18

the harbor where it cut into a right angle before the Empress Hotel and the Parliament Buildings.

Immediately below was the driveway, curving down from the house. I could look out upon one side to the steps by which I'd entered, and on the other to a rock garden that ran along the outside of the house. Daylight was nearly gone, and the evening was cool, so I went back inside.

When I stepped into the hall to look for the indicated bathroom, I heard a sound at the far end and saw that a man stood under a dim overhead light, leaning on a banister of the back stairs. I couldn't make him out clearly, but he seemed to be watching me.

"Hello," I called.

He didn't answer but hurried away up the stairs. Was this Mrs. Arles's younger brother, who had been referred to as "daft"?

When I'd washed in the old-fashioned bathroom that still displayed a tub on claw feet, I returned to my room to change from slacks to a gray skirt. A blouse came reasonably unwrinkled from my suitcase and the citron color cheered me a little.

It seemed to me that the reflection in the mirror as I combed my short brown hair bore little resemblance to the way I'd looked seven years ago, when Debbie was taken. I'd been heavier then, and my hair had hung below my shoulders. Now my eyes looked wide and shadowed in the glass and my expression had an anxious cast. I turned away, not liking what I saw.

Too much that was important hung on this meeting with Mrs. Arles, and a sense of panic was ready to stir in me at the very thought of meeting the child who lived in this house. So far I'd seen no one except the man on the stairs, and I wanted no sudden chance encounter until I had talked with Corinthea Arles.

On the first floor I walked past a spacious dining room, where the table was unset. At the rear of the hall I caught the flicker of firelight through an open door. Mrs. Arles heard me and called to me to come in.

The big room I stepped into was a library, now adapted to a different purpose because of need. Books still lined two walls, and walnut paneling around the rest of the room made it dark in spite of lamps and spears of flame in the grate. An old-fashioned bed had replaced other furniture, its headboard high and carved with grape clusters and leaves. A dressing table and bureau had further changed the room from a library. Near the fire that made the room seem overly warm to me sat a woman in a wheelchair. As I hesitated in the doorway, she turned her head to greet me.

"Thank you for coming, Mrs. Thorne. I am Corinthea Arles. Please come and sit down. No one else is home just now to interrupt us. I've seen to that."

Apparently the man I'd glimpsed on the stairs didn't count, any more than Dillow did.

Even in a wheelchair Mrs. Arles looked thoroughly in charge. Light from the fire played over her thin nose with its delicate aristocratic nostrils, and upon rouge-touched lips that might have been full, if the habit of suppressing all smiles hadn't long ago been imprinted. Her gray hair shone like dark silver and was waved high and pinned with amber combs. Cut in an ageless princess style, her garnet-red robe had been embroidered with touches of gold at the collar and in the looped frog closings. I had an immediate impression of pride that would probably govern this woman in all things.

As I took her outstretched hand, feeling its sculptured bones in my own, I was aware of a light scent of violets— sweet but faint. None of this perfection of grooming was for me, I was sure. I suspected that when Corinthea Arles was entirely alone she would give just such attention to personal details for her own satisfaction.

At her invitation I sat down in an armless slipper chair on the other side of the hearth and waited for whatever pleasantries about my trip would begin our conversation. I was to learn quickly that Mrs. Arles never bothered with such conventions. She studied me for a moment, her expression neither approving nor disapproving. She must have been in her early seventies, but her face was so surprisingly unlined that I was reminded of a mask. Only her dark eyes flashed with a light she couldn't altogether conceal.

This very lack of expression was unsettling, but I was to learn later that Mrs. Arles had long ago decided that animation could result only in lines and wrinkles, and she had banished all such aging outward emotions from her face. Her impassivity and fixed look made me uncomfortable, even though I suspected they were deceptive. Her voice, and sometimes the movements of her hands, gave her away.

When satisfied about me—though she betrayed no inkling of her conclusions—she plunged at once into the matter at hand. "I've sent the Corwins and the child away for the evening. I wanted to talk with you before you meet any of them. They know I have a visitor coming, but of course they have no suspicion of who you are or why you've come. The situation, as I've told you, is much too complicated to be explained on the telephone. I don't like or trust this pair and, as I also told you, I had an odd feeling about the child when I saw your little girl's picture in a magazine. It's because of the Corwins that I've asked you not to use your married name."

Because they might be the kidnappers who had taken Debbie? Questions seethed in me, but I held them back and waited, knowing she would tell me the story in her own way.

One thin hand moved to touch a comb in her hair, making sure every strand was in place, and the firelight caught the red of her garnet ring. Then she turned her head and addressed the shadowy room beyond the bed, where light hardly reached.

"Crampton, you may leave us alone now."

A large woman in a white uniform—of whose presence I'd been totally unaware—rose and went into the hall, moving lightly and quickly, in spite of her size.

———

"Crampton knows everything," Mrs. Arles assured me. "Just as Dillow does. She's been my personal maid and companion for twenty years. Lately, she's been my nurse as well. But I feel that you would prefer privacy in our first conversation."

"Thank you," I said, and again I waited, trying to control my impatience.

"I must warn you," Mrs. Arles went on, "that the little girl, Alice, is not an attractive child. Most of the time she seems sullen and unfriendly."

I found it difficult to swallow. Debbie had been a happy little girl. Even her tempers were only summer storms.

"Please tell me all of it," I said. "Why did you say you hoped this child wouldn't prove to be mine?"

"Because she is supposed to be my great-granddaughter," Mrs. Arles said impassively. "More than anything in the world I would like to be convinced that she's of my family's blood. Even if Alice Arles isn't the most pleasing child in the world, that might change if she were taken out of the hands of the people who claim to be her mother and stepfather."

"Claim to be?"

"It's undoubtedly true that this dreadful woman was married to my grandson. All her papers seem in order. Her present husband is a professional magician. He does tricks— magic!" Scorn cut through her voice, though her face remained still as a sculpture. "Their story is that they were working together in Brazil when they met my grandson. Farley Corwin had lived in that country when he was young and he spoke Portuguese. The woman performed as an assistant in his act and traveled with him, though they weren't married to each other then."

Mrs. Arles's hands moved in angry dismissal, as though she could hardly bear to speak of this couple who now visited her home.

"Edward, my grandson, had joined an expedition that was studying medicinal plants in the jungles along the Amazon.

He met those two in some small city where Corwin was performing. It is my conviction that they pursued him with a plot in mind. Of course Edward should never have gone out there at all. I raised him in this house from the time when his parents died in a boating accident, and I sent him away to good schools. He could have stepped into the family printing business and done brilliantly—he was capable and intelligent."

She paused to breathe deeply, quieting inner emotion. I felt a twinge of sympathy for her grandson, who might have been driven to escape.

"We quarreled, Edward and I. He did something unforgivable and I disinherited him. I told him I never wanted to see him again. Anyone who betrays a trust . . ." Ivory knuckles showed as she clenched her hands, and I watched her relax them deliberately.

"This is upsetting for you," I said. "Would you like to wait until tomorrow for the rest?" I didn't want to wait, but Mrs. Arles had been ill, and all this suppressed emotion worried me.

"I don't permit myself to be upset," she said quietly. "What I am telling you is long in the past. Edward went away nearly fifteen years ago. Eventually, he went to Brazil, where he married this dreadful woman, and she accompanied him on the expedition. There *must* have been some sort of plot between this magician and the woman, because Corwin signed on with the expedition as an assistant cook and went along too. My grandson"—for just an instant her voice quavered—"my grandson drowned in an accident on the river. It must have been a horrible death. There were alligators and piranhas in those waters. By that time Edward's wife was pregnant, or so she claims, and she sent Edward's things to me, and wrote me about the child she was to have."

Mrs. Arles was suddenly still, and a log fell in the grate, startling me.

---

23

"You saw the baby when it was born?" I asked softly.

"Indeed I did not. I didn't care to because I didn't want to believe this woman was carrying my grandson's child. It could just as easily have been the child of the magician. I guessed from the first that these people wanted money, and a child might be a means of getting it from me. After Edward's death the woman married Farley Corwin. Except for the pictures they kept sending me, I never saw the child until she was four years old. The mother had been writing to me all along, asking to bring her here."

I leaned forward eagerly. "Do you have those pictures?"

"Unfortunately, no. I threw them away. I'd wanted nothing to do with my grandson, and I wanted no child he might have had by this woman. I saw the little girl only once, as I say, when she was four years old, and then only because they brought her deliberately to my house and I let them in so I could see her. I felt no more than idle curiosity."

"Is this why you recognized the picture of my Debbie? Because you'd seen this little girl when she was four?"

"It's possible. I don't know. I was so angry with the effrontery of those people, and so suspicious of them, that I didn't allow them to stay for more than a few hours. I still couldn't believe that Alice was my grandson's child."

I thought about all this unhappily. If there had never been a baby, the early pictures the Corwins sent could have been of any baby at all. Later, still hoping to get through to Mrs. Arles, they could have needed to produce a real child of the right age—to be ready. They could have kept the child for a year or so—long enough to make her forget me, forget her grandparents. It was all unlikely, yet with a thread of possibility that made me uncertain.

"Where did their letters come from?" I asked.

"They'd returned from Brazil, so some came from the States. Sometimes from Canada. Or from St. Petersburg, Chicago, Los Angeles."

They wouldn't, of course, have written from the town, or even from the state from which Debbie had been taken.

"Why did you change your mind about seeing them?"

"A few months ago I came near to dying. That made a difference in the way I felt toward a child of Edward's, no matter who the mother was. There are no descendants left to me. My younger brother, Timothy, is unable to manage anything. He has never married and never will. I thought if I could find some way to be sure about this child—that she really was Edward's—then something might be done. They arrived as a family about two months ago, and hard as it is for me to have them here, I took them into the house where I could watch them, listen, perhaps learn something significant that would make me sure one way or the other. The child resembles my grandson to some small degree. Though she has fair hair, where his was dark. She has blue eyes like his, and her face is even shaped somewhat like Edward's. But who knows? If she was stolen, she might have been chosen for the resemblance."

"Debbie had blue eyes," I said softly.

Mrs. Arles turned her head away. "Recently, when I saw the picture of your little girl, as I told you on the phone, there was a moment when I believed that Alice Arles might be your child. That sort of quick recognition, however sharp, doesn't last when one begins to examine features, but it was a strong impression. I thought if *you* could be certain, then I would know all this was exactly the plot I've always suspected, and you might recover your child. If not, then I may be forced to accept their claim and do for this child what I could never do for my grandson."

"You've checked blood types, of course?"

"Yes. She could be my grandson's child. Her blood type also fits the records you sent. Which again proves nothing."

"What about the child's birth certificate?"

"She was born in Brazil, supposedly in some small place where record-keeping wasn't of the best. There are papers

———

25

and they seem to be in order. My attorneys have investigated, but I'm not sure that bribery couldn't have managed the whole thing."

"When will I see the little girl?"

"Not until tomorrow. I knew you'd be tired and anxious tonight, and I didn't want any chance meeting. You must be prepared when it happens. So I sent them all off to dinner and a movie, and they won't be home for hours."

I'd wanted to talk with Mrs. Arles first, but now further postponement didn't help my state of mind.

"If these are the people who kidnapped Debbie, then they may recognize me," I suggested. "They must have been watching me in the store that day, though my hair is short now, and I'm a lot thinner than I was then."

"That should help. Besides, you're out of context here. They aren't likely to expect the child's mother to turn up in Victoria in the same house. Not after all these years. I doubt if they saw the magazine article. I've kept it away from them."

"If they recognize me, they may run."

"Should that happen, they'd probably leave the girl behind, which could be proof of a sort. But I doubt that they'd give up their scheme so easily. The burden of proof would be on you, and they might brazen it out. The man strikes me as an adventurer—a risk-taker. So they might hold to their story. Unless you are absolutely sure, we can't even bring in the police. On the other hand—if *you* could recognize *them* . . ."

I no longer knew how sure I could be about anything. I might never have seen the man, and the woman had hidden her hair and eyes and been deliberately nondescript.

"Let's have supper now," Mrs. Arles decided. "This talk is tiring us both, and you must be hungry." She raised her voice slightly. "Crampton?"

The woman appeared from the hall instantly, and I wondered how much privacy we'd really had.

———

"Please tell Dillow we are ready to eat," Mrs. Arles said.

The meal arrived with such dispatch that he must have been hovering nearby as well. He set a small drop-leaf table with linen and silver, pulled up a chair for me, and pushed Mrs. Arles's wheelchair into place. A cart with silver-covered dishes was wheeled in, and we were served poached salmon with dill sauce, green peas perfectly undercooked, a leafy salad and hot rolls, whisked from an oven. Then Dillow stood back and waited.

That was the moment when I sensed that something was wrong between the butler-manager and his mistress. A clear disapproval seemed to emanate from Dillow. Not so much toward me as toward Mrs. Arles. Her look rested on him sharply, and he stared directly back for just an instant, so that I was aware of tension between them.

Then Mrs. Arles nodded. "Thank you, Dillow. Tell Grace everything is fine. And you might phone Dr. Radburn, since he is expecting a call. If he is here in an hour, everything should work out nicely. Crampton, I'll ring when I need you, so have your own supper."

The shadowy Crampton murmured something respectful and disappeared again.

Dillow said, "Yes, madam," stiffly and also went away. His behavior was again impeccable, and there was no further hint of stress between the man who ran this house and the woman he worked for.

While we ate, Mrs. Arles explained about Dr. Radburn. "Joel is a cousin, as you might guess from his name. Though distant. He's not in private practice as a doctor any more, since he has gone into research—quite important research. In a sense, he inherited me as a patient from his father, who died last year, and who was my doctor and friend for much of my adult life. Joel keeps a careful eye on me. He knows everything about you that I know, and he approves of my bringing you here. He agrees with my doubts about the child. He's also been looking after my brother whenever it was necessary. Joel is in his late thirties and is the son of his father's second marriage. He has been observing the child, Alice, and he can answer some of the questions about her you may have."

I couldn't think of any questions, except for the one that possessed me entirely—would I recognize her? Already I was steeling myself for failure.

"You may need to stay here for a few days." Mrs. Arles spoke quietly, perhaps aware of the anxiety that must have shown in my face. "When you talk with the child, some memory may emerge—though it might not come at once. You must sleep tonight, so try to relax now. Perhaps you'd like to take a book upstairs with you. We've a fine library here."

I'd noticed a thick volume on a table near her wheelchair. A bookmark showed her place, and reading glasses rested on the green jacket.

She saw the direction of my glance. "That book might interest you. I ordered it as soon as I knew it was published, since it's an account by Frank Karsten of the expedition he led into Amazon jungles all those years ago. The expedition on which my grandson died. Unfortunately, since my illness I've had trouble with my eyes, and I've only been able to read a few pages at a time. Karsten has died since the book was published."

"I wonder if the Corwins are mentioned?"

"I don't know. I didn't get very far. If you'd like to read it, take the book along to your room. Then you can tell me if you find anything interesting."

It wasn't Edward Arles's life or death that concerned me now and I was already thinking of something else. Mrs. Arles seemed to call Mrs. Corwin "the woman" when she spoke of her—a label of denigration. Now I asked her first name.

"It's such a ridiculous name that I can't bear to use it," she told me. "Though perhaps it suits her well enough. She's called Peony."

———

Peony. Yes, rather a silly name, except for a flower. I tried to remember the nondescript woman in dark glasses—an uncertain, nervous woman—but the dim memory would neither accept nor dismiss the name.

When the front doorbell sounded, I heard Dillow go to answer it. A deep voice greeted him cheerfully, and Dr. Radburn came quickly back to the library. Dillow had already removed our dishes and brought in small plates with Camembert cheese and wheat wafers. He busied himself pouring coffee, while Dr. Radburn bent to kiss Mrs. Arles's cheek. Dillow, I suspected, wanted to miss nothing.

The doctor was tall and rather slender, with dark brown hair conventionally cut. A slight line creased vertically between gray eyes that regarded me in friendly appraisal. The line, I thought, was probably not a frown but more likely grew from hours of concentration. His smile seemed warm in a pleasantly homely face that one might grow used to comfortably. No one had really smiled at me since my arrival, except for the impudent chauffeur.

"I'm glad you've come, Mrs. Thorne," he said as he took my hand. "I know this isn't easy for you, but we hope you can settle one part of the dilemma. Perhaps to your advantage, if you recognize the little girl."

Dillow brought another chair and Dr. Radburn sat down, accepting a cup of coffee.

"I have told Mrs. Thorne what I know about the Corwins," Mrs. Arles said. "At least I've prepared her for their unusual background, which has undoubtedly affected the child."

Dr. Radburn glanced at Dillow in a questioning way, and Mrs. Arles dismissed the butler with a casual "You may go, Dillow." When he'd left the room, she spoke to the doctor. "It will be done *my* way, Joel."

"I've no doubt," Dr. Radburn said dryly, and spoke to me. "You haven't seen Alice yet?"

I shook my head. "Will you tell me about her, please?"

His eyes were deep set and there was no smile in them as

he seemed to study me. "She's lonely, I think. Neither of the Corwins seems to have much imagination as far as Alice is concerned. Though the child is all imagination—maybe too much so. She and her mother have a sometimes affectionate, sometimes angry relationship, but Peony is under the domination of her husband, and Alice resents that and clearly dislikes her stepfather. For her sake, I hope that she can be taken out of the Corwins' hands, one way or another."

I looked at Mrs. Arles. "You mean they would give her up to you?"

Dr. Radburn answered for her. "I'm sure that Farley Corwin would accept a sum of money that he might regard as suitable, if the mother were to give the child up to her great-grandmother."

"What about this loss for the—the mother?"

"She'll do as she's told, as Dr. Radburn suggests," Mrs. Arles assured me.

I must have shivered, for the doctor spoke quickly. "You look tired, Mrs. Thorne. All this is distressing on top of your long flight. Would you like something to help you sleep?"

I shook my head. "I'd rather not. But you're right—I am very tired." I'd had all I could take. I wanted to get away before I found myself in tears.

"Of course," Mrs. Arles said. "I've kept you up far too long, considering the difference in time zones. So run along now, and sleep as long as you like in the morning. Breakfast will be on the buffet in the dining room, and you can go in when you like."

I remembered to take the book by Frank Karsten with me, though I doubted that I could concentrate on reading for long.

Dr. Radburn spoke to Mrs. Arles. "I'll look in on Uncle Tim before I leave. We have a serial chess game going. Good night, Corinthea. I'll see you tomorrow."

He came with me to the branching flight of stairs and we started up together, turning right at the landing.

———

"You've been told about Mrs. Arles's stroke?" he asked as we reached the second floor.

"Yes, it's been mentioned."

"We try to see that she doesn't get upset these days."

"That must be difficult with the Corwins here."

"I hope you won't add to the problem," he said gravely, and went off toward the rear stairs to the third floor.

I started toward my room at the front, where I'd left my door ajar. It was closed now, so probably Dillow had been up here. I opened it to a sense of movement inside—to something that slipped away just beyond my line of vision. The room was quiet—too quiet, as though it waited for something to happen. A single lamp I'd left burning was still on and the room seemed even bigger and more shadowy than I remembered.

"Is someone here?" I asked.

This time a faint breath was released. The sound came from behind a corner chair, and I went quickly to reach into darkness and pull out the girl who was crouching there.

# 3

The encounter was too sudden, too unexpected, My hands shook as I drew the child into the lamp's soft light. She was wiry thin. I could feel the bones of her arm in my hand, where my Debbie's arms had been soft, rounded flesh. Her face, tilted up to me with an air of defiance, had pointy features—a short nose and chin, and a straight mouth that wouldn't curve easily into smiles. Her hair was much fairer than Debbie's light brown, and it was short and curly, where Debbie's had been straight. Though hair, of course, could be changed, and very well might be if concealment were necessary. Her eyes were wide and very blue—but so were the eyes of thousands of other little girls.

Her whole body had tensed defensively, as though she expected nothing from me but anger. I knew with a sinking feeling that this wasn't my darling Debbie, but she was a child who had probably been mistreated by dreadful parents.

"Hello," I said, releasing her arm. "I've heard about you— you must be Alice Arles."

She'd started away as though she meant to run out the door, but now she turned and stood her ground suspiciously. "I bet the old lady told you. The one they say is my great-grandmother."

"Come and sit down so we can talk," I said. "Dr. Radburn

thinks you might be lonely in this house, where there aren't any other children."

"Doc's okay. But I don't like kids much and they don't like me. Anyway, I don't care. I don't have to go to school right now because I guess we'll go away pretty soon. The old lady doesn't want me, so she won't give Farley any money for me."

She was a mass of defensiveness, suspicion, and disturbing information that should have been kept from her. Waiting for my reaction, she stared at me without blinking.

"I don't know if any of that is true," I said.

"What do *you* know? You just came."

This was true, but at least she had decided not to run off right away. Perhaps the trait she'd best cultivated was curiosity, and for the moment she was curious about me. She seated herself on the edge of a chair, thin bare knees protruding beneath a too frilly skirt. One knee had scabbed over from a fall, and that bruised knee seemed the only familiar thing about her. I'd been used to skinned knees, both with Debbie and with the children I taught. I wondered how Mrs. Arles could ever have connected this child with the picture of Debbie.

"I thought you'd gone out with your parents to a movie and dinner," I said.

She shrugged elaborately, copying a grown-up manner. "That's boring. They never pick a movie I like, and at dinner they don't talk to me. Mostly they don't talk. Or when they do it's *about* me, and I hate that. Don't you want to know why I was hiding in your room?"

"Let me guess. I could be somebody interesting, and you wanted to learn about me. Am I right?"

"Maybe. Everybody's buzzing about you. The old lady doesn't have visitors since she's been sick. She doesn't want anybody to see her the way she is now. She can walk a little, but she won't try much, so her legs get weak. That's what Doc says. She gets Crampton to dress her up every day as if she was going to a party. Of course Dr. Joel wants her to be quiet and not see many people—so you're a—a—"

"A mystery?" I wondered who was buzzing—her awful parents, probably.

She could stare almost as impassively as Mrs. Arles, but some of her defensive anger had lessened.

"Do you like mysteries?" I went on.

"I like to read them. But mostly not the books in the old lady's library. Anyway, I'm not supposed to go in there unless she invites me. Even when she goes out for a drive, Dillow watches to see I don't go in. But sometimes I get even with him. It's easy to do."

Weariness struck through me again. Mrs. Arles had been right about the child not being attractive. Her unfortunate upbringing wasn't my problem. The answer I'd feared had been given me and all I wanted now was to go to bed and sleep—just to shut out the disappointment and letdown that had hit me like a body blow. Even though I'd told myself I was prepared, I *had* hoped, and the reaction left me limp—almost ill with the old despair.

Alice scratched her left arm absently, and my heart did a flop. Debbie had scratched her arm in just that way because of a rash that had resisted treatment for a long time. I went quickly to push up the left sleeve of the child's sweater. There was nothing there but a red mark from scratching.

"Do you always do that?" I asked.

She looked at me blankly. "Do what?"

I let it go. An itching arm was hardly identification.

"I'd like to go to bed now," I told her. "I've come a long way and I'm tired."

She took the hint and moved indifferently toward the door.

"Perhaps we can talk some more tomorrow," I said, disturbed by her quick acceptance of dismissal.

"Maybe." She turned and stared at me again. "What do *you* do?"

34

"Do? I'm not sure what you mean."

"Grown-up ladies do something. Peony—sometimes I call her Peony to upset her, but she's my mother—Peony is a magician's assistant." She spoke almost proudly.

"I see. Does she get sawed in half?"

"That's old stuff. Farley—he's not my father—likes to invent new tricks. Though sometimes they don't work—and then I laugh at him."

"What does he do then?"

"He hits me." She spoke matter-of-factly—not liking to be hit but accepting reality. "You still didn't tell me what you do."

"I'm a teacher. I teach boys and girls around your age."

Something about her gentled just a little. "Teachers aren't so bad. Except that we always move, and when I make friends with a teacher we go away."

In all my fantasies of finding my daughter I had clung to the dream of something that might identify her: one faint hope that she might remember how she had "talked" on her hands so happily to her grandparents when she was three.

"I teach deaf children," I said.

Her face brightened, and for the first time she looked interested. "What do you teach them?"

"All the usual lessons. And I teach them signing as well."

"What's signing?"

"It's a language the deaf can use with their hands and fingers—sign language. So deaf children can talk to each other, and to me."

"Show me."

I held back. This was the card I kept up my sleeve. If she could remember anything about signing, that might be a real test. But I hesitated to take this step, even though I'd told myself that I'd given up. Her reaction might be too final.

"Why are you interested?" I asked.

"Because of Uncle Tim—that's what everybody calls him. He can't hear and he talks funny—though I can understand

35

him pretty well. I write him notes when he can't read my lips, and he loans me books. Better books than the old lady has downstairs. Uncle Tim likes mysteries too."

This was an unexpected development. I'd been given the idea that the man hidden away upstairs was a little backward.

"Show me something in that sign language," Alice persisted.

I took a deep breath and risked it, moving my hands. She watched with interest but no recognition.

"What did you say?"

It really wasn't a test, I told myself. After all, Debbie had been three years old—only three. Of course she wouldn't remember.

"I said, 'I would like to meet Uncle Tim.' "

Her look was solemn, still suspicious.

"What do they call those signs?"

"They're part of a special language called Ameslan. You understand Ameslan by seeing everything in signs instead of hearing it in words."

"Anyway, I don't know if Uncle Tim would want to meet *you*."

"You could find out. Tell him I work with the deaf."

"Maybe. I'll think about it."

"Does he try to speechread? Read lips?"

"I guess he tries to. He gets mixed up a lot."

"That's because so many words seem alike when you speak them. Look in a mirror sometime and say 'bury' and 'marry.' Or try 'grouch' and 'ouch'—though there's a little difference there."

Alice snickered—not a real laugh. "That might look like 'He's a terrible ouch.' Maybe you could teach him some signs."

"I could try. But who would he talk to around here?"

"Me. You could teach me too."

"I'm afraid there won't be time. I'm going away soon. But

perhaps I can ask Mrs. Arles about this. If you stay here, perhaps you could both learn a few things that might help him. Has he been deaf all his life?"

"I asked Dillow that, and he said it happened when Uncle Tim was around fifteen."

"That's an advantage. It means that he remembers the sound of words so he's not like those who have never heard anything or learned how to talk. Both my parents are deaf, and my father was born that way. Because of that, I had to learn to sign when I was little."

I'd caught her interest now, but probably only because I was someone different.

"Uncle Tim may not need signing," I went on. "Though fingerspelling might help if there was anyone around to understand. That's easier. It's spelling words on one hand. It's good for when there are names, or words that are hard. People who live with the deaf really ought to learn these things."

"The old lady never would. She just thinks her brother is dumb. Once she sent him away to a bad place. Show me how to say my name."

I spelled "Alice" for her on my fingers and she imitated me quickly. Then she sighed. "Anyway, *she* won't help him —the old lady. And she hates me."

"Why do you think that?"

"I've heard her. One time when Dillow didn't catch me listening she told him I wasn't a lovable child." When I didn't react, Alice continued slyly. "Maybe she's right. I do mean things. I spilled your hand stuff in the bathroom, and I meant to."

"You mean so you could prove that you aren't lovable?"

She turned her stiff young back on me and walked out of the room. I heard her laughing, and the sound had an eerie ring in the empty hall. It was hardly the laughter of a happy child.

As I got ready for bed, all the old despair washed through

37

me. I must go home soon. There was no longer any point in my staying.

Still on Connecticut time, I woke up too early the next morning and couldn't get to sleep again. Since I'd left my flight arrangements open, I would call later today and make a reservation for home.

Right now I had no inclination to do much of anything. I still felt sore from my encounter with Alice last night, both because of the disappointment that I'd feared and also because of an unwanted tug of sympathy for the child herself. There seemed no point now in meeting her mother or stepfather. Whether or not the Corwins' story of Alice being Edward Arles's daughter was true, it still had nothing to do with me, nor was there any way in which I could affect the future for any of them. I could only hope that Mrs. Arles would take the child and remove her from those who had treated her roughly. Though I wasn't all that sure Corinthea Arles had much love in her to give a child either. There seemed to be a good many reasons for Alice to be unlovable.

Today I must tell Mrs. Arles that the girl was not my lost daughter. This, really, was what she wanted to hear, so that one doubt would be taken care of.

Since I was wide awake by this time I got out of bed and looked into the hall. No one seemed to be about, and I had no idea where Alice's room was, or that of the Corwins. When I'd showered and dressed in slacks and a cardigan, I went downstairs. Dark red carpeting softened the sound of my steps. The empty hall below was gloomy with the wood paneling that had been prevalent when this house was built, the only light filtering through stained glass windows on each side of the front door.

The lower hall that ran back from the foyer and behind the stairs was narrow and allowed for spacious rooms on either hand. Idly curious, I stepped into an enormous living room that would have been called a parlor, or perhaps a drawing room, in the great days of this house. A discreetly faded Chinese rug, fawn-colored, with a scattering of blue flowers around the border, stretched almost the length of the room, leaving well-polished dark flooring to show around it.

The furniture was old and worn, though not to the point of fraying. It was a room with character but no particular planned style. Chairs and sofas and small tables mingled Chippendale and Queen Anne, with a few pieces of homely Hepplewhite thrown in. Several lamps belonged to the art-deco period of the twenties. Again, stained glass had been set beside and above tall windows. Some of the patterns were geometric, while others presented designs of leaves or flowers or birds. In one corner stood an upright piano of no special distinction, its lid down over the keys, and no music sheets gracing the rack. Once this long, silent room, swimming now in jeweled light, must have known music and dancing and parties. Had Corinthea Arles grown up in this house, danced at such parties—and then forgotten what it was like to be young?

At the far end sliding double doors opened into the dining room I'd glimpsed last night. This morning the long table was laid with four place mats, china, and silverware—set probably for Alice, the Corwins, and me. The sideboard held electric plates for keeping food hot, but no dishes had been placed there yet.

Tall windows looked out upon shrubbery, rosebushes, flower beds, and hedges. Again, panes of stained glass filtered light through amber, peacock green, fiery red, and the special blue of a dark sea.

"Would you like breakfast now, Mrs. Thorne?" Dillow spoke from the doorway behind me.

He looked even smaller than he had last night, as though he'd shrunk in his black suit, though he seemed every bit as dignified and proper as before. His fringe of gray hair had been smoothed down damply around his head, and it was possible that his bald pate had been touched with talcum powder to cut down its shine. I liked the hint of vanity—it made him seem more human.

"Thank you, Dillow," I said. "I'll have breakfast later. I thought I might go for a walk first."

"Very good, madam. The garden out in back is pleasant with the sun coming up, though the grass will be wet from rain during the night. The rear door down the hall will take you out to the terrace."

He stood back to let me pass, and then followed me. "I'm sorry if the child bothered you last night, madam."

Clearly, Dillow knew everything that went on about the house. In his dark suit he could flit through prevailing shadows and lose himself discreetly. His ears, a bit large for his small head, were set neatly for listening. Nor was he as meekly servile as he sometimes pretended. The look I had caught last night between him and Mrs. Arles had told me that.

"Alice didn't bother me," I said.

"She can be—" He shook his head, not finishing, and I suspected that he would make a perfect target for Alice, who had never been taught to be kind.

Not only had she spilled my hand lotion on the floor, but she'd smeared some of it on the mirror as well, so I'd had to clean up the bathroom this morning. I remembered Debbie's love of fun and mischief, but this child was older, and her mischief was malicious.

I went out the rear door and down to a flagged terrace, where several mallard ducks were feeding on grain that had been tossed out for them. The birds seemed tame and unafraid of my presence. On a lower level a small pond had been set among rocks, its water shining in early sunlight, with more ducks paddling about on the surface.

From the rear of the house I could look north to where a lone mountain would probably be Mount Tolmie, Victoria's own nearby mountain that I'd seen on a map.

---

Now, however, it was the near vista that held my attention. An enchanting garden dropped away from the terrace and ran along below the pond. The hilltop's granite outcroppings had been tamed and used affectively, so that great lawns were cradled in rock that was itself contoured by plantings. Moss and pink heather, broom and fern crept over hard gray surfaces, blending their soft colors.

I followed winding stone steps down past the pond to a lower level of unbelievably green lawn. Victoria's climate is moderate and moist, rather like that of England, so that plant life thrives. Wide spreads of green curved around the base of rocky mounds, offering turns that led to continued pleasant surprises. The air had a fresh morning scent that mingled flowers and sea air.

Circling this secret world, and protecting it, rhododendrons grew tall, and other green shrubbery and trees hid lower houses and streets, so that this was a space set apart. Even the sound of the city seemed distant in so secluded a spot, and I thought of how much my father would love this beautiful garden.

The lawn flowed like a green stream, lapping rocks that accommodated its width. Clipped green edges might have been cut with a child's shears to form interesting patterns around the base of granite mounds, and two tall oak trees cast lacy shadows over lawns and upon cedar stepping blocks. I found that I could follow the rounds of cedar without wetting my feet, though everything around me was moist to the touch. Raindrops still glistened in early sunlight, lending their own jeweled touch, and I heard the gentle sound of dripping everywhere.

All of this must bloom riotously with azaleas and rhododendrons in the spring. Now the dark red of Japanese maple contrasted with borders of winter-blooming heather and the gray-green of mosses. These must seem peaceful colors, after the intensity of earlier seasons. In rocky grottoes maidenhair fern coiled its delicate tendrils, and the whole effect was wild, natural, soothing to my all too troubled spirit.

I walked on around a mass of creeping broom that edged another drainage pond, where phlox and marigolds bloomed. The house, high on its summit, was no more than a ghostly presence, and I could almost forget about its disturbing occupants. *Almost.*

As I came around a curve of lawn, the sense of peace vanished. The chauffeur—Kirk whatever-his-name-was—sat smoking on a rustic wooden bench. I promptly sneezed, as I often did at any whiff of tobacco smoke. This early in the day, he hadn't put on his uniform and billed cap, and no longer wore dark glasses, so that for the first time I saw how deep a blue his eyes were—almost a navy blue. Again, I was aware of his interest in me as he stood up and took the cigarette from his mouth. He looked even more muscular and broad-shouldered in a turtleneck sweater and the jeans that fitted his legs snugly. The mustache with the movie-pirate droop was one of the things I disliked about him. It hid his mouth, and mouths were always an indication of what lay behind.

He rose courteously enough to greet me. "Good morning, Mrs. Thorne. You're up earlier than the rest of the house."

I sneezed again and he grimaced. "Sorry. Smoking's a filthy habit, even outdoors. I've been promising myself I'd quit. So now I will."

He didn't throw the cigarette away but bent to bury it carefully under an azalea bush.

"There," he said, "no desecration. Would you like to sit down, Mrs. Thorne?"

He was not only out of uniform but out of the role he seemed to play as the Radburn House chauffeur. I sat down uncomfortably, my moments of enjoying the lovely garden gone. This man left me with a feeling of uncertainty that I disliked. I never worried about conventions and what was considered "proper," but I was a guest of Corinthea Arles, and I didn't entirely trust her chauffeur's behavior. Perhaps I would ask Dillow about him later, but for now I'd play this by ear.

"Can you stop smoking just like that?" I asked idly.

"I usually do what I set out to do. So I've stopped—as of now. We can't have you sneezing like that."

He was much too readily personal. Once more he'd managed to disturb me, and as usual my face gave me away.

"Of course Mrs. Arles would approve if you got up and went straight back to the house," he said.

"I'm not Mrs. Arles. I came down here to enjoy the garden, and that's what I'd like to do."

It was a clear invitation for him to leave, but he continued to stand beside the bench, looking down at me. When he spoke again he seemed unexpectedly kind.

"Things aren't going very well for you up at the house, are they?"

"I don't know what you mean," I told him stiffly.

"And besides, it's none of my business, is it? I suppose I just enjoy watching the resident comedy wherever I take on a job."

I didn't believe him. There was something more here, something that ran deep behind the "character" he'd adopted. I had a curious sense of quagmire under my feet. Better not to answer, not to get caught up in this fiction he was playing out—whatever it was.

He stepped over to a patch of sunlight and stretched luxuriously, reaching toward the sky with long arms. I watched him, listening to the light dripping all around me—moisture not yet sucked up by the sun. When he turned back he smiled at me easily, naturally.

"I'm sorry that I've upset you. I didn't mean to. Whatever it is that brought you here, the answers haven't been happy for you, have they?"

This was more perceptive than I liked to admit. He could be appealing when he chose, and I wanted none of that.

———

"Why did you use the word 'comedy'?" I asked. "Why should you think whatever's happening at Radburn House is funny? So far, I haven't found anything up there to make me laugh."

He came to stand again before my bench, looking down at me a little too intently for my comfort. "As a matter of fact, I expect what may be happening is a lot closer to tragedy. So maybe it's safer to laugh and not get involved."

"Why should you be involved at all? Are the dark glasses and the mustache some sort of disguise?"

His laugh was unamused. "Let's just say I can disappear behind them more easily."

Whatever intrigue he was engaged with had nothing to do with me. I didn't like his abundant male arrogance, and I didn't trust the faint stirring in me of something that had been asleep for a long time—a purely female response that I wouldn't accept in myself. Not with a man like this! I had always liked gentle men. Larry had been a dreamer, with his eyes on mountaintops, and I'd loved him very much. With Debbie's loss, there seemed no comfort for me anywhere, and I'd kept my relationships with men friends casual. Only through my work could I really deaden pain. So in a moment I would return to the house—get safely away. The very fact that I could think of leaving in terms of safety was a warning. But I wouldn't run precipitately and have him laugh to himself.

"What I'm more curious about right now is *you,*" he went on. "The mysterious guest who appears suddenly, when Mrs. Arles is still recovering from a serious illness and doesn't see anyone. Yet she's entertaining those Corwins, and now you. A bit strange, isn't it?"

"No more strange than your being here." At least my defenses were up. "The mysterious chauffeur who doesn't have a last name! Why do they call Dillow and Crampton by their last names but call you Kirk?"

"If you need another name, McKaye will do. But I asked Dillow to use my first name, and no one seemed to mind."

*Will do?* I wondered. "Why do you think things aren't going well for me at the house?"

"That's easy. Your face gives you away. It's an interesting face, really. But all the lines turn down, instead of up, and you're too young for that. Besides, I have my spies who report to me."

"For someone who's worked here for such a short time, you've settled in pretty well."

"I can settle in anywhere. I've had a lot of practice. Besides, I have a friend up there. Not either of the Corwins, I might add."

"And certainly not Dillow. Though I still wonder why he was willing to hire you. Uncle Tim, perhaps?"

"Tim's okay. I've played chess with him a couple of times. His deafness is no handicap there."

How, I wondered, had he managed to meet the elusive Timothy Radburn? How had he managed to get into the house and up to the room on the third floor? Kirk McKaye seemed to attract unanswered questions.

"I mean Alice," he went on. "The little girl. She's full of words that nobody listens to. So I'm somebody for her to talk to. Since Mrs. Arles probably wouldn't approve of her talking to me, that adds to my attraction. She tells me she played a trick on you last night."

"I see what you mean about spies."

His laugh was so sudden and so unrestrained that he made me jump.

"*You* really shouldn't be talking to me, you know," he said. "I'm probably subversive and off limits. But at least they can't fire you. And my time's sure to be short. Just so I have enough for something I might want to do. When I make up my mind what it is." Something in his voice had changed, and he wasn't laughing now. "In the meantime, I try to please Dillow. Mrs. Arles regards me as part of the scenery and she doesn't hobnob with the hired help. So I take care to behave myself perfectly when anyone is watching."

"How do I happen to be in a different category? Why are you talking to me? How do you know I won't tell Mrs. Arles everything you've said?" I glanced up at the house uneasily, wondering if we were being observed. Only the roof and a third-floor room peaked above the trees.

"Don't worry," he assured me. "They can't see this spot from most of the house. I've checked. And if you want to tell them, of course you will. Though what will you tell? That the chauffeur has been fresh and out of line, and you've been listening? Anyway, it doesn't matter."

He could really get under my skin. "What *does* matter to you?" I asked sharply.

"A lot of things. This garden, for instance. I live up the little hill there in what they call the potting shed. It's a decent enough building, and since the gardener doesn't stay in it these days, I have the rooms at one end. So I can come down here whenever I like. I heard about the Radburn garden long before I came to Victoria."

It seemed surprising that this rather hard, derisive man should be sensitive to the gentle beauty around us. But as I watched him I saw that his feeling toward the garden was different from mine. Something cool had touched his eyes. The thought struck me that this might be a dangerous man —even moving outside the law, if he chose.

"How did you learn about the garden?" I asked.

He considered my question as though I'd handed him a challenge.

"I heard about it years ago, Mrs. Thorne. Edward Arles described it to me. Alice's father. We were both in our early twenties then."

This silenced me completely. If he had known Edward Arles, a whole range of possibilities might open up. He was certainly no ordinary chauffeur, and there would be some strong secret purpose in his working here.

46

He went on more lightly. "I don't know why I should trust you with this momentous announcement, but I have the feeling we may be in the same boat in some ways. I'm not sure where my voyage is heading, but it may be interesting to find out."

"Go on," I said. "What brought you here? Not just idle curiosity about a garden?"

He looked away from me. "I met Edward Arles first when we worked together at a lumber camp in the States—in Washington. That must have been fifteen years ago. He'd just left Victoria, and he wasn't up to that rugged job at first. We hit it off pretty well, and maybe I helped him to grow out of an adolescence that had lasted too long. We kept in touch after that, and I saw him once in a while. When he went off on that Amazon expedition, he wrote me a letter that reached me after his death."

Now I listened with growing interest. Anything that touched Edward Arles might be on my main road. If Alice was Edward's child, that would be that.

"What was in the letter to bring you here?" I asked directly.

He shook his head. "You move too fast, Mrs. Thorne. As you say, I've no reason to think that you won't go right to Mrs. Arles with what I've told you."

"Why shouldn't I?"

"That's up to you." He was serious now, all trace of pretense gone. "Only it might be better for her if you would wait. I'm not planning anything that will hurt her, and it's better not to add new shocks until she's stronger. Later, perhaps it won't matter."

"What I don't understand is why you've opened up to me like this. *Why?*"

"Maybe I do some things on impulse. You're inside the house. You'll meet Edward's wife and her husband. What if those two had something pretty vicious on their minds out there in Brazil?"

I stared at him. "Is that what Edward wrote to you? That he expected trouble?"

Kirk sat down on the bench beside me. "No more now. But you can see why it wouldn't be kind to blurt out any of this to Mrs. Arles. Not until—well, until I know what needs to be done. In the meantime, Mrs. Thorne, what I said about your being a mystery guest isn't true. Dillow told me why you've come. He told me about the kidnapping of your daughter and why Mrs. Arles invited you to visit her."

This was even more upsetting. "Why would he tell you?"

"He knows about my connection with Edward. At least, he knows part of it. He'd never have hired me otherwise. Of course Mrs. Arles has no idea of any of this. I'm just a cap and a uniform to her. Her eyes aren't all that good since her stroke, and she hasn't spotted that I'm a fake. A pretty good one though—don't you think?"

"I've never been convinced," I said. Too many revelations were coming too fast, and I wasn't sure what I thought.

"Don't be upset. I told you we might be on the same voyage—of discovery. That is, to find the truth about Alice. Though she's only part of why I'm here."

The Corwins, I thought. They were the real reason why he'd come. To pay a debt for his friend.

"Did Edward's letter talk about the Corwins?" I asked.

"Some. It's possible we could help each other get to the bottom of this—if you're willing."

"How?"

"I'm not sure yet. What do you feel about Alice? Do you believe she's your child?"

I shook my head unhappily. "From what I've seen, I don't think she can possibly be Debbie. I'm planning to fly home in a day or two. So none of this really affects me. There won't be any voyage for one. Do you want her to be Edward's daughter?"

"I suppose I do. Because of something he wrote, I couldn't let this pass. I owe him that."

---

"After all this time? Why now?"

"The Corwins haven't been easy to find. They move around a lot. I gave up for a while. Then I saw a Victoria newspaper a couple of months ago that spoke about Mrs. Arles's great-granddaughter coming to visit Radburn House, along with her mother and stepfather. So I came—and talked Dillow into taking me on. Right now I'm waiting to see what will happen next."

There was a lot missing in his story. But as I'd told him, none of this mattered to me. I'd be gone soon, with nothing to hold me here.

Kirk looked around. "Here she comes now—probably sent to look for you."

I saw Alice as she came toward us, hopping from one cedar round to the next. When she discovered us sitting on the bench she came to a halt, staring. Her look defied me to mention hand lotion. This morning she wore jeans and a pullover blue sweater, and her short fair hair had been tied with a yellow ribbon on top of her head.

"Hi," she said to Kirk, and then spoke to me. "Uncle Tim says he'd like to see you, but I'm not to tell the old lady if I take you up to his room."

"That's fine," I said.

"Couldn't you call Mrs. Arles something else?" Kirk asked her. " 'Old lady' sounds so—"

"I know—disrespectful. That's the way I mean it. I don't like her and she doesn't like me. How can I call her Great-grandmother?"

"What do you think, Mrs. Thorne?" he asked solemnly.

"I think Kirk is right," I told her. "If someone called you 'child' at every other breath, you wouldn't like it either."

She considered that. "But I am a child, and she's an old lady. Your name's Jenny, isn't it? I think I'll call you that. Dillow sent me to tell you to come to breakfast. The old . . . *she* is having breakfast in her room, like always, but you're to go to the dining room. Dillow says she wants to see you as soon as you've eaten. And, McKaye, Dillow says she'll need the car this morning."

"So it's McKaye now?" Kirk said. "Well, I'd better get going. So long, Mrs. Thorne. See you later, Alice."

Before he could leave, Alice spoke again. "I know! I can call her Corinthea." She rolled the name through all its vowels, relishing the sound. "That's a great name, McKaye. Don't you think so?"

"I'd like to see you use it to her face," Kirk said as he walked off.

That struck Alice as funny, and she looked after him, smiling for the first time since I'd seen her. It was a smile that lighted her whole face and showed even teeth. For once, she looked almost friendly.

My heart didn't do a flop this time. It began to beat hard right up in my throat. For the instant of that smile I saw what Mrs. Arles had seen in the picture of Debbie—the flash of recognition, the clear resemblance to that younger child who had always smiled so readily.

"What's the matter?" Alice asked. "You look funny-peculiar."

The flash was already gone, and Alice Arles didn't in the least resemble the small daughter I remembered. Nevertheless, for an instant I had seen the likeness too, and I was shaken by an uncertainty that was terrifying—because it wouldn't be easily resolved.

"Are you going to be sick?" Alice asked with interest. "Sometimes I get sick, and I don't even know when it's going to happen. Once I threw up all over Farley. But that was when I was little. And after that he didn't shake me so much any more."

"I'm not going to be sick," I said, and stood up.

"Then come along," Alice ordered. "I haven't had breakfast yet either, and I'm hungry." She went skipping off ahead of me.

I followed more slowly, trying to get myself in hand. A smile meant nothing, I told myself—it wasn't *proof.* Yet my heart went right on thumping against all reason. A heart was for hoping, and that was what I'd begun to do.

# 4

By the time I reached the dining room I'd recovered something of my outward control, though I was still churning with uncertainty. I paused in the doorway before going in. *If* that flash of recognition meant anything, then these were the people who had taken my child, and I wasn't sure I could face them without giving myself away. Nor was I convinced that they wouldn't recognize me, in spite of the years and the changes in my appearance.

The man stood at the sideboard helping himself to food, while the woman sat at the table staring at her plate. In a moment they might look around and recognize me, so—*be on guard!* In this one moment, while they were still unprepared, I must watch intently for any reaction that might give them away.

Alice bounced into the room and went to the sideboard to serve herself, and both of them looked at me. The man seemed interested, the woman indifferent. She returned her attention to her plate after a single glance, and there seemed no betrayal of recognition in either of them.

I moved toward the woman, watching for any detail that would remind me of the moment in the store seven years ago. But that woman had worn dark glasses and her hair had been hidden by a kerchief tied under her chin—to add to the difficulty of identification. I could recall only an impression of someone rather young who had seemed nervous and helpless. If Debbie *had* been chosen because of some resemblance to Edward Arles, finding her must have been happenstance. Planning could have been only a general sort of thing. They must have been ready to improvise when an opportunity opened. As far as I knew, I'd never seen the man. For all that was really known, it might have been another woman instead of a man.

If this was the woman I had seen, she had added several pounds of flab that gave her a rather blowsy appearance. Her blond hair, frizzed to a bush around her face, had been bleached to the thinning point, so that it looked brittle and dry. Her eyes were a paler blue than Alice's. While she must have been in her mid-thirties, she already looked older. Her first glance in my direction seemed furtive, though that was probably because of the man who stood at the sideboard, helping himself to breakfast. She wasn't interested in me, but she would take her cue from him. Perhaps *she* was the rabbit the magician had pulled out of his hat. She seemed about as self-assertive.

The man spoke to me first. "Ah, Mrs. Thorne, isn't it? Mrs. Arles's new guest? Good morning. I am Farley Corwin, and this is my wife, Peony."

He was considerably older than his wife, tall and rather lanky, with the once carved but now blurring profile of an actor who was losing his youth and liked his liquor. His long fingers continued to move gracefully as he served himself— the hands of a man whose sure movements were his livelihood. Only when he turned toward me full face did I note the impact of his eyes—large and very dark, with long lashes, and fierce black brows. Compelling eyes that he used to good effect, so that for just a moment *I* was the rabbit, fixed under his penetrating gaze.

I managed to say, "Good morning," to them both. Peony Corwin responded with a listless "Hi," and continued to push scrambled eggs around on her plate.

"May I serve you, Mrs. Thorne?" Farley Corwin asked gallantly, quite aware of the effect his look had had on me. Though he couldn't have known that what I felt was nausea.

"Thank you, I'll manage." I dropped bread into a toaster, and when the toast was ready and buttered, I poured coffee and sat down beside Alice, who shoved a container of marmalade toward me.

"It's English," she said. "They get lots of English things here in Victoria." She had filled her plate generously and began to eat with a good appetite.

"Are you Canadian or American?" I asked, trying to sound casual.

Farley, who had seated himself at the head of the table, as if by right, said, "She's Canadian," and Peony, without looking up, said, "American," and winced when Farley scowled at her.

Alice waved a piece of toast, explaining, "I was born in a jungle in Brazil, wasn't I, Ma? So I could be anything."

"On the Amazon," Peony Corwin added as though by rote.

"Only I don't remember that," Alice said. "I wish I did. My mother's Canadian, but he's American, so they never know what I am. I guess I must be Canadian, because that's what my *real* father was."

"You must have had an interesting life." I was still trying to speak with an ease I didn't feel. "Do you remember anything about when you were little?"

"Not much," Alice said, and I was aware that they were both watching her. "It's mixed up because we moved around all the time. Whenever *he*"—she seemed reluctant to call her stepfather by name—"whenever *he* got jobs, that's where we stayed."

"Where are you from, Mrs. Thorne?" Farley broke in smoothly.

I didn't want to give anything away, though in the short

time that had passed since my first shock of recognition in the garden I was becoming less sure about Alice all the time.

"I'm from Vermont," I said, and named the town where Larry had been killed in the climbing accident. That shouldn't give them any clues.

"A beautiful state," said Farley sociably. "I've traveled through it when I was young."

He seemed curious about me, but not particularly suspicious. Peony seemed watchful of her husband, but nothing more. I had the feeling that there had been a quarrel just before I walked into the room, and that Peony was still sullen as a result. Perhaps not wholly a rabbit, though Farley didn't strike me as a man who would lose many arguments with his wife.

I was relieved when Dillow appeared in the doorway.

"If you are finished with breakfast, Mrs. Thorne," he reminded me, "Mrs. Arles would like to see you in her room."

"I've just finished, so I'll come now." I rose from the table. "Excuse me, please."

No one said anything, and Alice went right on eating. With that sort of hunger, it was remarkable that she stayed so thin.

I went ahead of Dillow down the hall to the library. Once more, he appeared the proper butler, but I remembered the moment last evening when I'd sensed some clash of wills between Mrs. Arles and this man who served her. Certainly, he'd gone behind her back in hiring Kirk, and I didn't trust him at all.

This morning Mrs. Arles sat before her dressing table, while Crampton's stubby hands moved with surprising agility, pinning up silvery strands with the same amber combs I'd noticed last night. Her mistress had changed her garnet robe for one of old gold, and again I was aware of her unlined face, with only her dark eyes hinting at a depth of emotion carefully held in check.

She looked at me now in the mirror. "Good morning, Mrs.

---

55

Thorne. Please sit down, and we'll talk for a few moments. I've made some plans for you today—I hope you won't mind. Crampton, help me to my chair, will you? Then go and see that Alice is made presentable."

Crampton was a woman of few words, and apparently of implicit obedience. She helped Corinthea Arles to her wheelchair, positioned her near an open french door that overlooked the garden, and went silently away. I found myself wondering how she got along with Dillow. The two seemed mostly to ignore each other.

Bright morning sunlight poured in, and Mrs. Arles breathed deeply several times, as though this was her usual ritual. The room looked less gloomy than it had last night, with light flooding through. Again there was stained glass beside some windows, turning shafts of light into a gemlike glow. This morning no fire burned in the grate.

I pulled over a chair and sat down to face Mrs. Arles. She looked at me, her deep-set eyes searching. "Dillow says you met the child last night, Mrs. Thorne."

"Please call me Jenny. Yes—when I returned to my room Alice was there. She didn't go out with the Corwins after all, because she said it would be boring. And I suppose she was curious about me."

"You sound as though you'd made up your mind?"

I shook my head. "Last night I was certain she couldn't be Debbie. I was equally sure this morning when I saw her in your beautiful garden. Until she smiled. Then I caught exactly what you must have seen in that picture taken of my daughter when she was three."

"Then you are sure?" Mrs. Arles sounded disappointed.

"I wish I were. The sense of resemblance faded so quickly. It might not mean anything, and it isn't something to count on."

"Then you'd better stay a few more days and give yourself an opportunity to judge. I am a woman of principle and I want to give you every chance."

---

People who boasted about principle made me uneasy. It often meant an iron inflexibility. I heard my own long sigh. After meeting the Corwins I didn't know any more than I had earlier, and they'd given no sign of recognition toward me. Alice herself believed she'd been born on the Amazon and that Edward Arles was her father. Which again proved nothing. Three was too young for memories that could be expressed. All she knew was her early life with those two. Kirk McKaye, as Edward's friend, wanted to believe the child was Edward's, and there was still the matter of the letter from Edward Arles to be explained. I wondered if I could persuade him to show it to me.

"I don't know how I can ever be sure," I admitted. "For just that one moment this morning I felt elated, excited—positive. But now so many doubts have moved in."

"I know. I had a similar experience when I saw the child's picture. The impression was lost at once—yet we both saw the same thing, and if you leave too soon neither of us can be sure of anything. The story of this woman's child being my grandson's can easily be a lie that I don't want to be trapped into accepting. If this child they call Alice isn't my grandson's child, then where did they get her? That's the question that might turn everything in your favor. *If* you could make an identification."

"I don't know how that will be possible," I said helplessly. Everything had seemed so much simpler from across a continent.

"You must give yourself more time," Mrs. Arles said. "I've arranged for you to have some hours with Alice away from the house today. Joel—Dr. Radburn—will arrive shortly, since this is Saturday and he's not at the lab. His mother wants to meet you and see the girl. I'm not sure why, and I'm not sure I approve, but I've sent my car to pick Joel up. The new chauffeur will drive you all to Oak Bay."

I would be glad to have more time in which to watch

Alice, and perhaps I could talk to Dr. Radburn more easily away from the house.

"Before you meet Joel's mother," Mrs. Arles went on, "I should tell you a little about her. Warn you. His father, Dr. Lewis Radburn, was much older than his second wife, Joel's mother. His first wife, Louise, was my dear friend. After she died I tried, for Lewis's sake, to be friends with Hazel Schmidt. That was her real name, but she dropped it when she was young and called herself Letha Janova when she became an actress on the London stage. Now she uses Letha Radburn as her name."

Mrs. Arles's emphasis on the word "actress" put the profession in the same class as "magician."

"She made quite a success touring in *Bell, Book, and Candle,* I believe, and it typed her forever. After that she always played witchlike roles—even in a film or two. Only B pictures, I might add. Anyway, the witch thing went to her head."

Mrs. Arles paused, and I said, "Oh?" rather blankly.

"I mean—of course it sounds ridiculous—but I think she rather fancies herself as possessing certain—powers, you might call them."

I couldn't picture Dr. Joel with a witch for a mother, and I smiled.

Mrs. Arles flicked a hand at me. "Don't dismiss this, Jenny. People can become what they believe they are, and sometimes that makes them capable of disturbing actions. Of course my early attempt to befriend Letha was sure to fail. Our interests and tastes are too far apart. I thought her a silly young thing at the time, and not worthy of Lewis. She may still be appealing in certain ways, if you like her sort. But she is no longer either silly or young. I'm not sure you should see her at all, but Joel has insisted."

"What does her son think of her—uh—talent?" I asked.

"I'm afraid he's under her spell. Perhaps he's a little amused, but he's also tolerant and affectionate as well. Of course he grew up with all that eccentricity, so he's used to it."

Under her calm words and even tone I sensed a welling of deep resentment in Corinthea Arles. Perhaps I was the accidental recipient of words she would never express to those closer to her.

I asked another question. "Dr. Radburn isn't married?"

"Most wives wouldn't put up with Letha. She'd give them too much competition. I don't mean in the sense of all those psychological complexes that have become so popular, but only that she likes her own way. Women enjoy Joel and he enjoys them. But he is truly married to his research, and he always puts his work first."

I'd had a husband who'd been married to an all-absorbing hobby—mountain climbing—and while Joel Radburn's interest seemed more significant, I felt a little sorry for the woman who fell for him.

"Right now," Mrs. Arles continued, "the important thing is that Letha has asked Joel to bring you and the child to see her. For whatever the reason may be, I wanted you to be warned. She has even invited me, as well, though she knows I would never come. Letha and I haven't spoken for years. Not since my grandson was thirteen and she accused him of stealing some trifling object she treasured."

Mrs. Arles broke off and was silent for a moment. Then she went on more quietly.

"These are things I haven't talked about in years, but if you are to meet Joel's mother you must know my side of our falling out. Her accusation seemed ridiculous, and after what happened, I kept Edward away from Oak Bay. The boys went in different directions as they grew up and I didn't realize for many years that Letha might have been right. Joel is a dear, and he would have nothing to do with what he called our feud. Of course, he has always been devoted to me."

None of this seemed relevant to the matter that con-

---

cerned me, and I tried to draw her away from unhappy reminiscences.

"Do you have any pictures of your grandson?" I asked.

"I disposed of most of them because I didn't want to be reminded of him after he went away."

Just as she'd destroyed pictures of Peony's baby, I thought. As though she could wipe out portions of her life in such futile gestures.

"However, I did find a few snapshots I'd overlooked. After Alice came I wanted to check any resemblance. But they're not very good. You'll find them in that envelope on the table near you. They won't tell you much."

I picked up the envelope and drew out three small snapshots. One had been taken in the garden at Radburn House. The young Edward stood beside his grandmother, almost as tall as she was. He looked sullen—a thin, sharp-faced young man. The next picture showed him in white tennis shorts, with a racquet in his hand and a girl beside him. This was a color shot, and his dark hair shone with highlights in the sun, but his features were blurred. The third was a profile shot, and too indistinct to mean anything. Perhaps there was some slight structural resemblance to Alice in the pictured faces, but they were anything but conclusive.

"Do you think Alice looks like him?" I asked.

She moved her hands vaguely. "Not really. Perhaps sometimes—I don't know."

"What was your grandson like?"

"In appearance, he was rangy, wiry, always too thin, and not very strong. He was sick a lot as a boy. After his parents were lost in a boating accident and he came to live with me, he nearly died of scarlet fever."

I remembered what Kirk had said about Edward not being very strong. What would happen, I wondered, if I told Mrs. Arles what Kirk had said this morning in the garden? But I couldn't take that chance until I knew more about what he intended. I really needed to have another talk with

---

60

Kirk McKaye soon. I put the pictures back in the envelope and set it aside.

"Perhaps you'd better go and change before Joel arrives," Mrs. Arles suggested. "I just wanted a few words with you alone first."

"I'll hurry," I said.

As I reached the upper hallway, a door opened cautiously, and Crampton peered out. Her behavior seemed secretive and strange. When she saw that she'd been observed, she went quickly past me and up the stairs to the third floor— where, as I later learned, she had her own room.

Odd, I thought, but dismissed her behavior as I went into my room. I changed to a beige skirt and jacket, with a navy blouse, and clasped a gold heart locket that had been Debbie's about my neck for luck. Then I went downstairs again.

Crampton appeared shortly after, pushing a reluctant Alice ahead of her. At least the girl had not been put into frills today. She wore a denim skirt and jacket with a white blouse, and knee socks on her thin legs.

"Why do I have to get dressed up like this in the morning?" she demanded of Mrs. Arles. "Old Crampton won't tell me anything."

"You are not to say 'old Crampton,'" Mrs. Arles reproved. "To you she is Mrs. Crampton. Please remember that. You are going to pay a visit to Dr. Joel's mother in Oak Bay. Mrs. Thorne will go with you, and it will be a pleasant trip. I want you to behave properly and be a credit to me as my great-granddaughter!"

Alice looked rebellious, but she didn't argue. Perhaps she recognized a greater stubbornness than her own.

When she caught me watching her, she scowled. "You're always staring at me," she accused, and I looked quickly away. Debbie had never been a sulky, resentful child. With all the love she'd been given by the time she was three, surely she wouldn't be like this now. I didn't want her to be mine, I thought, and felt guilty at once. Alice Arles had been

61

formed by circumstances to become the way she was. Someone needed to understand and help her to be different. But
that wasn't my task. I would go home soon and I'd never see
any of these people again. Whatever mysteries were here
would remain mysteries—and I didn't really care. I must
keep telling myself that and not become involved.

Dillow appeared in the doorway and spoke to Mrs. Arles.
"Kirk has arrived with Dr. Radburn, madam."

"Ask them both to come here," Mrs. Arles instructed.

Dr. Joel came in first, and I felt glad to see him, in spite of
all that had been said about him and his mother. He stood for
sanity, at least, and I liked his rather homely face and clear
gray eyes. I could see that he would be attractive to women,
though with a different sort of assurance from Kirk's. Joel
Radburn appeared to know who he was without any mock-
ing bravado. So why did bravado intrigue me, make me
curious?

Kirk stayed in the doorway, cap in hand, awaiting instructions, correct in his uniform and manner, and once more
wearing dark glasses. Dr. Radburn came to stand beside
Mrs. Arles's chair, and she looked up at him in greeting
before she spoke to Kirk.

"Come in, please," she said to the chauffeur. "I want you
to do something for me." She picked up a small cardboard
box from a nearby table and handed it to him. "You are to
drive Dr. Radburn, Mrs. Thorne, and Alice out to Mrs. Letha
Radburn's home in Oak Bay. After the visit, and *only* when
they are ready to leave, you are to give this box to Mrs.
Radburn and tell her it is from me."

"With your compliments, madam?"

"*Without* my compliments. Don't add anything. Just give
it to her."

"Yes, madam." He sounded letter perfect in his role, but as
he went out of the room, he glanced in my direction, and I
suspected there would again be that strange challenge be-

hind the dark lenses. Then he touched a forefinger to his temple and went off, putting on his cap.

Alice followed Kirk out of the room, and when she'd gone, Mrs. Arles spoke to me.

"Don't be taken in by Letha, Jenny. She's up to something, of course, so be on your guard."

Again I must be guarded—what else?

Joel Radburn smiled as he bent to kiss her hand. "You don't trust me, do you, Corinthea?"

"When it comes to your mother, you're prejudiced," she told him crossly, and pushed him away. "*I* take Letha very seriously."

"So do I," he said. "Of course you've prepared Jenny?"

"As much as I could." Mrs. Arles turned her chair so that she could look into the garden. We had been dismissed, and Dr. Radburn and I went out to the car together.

Alice was waiting outside. "I want to sit in front," she announced, and climbed into the seat beside the chauffeur.

"We can take the Marine Drive," Joel suggested to Kirk as we started off.

Our road followed the irregularities of the shoreline along the Strait of Juan de Fuca. Victoria is a city built upon water. The splendid harbor has always attracted shipping to the city, and in the last century fur trading had been very important. This lower tip of Vancouver Island had been settled (after the Indians) by the Hudson's Bay Company as a grant from Great Britain, providing that a colony would be established here. So Fort Victoria was built, and a town grew up around it. Once this had been a stopover point on the rush to the goldfields on the Fraser River, and miners' tents would have lined the shore. Eventually, there was no more need for a fort; the fur company sold off the land to private citizens, and suburban communities began to spring up. Now there were little towns scattered all the way up the island.

Across the strait, I could see the Olympics standing clear this morning, their snow-capped peaks visible. Nearby, little

63

green islands floated on the water, and sailboats skimmed among them, with an occasional large white cruiser moving at a more stately pace.

Alice had never made this trip, and she seemed interested in everything and no longer sulky. She was clearly curious about the box Kirk had to deliver, and after a time of restraint she picked it up from the seat between them.

"I wonder what's in this box Corinthea gave you?" she remarked to Kirk. "It's not tied up, so maybe I could look inside."

"Leave it alone," Kirk told her. "It's not for you to open."

Reluctantly, she set the box down on the seat, apparently more willing to listen to Kirk than to others. No one commented on her use of Mrs. Arles's first name, though Joel Radburn raised an eyebrow at me.

Interesting place names came up along our route—like Foul Bay, which of course dated back to sailing days on these treacherous waters along the island shore. The road ran past small houses built early in the century, enchanting in their architecture. Their styles were a mixture of Victorian Gothic and anything else the architect chose to incorporate. Shingled roofs peaked above windows and doors, and the colors were cheerful—pink and gray, yellow trim on white, touches of green or blue that matched the shadings of the sea. And always, no matter how small the plot, there were gardens. I glimpsed geraniums everywhere, and late-blooming roses, as well as the yellow flowers of fall.

"We call these Traditional Houses," Joel said, "and they give a special flavor to Victoria and its suburbs. The houses are protected now by law to keep them just as they were early in the century. Larger homes are farther ahead in Oak Bay."

In the front seat Alice continued to look and exclaim, and I found myself watching every turn of her head, listening to her voice—trying to find something that would speak to me as her smile had done. But this child seemed only a stranger

—not my Debbie. Yet she was a child in need and I felt sad and helpless when I thought of those two who had brought her to Mrs. Arles.

Aware of the way I watched Alice, Joel spoke softly, so she couldn't hear. "You're beginning to take her on, aren't you, Jenny? Better not, until you're sure. I think she'll be all right, no matter what. She has the sort of spirit nothing's likely to quench. Some kids have that from the beginning. They can grow up under terrible circumstances and surmount everything. Alice has that core of strength, so don't worry about her. She may not be your problem. She may even be able to hold her own with Corinthea. For one thing, she's learned how to bluff and cover up her fears."

His words encouraged me unreasonably. Debbie had shown a special spunkiness and independence from the beginning. Perhaps this trait might be more recognizable in her than anything else. Though nothing really offered the conviction I needed. I held back from telling him about my experience in the garden, less certain of it now.

When, at Joel's suggestion, Kirk detoured into a maze of quiet, winding streets, the houses became mansions, many of them built in the Tudor style, with half-timbering that was sometimes used in fanciful patterns against pale cream walls. These houses were built by people who remembered their English heritage.

"Sometimes people say that Oak Bay is behind the Tweed Curtain—a bit of old England," Joel told me. "There's more of a clinging to British roots and customs here, and you can still hear English accents. Though it was once a toss-up whether Victoria would belong to Canada or to the United States."

I remembered reading about the arguments that had arisen concerning a boundary between the two countries. When the 49th Parallel was finally chosen, the dividing line ran through the center of the Strait of Juan de Fuca, so that Victoria and some of the islands fell on the Canadian side.

With borders so close, a great deal seemed interchangeable between the two countries—neither one completely foreign to the other. But as I paid closer attention, differences were to be found. In uniforms, of course, in the flying of the Maple Leaf flag, in pictures of the Queen. Occasionally words were used in a different way, and pronunciations could vary, but mostly we were close cousins. The many gardens had come directly from an English delight in ordered growth—to become Victoria itself, the garden city.

Back again on the road that followed the water, we drove between stone gateposts into an exclusive section called The Uplands, and here the houses were even more spacious and the grounds still larger. Low stone walls and hedges protected the properties and separated them, and there were a great many tall trees. Shrubbery was carefully landscaped and I thought of the appreciation my father would feel if he were here.

At Joel's direction, Kirk turned the car into a winding driveway that circled wide lawns and led toward another great Tudor house. Again there were peaked roofs and high windows, but this house was far wider than it was tall. A porte cochere offered shelter for those arriving by car—or carriage, as used to be the case when the house was built. A long, wide flight of shallow stone steps ran down to a lower lawn, where two enormous black birds pecked at the edge of a flower bed. They were almost as large as chickens, and I stared at them in surprise.

"Those are ravens," Joel said. "They can be a scourge around here, though the Indians considered them sacred birds. All sorts of legends about them have been handed down. Uncle Tim's an expert on ravens."

The more I learned about Timothy Radburn, the more interesting he sounded.

When Kirk would have come around to open the door for us, Joel stopped him.

"I want to talk with Mrs. Thorne for a moment before we go in. Alice, would you like to look around outside?"

Alice gave Joel a knowing glance but left the car and ran down the steps toward the ravens, who edged slightly away, not especially afraid. Kirk got out and stood beside the car, but I noticed that he left the door open—in order to listen, of course. Joel seemed not to notice, and I wondered if he should be warned about this chauffeur Dillow had hired. The fact that he had known Edward Arles didn't explain everything.

"My mother has given me exact directions about how this meeting with Alice is to be managed," Joel said. "She's really a darling, and we mustn't laugh, no matter what happens."

I said I didn't feel like laughing, and Joel went on.

"She'll be waiting for us in her meditation room, and she wants to see you and Alice appear together without any introductions or preparation. Quick first impressions are important to her, and she believes that she'll know at once about Alice."

"You mean she thinks she can tell whether Alice is my child? Just by looking at us? When I can't even tell myself?"

"I don't necessarily believe any of this, but Mother is right in her instincts so much of the time that I listen to her hunches."

I felt increasingly uneasy. "Tell me a little more before we go in. Why doesn't Mrs. Arles like your mother?"

"That goes back a long way, and it's no secret. After my father's first wife died, and Mrs. Arles's husband died, Corinthea would have liked to marry my father. They were old and dear friends and it might have worked out—but then Letha came along and captivated him. Corinthea couldn't easily forgive a defeat like that. Though she tried to be nice to my mother at first—until something unpleasant happened. These days she ignores my mother's existence and thinks of me only as Lewis Radburn's son. But that's all ancient history, and you needn't concern yourself with it.

---

67

What happens now may be a bit of an act—I don't expect it to prove anything. But, with my mother, one never knows. So be patient, and don't let anything she says upset you."

"Among other things, I hope she won't upset Alice," I told him. "That's a pretty delicate situation, and I don't know how much affection Alice may have for Peony."

"I don't think you need to worry," Joel said. "My mother's sensibilities won't let you down. Let's go in now."

We got out of the car and faced the enormous house. Down the steps Alice called to Joel, and he went to see what she wanted to show him. For a moment I was left alone with Kirk McKaye, and I spoke urgently.

"I need to talk with you. I want to know more about that letter from Edward Arles and why you haven't told his grandmother you have it."

He took off his dark glasses, and I could see the intense dark blue of his eyes again. "Thanks for not giving me away. It's important to wait. Edward wrote some pretty strange things, and maybe I feel that he left me with a mission. But we can't talk now. Suppose you come down to the bench in the garden later this afternoon? Say around four-thirty? If I'm free, I'll be there."

"I'll try to get away," I said.

"Isn't that up to you? You're not a prisoner."

"Of course not. I'll come down to the garden at four-thirty and look for you."

"There's a back gate out of the garden. We can sneak off without Mrs. Arles ever guessing that you're meeting her chauffeur."

He was laughing at me again, but while I hated to offer any new opening for his devious schemes, I needed to know about that letter.

Joel and Alice were coming toward us from the lower lawn, and Kirk replaced his dark glasses. Who was he hiding from? Joel?

"You've been here before, haven't you?" I asked softly.

He grinned at me and walked away. I was beginning to feel sure that he hadn't met Edward Arles for the first time at that lumber camp, as he'd claimed.

As we walked into the shadow of the big house its dark roof seemed to block out the sunny sky. On the far side, the grounds would slope down to the water, and the wind from that direction was cool. I shivered in my light jacket, but only partly because of the wind. I was beginning to dread what was about to happen.

# 5

A young English maid in a neat uniform admitted us, and Joel called her Iris. Mrs. Radburn was waiting for us— "Back there," she said.

The spacious entry hall seemed almost baronial, partly circled by a wide gallery. The ceiling rose three stories high, timbered with heavy beams, and a wide staircase rose four-square to the floor above, with no feminine curves—strong and impressive in its gleaming golden oak. Leaded glass windows on either side offered gray light.

"This is a Maclure house," Joel said. "He was a Scotsman who built some of Victoria's greatest homes. He and Frank Lloyd Wright were friends, and probably influenced each other."

We moved past the stairs and down a hall, where big rooms opened on either hand. At the back of the house, windows looked out toward the water and more sunlight reached in. Before the last open door we stopped.

"We're here, Mother." Joel spoke quietly, as though he remembered the hall echoes and didn't want to rouse them.

The answering voice was musical—the vibrant voice of a woman who had spent years on the stage. "Come in," she called.

Joel pushed Alice and me gently ahead of him and let us go alone into a room that was dimly lighted. Here the windows were covered by long purple draperies, and several floor lamps dripped gold fringe, casting localized pools of amber here and there. Only the woman across the room was dramatically lighted from some invisible source.

She sat in a woven wicker chair that might have come from India and that rose above her head in a great peacock swirl, framing her effectively. Her eyes were closed, her hands lightly clasped in her lap, as if she meditated—or perhaps prayed for guidance. I had a feeling that it was the latter.

Her long black gown of sheer wool flowed from its boat neck to the floor, with a Grecian key in green and gold threads embroidered around the hem and banding the full sleeves. Around her neck hung a golden chain, its length interrupted at intervals with green jade beads. Her hands shone pale against the black gown, the fingers long, slender, rose-tipped, and without rings. Her black hair, parted in the center, had been drawn over her ears in two sleek wings, and gold and jade earrings trembled from invisible earlobes as she opened her eyes and inclined her head to acknowledge our presence.

Once I had taken in all that was theatrical and extraneous, it was her eyes that held me. Gray eyes, like her son's but carefully made up to emphasize with mascara and eye shadow how large and luminous they were. I didn't know what had become of Joel, since he had slipped back into shadow near the door.

"Stay right there, please." The woman in the chair spoke the command clearly in the quiet room, and we stopped at once.

She moved her hand, and light came on magically, illuminating the entire area from a central chandelier. In this sudden flood of radiance, Mrs. Radburn studied us. Alice pulled at my hand. I sensed that she was about to bolt, and I tightened my grip.

"Where are you, Joel?" Mrs. Radburn asked. "Perhaps you

71

can show Alice your father's Indian room across the hall? Then come back here. I've seen what I needed to see."

Joel emerged from the shadowy area near the door, and the child beside me recovered enough to protest. "People always send me away when they're going to say something interesting!"

Letha Radburn smiled. "I know. They did that to me too when I was young. You'll get even someday. But for now, go with Joel."

Alice went off without further argument, and Joel took care not to catch my eye.

"Come and sit down, Jenny Thorne," his mother said, and I sank into a deep red velvet chair that swallowed me in a gulp. Now, in light from the chandelier, I could see a room of low, cushioned furniture—rather Turkish in its effect. Small console tables abounded, with fragile ornaments collected on dark wood and inlaid surfaces.

Once more Mrs. Radburn touched some remote control on the table beside her, and the brilliance dimmed a little, though the room was not returned to its original darkness.

"I'm sorry for the theatricality," she said in a voice that drew the vowels out in rounded tones. "It was necessary if I was to receive any sort of immediate message."

I wished she would drop the suspense and tell me what the message was, if any.

Joel returned and went at once to kiss his mother on the cheek. "Now that you've frightened the child," he said, "you'd better tell us your conclusions."

"Sit down and don't chatter," Letha Radburn commanded. "This isn't to be treated as frivolity. I had no idea if anything would happen—but it did. And very quickly. I've never had an impression come through that was as strong and vivid as this." She leaned toward me, serious and intent. "The little girl is yours. There's no mistaking this. So you must take her away as quickly as you can and go back to wherever you came from."

---

Joel coughed gently. "That's fine, Mother. But it isn't as simple as that. Alice already has a mother—Peony Corwin, who comes complete with birth certificate and the fact that she was undeniably married to Edward Arles for a short time before his death. Jenny can't just walk in and say, 'This is my daughter,' and take her away. There has to be proof."

Letha Radburn waved slim fingers in dismissal of such irrelevant details. Unlike Corinthea Arles, she had a mobile and expressive face, and while she was probably in her early sixties, she possessed an air of youthful excitement that was stimulating.

"I have no information about any of that," she said. "Of course something more may come through later—I don't know. My guides don't always answer my questions immediately. They must always turn to a higher source. If I learn anything I'll let you know at once. In the meantime, I have something for you, Jenny Thorne."

She picked up a swirl of tissue paper from a crystal bowl and handed it to me. I opened the paper and took out a black feather that was nearly twelve inches long. I held it up, questioning.

"It's a raven's feather," she said. "The raven is a magical bird—our Indians of the Northwest have always known that. I picked that one up myself, and it's perfect. Some feathers should never be picked up, you know—like the owl's or the peacock's. The owl can come looking for you if you hold his feather. And the eye in the peacock's feather can watch you in an evil way."

"Mother," Joel said, still gentle with her.

The huge feather was beautiful, with its satiny black comb, and I stroked the hard, shining spine.

"What am I supposed to do with it?" I asked.

Letha studied me thoughtfully. "I'm not sure. I was prompted to give it to you—so it must mean something. Perhaps it's an omen. Perhaps it's for protection. Can you remember anything about a feather in the past?"

---

I shook my head, though some hint of memory I couldn't place tantalized me as I folded tissue around the black plume. My handbag was just wide enough to accommodate its length.

Joel had listened to enough about feathers.

"Since you've had such a strong impression about Jenny and Alice, Mother, perhaps I should arrange for you to meet the Corwins? If you see Peony and talk with her, perhaps something more may come to you."

Letha shook her head. "Not yet. There's something blocking the way—I'm not sure what. Besides, it isn't necessary, since I already have the answer."

She broke off as Alice appeared in the doorway.

"Can I come back in now?" Alice asked.

"Of course." Mrs. Radburn smiled at her. "Did you find anything interesting in the Indian room?"

"It was all interesting," Alice admitted. "But I wanted to be where something important was going to happen. *Did* it happen?"

Mrs. Radburn nodded. "It happened, Alice. But for now it's another one of those grown-up secrets that you'll have to live with. Come here, please."

Now that Joel's mother had dropped the air of a seeress, she seemed more relaxed and approachable, and Alice lost her uneasiness. She went without hesitation to stand before Letha Radburn, who took both her hands and drew her close, her luminous, slightly nearsighted eyes peering into the child's intently. Then she looked at me and sighed, shaking her head. I knew what she meant. Whatever first vivid impression had communicated itself had now dissipated, dissolved, and she had nothing more to offer.

She shrugged and spoke to Joel. "Are you taking these ladies to lunch?"

"That's what I plan. Will you come with us, Mother?"

"I'd love to. Just let me go and change. Show Jenny the Indian room, Joel. And I'm sure Alice would like another look, now that she's no longer curious about what's happening in here."

Mrs. Radburn floated away with a chiming of beads and bracelets, and we crossed the lower hall to a room where no draperies had been pulled and sun flooded in. From the rise of ground this house would offer views of Haro Strait, and I paused to look out before I stepped into the room across the hall.

Joel waited, while Alice ran on ahead. The peaceful view calmed me and I joined him in a moment.

The Indian room was filled with carved ivory and brass and cinnabar. Little tables inlaid with mother-of-pearl stood about, with ivory and ebony elephants clustered on them in groups of seven. Brass trays and bowls and incense burners, along with carved statues from the Hindu pantheon, crowded the room. Alice stood before a goddess with several intricately arranged arms and tried to imitate her position.

"This was my favorite room when I was a kid," Joel said. "I had special names for some of my friends in here. All of this came from Dad's days in British India, when he was an army doctor. Corinthea went out to visit them once, when he was married to Louise. Look over here, Jenny—this lady is one of my favorites. She used to get into my nightmares, but she fascinated me anyway. There's something hypnotic about her."

The "lady" in question had been carved of black teak, her seated figure a foot or so high. She held a skull in her hands and wore a girdle of writhing snakes.

"Kali," Joel said. "The blessed dark one, they call her. She's Siva's wife and, like him, she can be a destroyer. They always portray her with blood on her hands, and she's the goddess of disease, among other things."

Alice spoke unexpectedly. "But she cures diseases too—she's not all bad."

"How do you know about Kali, Alice?" I asked.

"I read about her in a book Uncle Tim has—all about

75

Hindu gods. Siva and Kali had a son with an elephant's head."

Joel looked startled. "Well! You seem to have learned a lot since you came to Radburn House."

"I don't have much to do, and I like spooky things. Your mother's kind of spooky, Dr. Joel."

He laughed. "You should see her when she puts on a sari and does Indian dances. She really took to this room, though she's never been to India."

Mrs. Radburn spoke from the doorway. "I'm ready, if you are." I was quite willing to leave Kali and her relatives, and relieved to see that Joel's mother had dropped her theatricality. She wore beautiful tweeds in a weave of pale lavender shot with heather. Scottish tweeds, undoubtedly. And her jade earrings had been changed for small amethysts. She looked trimly elegant as she came into the room and stood gazing around for a moment.

"I will never forget the last time poor Edward Arles was in this room. After what happened, I was relieved when Corinthea wouldn't let him come here to visit you any more, Joel. You remember that he actually took a valuable jade carving of that elephant god Alice just mentioned."

Clearly, Joel didn't want to talk about Edward Arles. "Let's go to lunch," he said. "I've made a reservation at the Oak Bay Beach Hotel."

"One of my favorite places." Mrs. Radburn brightened. "But first I would like Alice to have something from this room, something to remind her of her visit here."

She moved about, touching several objects lightly, then moving on. "Ah—here we are." She picked something up from a lacquer dish and held it out to Alice. The child took it carefully and balanced it in one palm—a tiny lotus blossom brooch, delicately carved in pink coral.

"Be sure to show it to Mrs. Arles," Letha Radburn said, and I sensed some underlying meaning in her words, though she didn't explain.

"Do you want to wear it, or shall I put it in my bag until we get back to the house?" I asked Alice.

She gave it to me at once. "I don't want to lose it. Thank you, Mrs. Radburn. It's very pretty." Considering her frequent rudeness, it was pleasant to find her polite at times.

When we went outside, Kirk was waiting near the Mercedes. He reached at once into the front seat for the small box Corinthea Arles had given him to deliver. He handed it to Mrs. Radburn, along with the accompanying envelope, explaining his instructions. I thought again of how much that mustache made him look like a pirate, and wondered idly what he would be like clean shaven.

"How strange," Mrs. Radburn said as she took the box. "I can't imagine why Corinthea should send me anything. I haven't spoken to her in years."

"All very foolish," Joel said, "but I never argue with Corinthea. Or with you."

Kirk opened the car door with a slight flourish—something Mrs. Radburn noticed with a quick look, though she didn't comment.

I wondered if one of her spirit "guides" might tell her something about Kirk McKaye. Or perhaps this had already happened, because she spoke to him directly.

"You're new in Mrs. Arles's employ, aren't you?" she asked.

"Yes, madam," he said, waiting for us to get into the car.

Alice climbed in front again, preferring Kirk's company, and Joel sat between me and his mother in the back seat. As we drove out to the road, Alice was already telling Kirk about the room of Indian treasures. He, at least, seemed to listen to Alice without brushing her off, as the Corwins did.

Under cover of the child's chatter, Mrs. Radburn spoke quietly to her son. "I think you should advise Mrs. Arles to get rid of this new chauffeur. The vibrations around him are wrong. There's something—something that promises trouble."

---

77

"I'll report your impression," Joel said. "Though I don't think Corinthea will pay much attention. She trusts Dillow, and he always hires anyone new with great care."

Only this time he had connived behind Mrs. Arles's back.

"Well, the chauffeur isn't my problem," Letha said. "Now I must look at what Corinthea has sent me." She opened the box and spread back the tissue inside, her movements quick and sure. When she saw the contents she exclaimed, "Joel! Do you recognize this?"

Joel took the box from her and lifted out a small carving of mutton-fat jade, its yellow-white delicately veined in green. As he held it up, I saw that it represented the son of Siva and Kali—the god with the elephant head.

I glanced at the two in the front seat. Alice was still talking to Kirk, and his attention seemed to be on his driving as he listened to her, sometimes responding. Yet I couldn't be sure he wasn't listening to us as well. His dark hair grew tightly against his neck beneath the cap, and the back of his head told me nothing.

"What a lot of trouble this caused," Joel mused, staring at the carving.

His mother's excitement grew. "This is what Edward took that day! I saw him looking at it, and I knew how much this piece fascinated him. When it disappeared the very same day he was here, I had to call your father, Joel. No one else could have taken it. Of course Lewis was angry. In fact, he was so furious that I was afraid of what he might do or say if he saw the boy himself. So *I* went to talk to Edward's grandmother."

"I remember," Joel said soberly. "The whole thing was pretty awful—especially since I was never allowed to see Edward again. We were only kids—thirteen—and Dad shouldn't have made so much of it. I was pretty scared of him in those days."

Mrs. Radburn went on quietly. I knew she too was aware of Kirk and Alice in the front seat. "Of course Corinthea was furious when I told her what Edward had done. Furious with me too. She didn't like me anyway, and she said she would never allow her grandson to be accused of stealing. Though I think she knew all along that he must be guilty. When some things were missing from her house years later, she simply threw him out. From early on, that boy was no good. Let's see what she has to say."

Letha opened the note from Corinthea and read it through.

"Imagine! She's known for a long time that he took this. After Edward died in Brazil she was going through things he'd left at the house, and she found this. Yet she's kept it all these years without saying a word. Why does she send it back to me now?"

"Perhaps because she's been ill," Joel said. "Perhaps she wants her conscience clear and she's sorry for what happened."

"That woman's never been sorry for anything!"

Joel answered his mother quickly. "There's something you ought to know about this. Something I never told you— though I should have. Edward didn't steal that piece of jade. I gave it to him."

"You *gave* it to him?" Mrs. Radburn echoed. "And you let him take the blame?"

They'd both forgotten me, and I kept very still so my presence wouldn't matter.

"I was a kid, and I only meant it as a lark," Joel went on. "I knew how much Edward liked the carving—and I enjoyed making a grand gesture. Maybe I thought it would never be missed. Afterward, I was afraid to admit what I'd done because I knew what a thrashing I'd get from Dad. I didn't think through to what might happen to Edward. In fact, I never thought anybody would guess that he had it."

His mother was shaking her head. "I don't understand why Edward didn't tell the truth. Why should he take the blame to spare you?"

———

79

"He was like that. Stiff-necked. Angry and proud. He wasn't very strong physically, so maybe he compensated with another kind of strength. He'd have said, 'Let them think what they like if they're that stupid!' Besides, he knew what Dad would do to me whenever I stepped out of line, and he wouldn't have wanted me to get a licking when I'd been generous to him. I should have told you, but you'd have told Dad, and I was a coward. Afterward, Edward and I went in different directions, but it always bothered me. I always thought I'd make it right someday—and then it was too late and he was gone."

Letha rested her hand gently on her son's arm. "Who doesn't play the coward a few times in every life? At least Corinthea must be told what happened—since she has made this gesture." Letha took the jade figure from her son, wrapped it in its tissue nest, and covered the box. "I owe Corinthea an apology. I'm glad she's had the grace to return this, even though she kept it too long. I'll thank her myself one of these days, and tell her I'm sorry I blamed Edward. Perhaps the old wound can be healed."

"I wouldn't count on that," Joel said.

"In the long run, of course," his mother went on, "Edward wasn't all that innocent. He might not have been guilty that first time, but years later, when valuable art objects that belonged to his grandmother turned up in pawnshops, he turned out to be a real thief."

"None of it matters now—not with Edward long dead in a senseless accident."

"Nothing is accidental," Letha said.

I thought of the ominous letter Kirk had received, and asked a question. "Mrs. Radburn, have you ever had any—I don't know the word—any message about Edward's death?"

"Please call me Letha, since I shall call you Jenny. There is always a mist when I think of Edward—something that frightens me. Perhaps something threatening."

———

Joel looked at me curiously. "Why do you ask? Have you heard anything around the house?"

I'd have liked to tell them both about Kirk and the letter, but something still held me back. Perhaps the very fact that Kirk might be listening. I would need a private time to talk about this.

The car had turned into the wide driveway in front of the Oak Bay Beach Hotel, and I looked out at the impressive building. It was very wide, with peaked brown roofs, creamy walls, and again the Tudor half-timbering. The windows were small-paned and spaced well apart across the front— probably not letting in very much light. Tall oak trees surrounded the entry court, and I could glimpse water beyond the garden at the side.

Mrs. Radburn slipped the small box into her handbag. "I'm sorry about all this, Jenny. We must cheer up now and let old mistakes go. This hotel is one of Oak Bay's touches of old England, and it dates from the twenties. There's a pub here called the Snug that's still popular, and the whole place has a special character I'm fond of."

We crossed a spacious old-fashioned lobby and went back to the Tudor Room, where a headwaiter in a red jacket and bow tie greeted us. The room had been opened up on the tremendous view, part of it surrounded with glass. We were seated on a platform that overlooked lower tables and was guarded by a brass rail. From here we could enjoy the sight of water and islands and distant mountains. I liked the Victorian touches of wallpaper, a red-figured carpet, and red velvet chair seats, contrasting with snowy linen. Vines grew along the tops of the windows, dripping graceful green tendrils, and paintings of river scenes hung in the spaces between windows.

Letha looked up at one of the paintings. "Maclure was an artist as well as an architect, and that's one of his landscapes over there."

Though the room interested me, it was Alice who held my

81

main attention. I kept watching her with a mingled sense of loss and doubt and hope that I couldn't deal with. She sat across the table between Joel and his mother, obviously on her best behavior. Though when she caught my eye I saw a dancing light in her eyes that stabbed through me with a reminder of Debbie. If Alice was awed by this room, or by the large menu folder that was handed to her, she didn't show it, and I admired her aplomb. Perhaps, as Joel said, she had learned to bluff.

We all chose the buffet luncheon and walked over to the long table.

An assortment of salads and hot dishes made a colorful display. I helped myself to a creamy clam and scallop chowder, cold salmon, green salad, and hot rolls. Alice chose with moderation (for her)—obviously an experienced diner. She whispered to me that we could return for more as often as we liked—her favorite kind of meal.

Back at the table, Mrs. Radburn told me something about Oak Bay. Her lavender tweeds had put her into a more prosaic world than she'd occupied at the house, but she still retained an aura of the exotic. I marveled at the contrast between her animation and the quiet manner of her son. Perhaps Joel had grown up with so much excitement around him that he was willing to be subdued in the shadow of his mother's vivacity. When I'd seen him with Corinthea Arles, his manner had been more authoritative—both that of a friend on an equal footing and of a doctor in charge. Now he listened attentively, sympathetically, to his mother, enjoying her and allowing her center-stage.

"Of course the native Indians were here for thousands of years before the white man came," she told Alice and me. "A great many of their rock cairns have been found, and each one marks a single grave. So archaeologists have made valuable finds. Probably some of our finest homes have Indian warriors buried under their basements and lawns. There are always ghost stories. Sometimes in early morning

82

mists I've sensed those warrior spirits out there, wondering about us, perhaps hostile to the way we've taken over."

This idea appealed to Alice. "Do you think they come out with their tomahawks around Corinthea's garden?"

"The Nootka didn't use tomahawks," Letha Radburn said. "They made clubs and daggers out of whalebone. But I like the idea of their haunting Corinthea's garden."

Though I listened to all this, my focus was always upon Alice. Even if she was bluffing a little, and not as certain as she seemed, I liked her behavior under strange circumstances. In spite of the treatment she must have received at Farley Corwin's hands, and perhaps neglect from Peony, she had kept her own special adventurous quality that brimmed with life and wouldn't be put down.

I was ready to do more than like her, and that made me afraid. For these past seven years I'd spent my love and longing on my charges in the school. There was satisfaction and reward in helping children who needed me. But that was different. This child might be my own.

While I couldn't set much store by Mrs. Radburn's immediate conviction that Alice was my lost daughter, neither could I discount it. Or discount that flash of recognition I'd felt. But if I let down all the barriers, if I allowed myself to pour out too much ready affection, and then had to give her up and go home, the pain would be more than I could face. This was what Joel's warning had meant. Unless I could prove her identity one way or the other, I was fearful about what lay ahead.

In a few days Mrs. Arles might decide that I couldn't prove anything, and then she would take the action she wanted, having assuaged her conscience. She would claim Alice as her great-grandchild and heir. Unfortunately, I felt that she desired this, not because of any affection for Alice herself, but because she was old and ill and possessed by that strange human drive to pass on all she owned to her own flesh and blood. Once she made her decision, I wouldn't figure in the picture at all.

I knew there were artists who claimed that from an early photo they could project what a child would look like years later. But even though such a drawing might come surprisingly close, it still wouldn't provide the legal proof I needed.

Across the table, Alice regarded me doubtfully, and I knew I must have fixed my attention upon her too openly again. Letha, with her special sensitivity, seemed to notice this, and she began to talk to Alice, inquiring into what the child might remember.

"Did you have any pets when you were little?" she asked.

Alice thought about that, and shook her head, her fair curls doing a lively dance around her face. "No, I couldn't have a dog or a cat or anything, because we were always moving around. I had a turtle once."

My heart did its usual senseless start. Debbie had had a turtle but so had millions of other children.

"What was his name?" I asked, carefully casual.

Again she shook her head. "I don't remember."

I dared another question. "Is your hair really as fair as—as your mother's?"

"I don't know what color my hair is," Alice admitted frankly. "Ma likes it to look like hers, so she always puts something in the rinse for both of us."

"And is it curly, really?"

"Oh, we both have permanents. Ma says curly looks better."

I caught Letha Radburn's eye and she nodded at me, noting possible new confirmation. But what good it would do me I didn't know.

Joel asked his own question. "Do you remember your grandparents, Alice?"

Clearly she enjoyed being the center of attention, and I hoped she wouldn't be tempted toward an imaginative answer.

84

"I don't think so. Ma said her mom died when she was little. She didn't like her father much, and she won't talk about him."

"And Farley's parents?" Joel asked. "Did you know them?"

Alice's laughter had a scornful ring. "I don't think he ever had any parents. Maybe a rabbit pulled *him* out of a hat. When I was little I used to think he was my father. I used to call him Pa. But one time, when Peony was upset, she told me he wasn't my father, and I didn't have to call him that. I guess the only ancestor I've got is old Corinthea."

There might be another approach, I thought. "Do you remember anything about a wide river in a very hot country? Do you remember a jungle?"

"Where I was born?" She had denied such memories before, but now she picked up the challenge. "Maybe I can remember. Sometimes I think I can, though Ma says I was too little. There were bugs and mosquitoes and alligators in the water. Alligators ate my father."

"Not with lunch, please," Joel said dryly. "Anyway, I don't think it happened like that. You'd have been too little to remember the Amazon country—your mother is right."

Alice looked crestfallen. "I guess it's just that Ma talks about the river and the jungle sometimes—especially when she's mad at Farley. And sometimes she tells me stories of those days that she hated so much. So I feel like I remember."

"Do you think she hated your father?" Joel asked.

"My real father? Oh no! She loved him a lot. She said he was kind to her. She throws that up to Farley all the time."

Letha Radburn had been listening thoughtfully. "It's possible," she suggested, "to go back farther in our memories than we think we can. Would you like to try that sometime, Alice? We would do it together and see if anything interesting comes out."

"I don't think so," Alice said again, drawing back. "I was

85

sick a lot when I was little. And I cried all the time. And got spanked. I don't want to remember. It makes me afraid."

I felt sick myself—because the memory she feared might be of the awful time when she had been stolen and had lost me. Perhaps this was the way the truth would be found. Not with sudden illumination, but with bits and pieces that began to add up. Though whether the law would ever accept such vague memories as legal, I didn't know. How could they stand up against Peony's documents?

When we'd finished our first helpings and returned to the buffet table, Letha Radburn walked beside me, letting Alice go ahead with Joel.

"It might be possible to take her farther back than that time when she was unhappy. Back to when she was three and even before."

I felt doubtful. "What if she only remembers alligators?"

"Isn't it better to know? Besides, that won't happen. I am *sure.*"

I felt confused, torn either way. "Would you use hypnotism on a child?"

"It's not that. We'll talk another time."

While we were finishing our pastry and coffee, the headwaiter came to tell Joel that he was wanted on the telephone. He went off at once to take the call.

When he rejoined us, he looked grave. "Dillow tracked me here through Iris. I'm afraid we'll have to go back right away. There's been an accident and Corinthea had Dillow call me. We'll drop you off, Mother, and then I'll return with Alice and Jenny."

We went outside and Kirk brought the car to the front door. Joel gave him quiet instructions, and this time Alice was much too curious to sit in front. I took her onto my lap, almost afraid to hold her, aware of long thin legs dangling beneath her denim skirt. Debbie's legs had been short and plump—baby legs.

When we were on our way, Joel told us what he knew.

———

86

"Dillow says that Farley has had a bad fall down the back stairs."

"Oh, good!" Alice said.

Joel shook his head at her. "Dillow told me that Uncle Tim pushed Farley down those steep stairs, and he was knocked unconscious."

Alice's enthusiasm increased. "That's even better! Good for Uncle Tim!"

"I don't think we should wish for other people to be injured, even when we don't like them," Letha Radburn said quietly.

If Alice was in awe of anyone, it might be of Joel's mother, who must seem rather magical to her young eyes. Nevertheless, she protested.

"What if that's the way I feel inside? Why do I have to pretend?"

Joel laughed. "You're right, Alice. Your way is more honest. But in order to be what is called civilized we sometimes try to see other people's viewpoints. I expect even Farley Corwin has one."

Alice remained defiant. "I hope he goes to the hospital and stays there a long time. Do you think that will happen, Dr. Joel?"

"I'll have a look at him and see what's necessary," Joel told her.

"I wonder if I could help in this crisis?" Letha asked. "I want to thank Corinthea for telling the truth—finally—and reassure her besides. Since *you* caused the whole thing, Joel."

Again he shook his head. "Not now, Mother. Here you are home—and I'll leave you there now. I'll phone you as soon as I know something. You can talk to Corinthea another time."

Before she got out, Letha touched my hand. "We'll meet again soon. In the meantime—just *believe.*"

"Believe what?" Alice demanded, as Kirk opened the car door for Letha.

I let Alice slide into the place between Joel and me, and he managed to distract her from the question as we drove off.

Kirk took us back to Victoria by a quicker, less scenic route, and since distances in these near suburbs were never great, we were soon rolling up the drive to Radburn House.

"Why didn't your father live here, since his name was Radburn?" I asked Joel.

"It's Mrs. Arles's maiden name as well, of course, and the inheritance was more direct in her branch of the family. When she married, she and her husband came to live here, where she'd grown up. Though I guess Dad was always miffed because he wasn't in the direct line."

From low on the driveway, the house seemed to block the sky, its decorous gray paint giving it a certain dowager air of dignity, austerity.

Dillow was already hurrying down the steps, and Alice squirmed beside me. "I don't care about Farley, but I hope Uncle Tim won't be in trouble. Old Corinthea's always talking about sending him away."

Dillow stood waiting for us, looking displeased and very much on his dignity as we left the car.

---

# 6

"Mrs. Arles is waiting for you in the parlor," Dillow told Joel. "We've put Mr. Corwin in there for now."

Alice was the first one through the front door, and Joel followed. I paused at the top of the steps and looked down at Kirk McKaye, who stood beside the Mercedes, waiting for instruction.

Dillow said, "Leave the car out for now, Kirk. You may need to take Mr. Corwin and Dr. Radburn to the hospital."

Kirk nodded soberly, and I had the feeling that he had heard everything we'd said on the drive from Oak Bay. More than that, I had to talk with him. Everything had changed since this morning in the garden. He met my eyes for a moment and then turned away. His look said, "Later." So I would have to wait until four-thirty.

I went inside and stopped in the parlor doorway, feeling myself a somewhat unwelcome guest. Across the room, a large man sat on a sofa, and Alice had gone to stand beside him. He wore a green plaid shirt and jeans, and his raw-boned hands rested on his thighs, seeming somehow separate from the rest of him, as though these instruments of a vicious deed were possessed with a life over which he had little control. He looked older than his older sister, his thick hair gray and combed straight back without a part. Beneath a broad forehead his eyes seemed the only live thing in his face, and I sensed that his stillness was different from his sister's—more like a wary, waiting stillness. Tim, of course, would have difficulty understanding what was being said in a group. Speechreading, when everyone spoke quickly, would be nearly impossible. So he simply stared off into space and shut out the world of alien sound and spoken words. I'd sometimes seen my father do just that when there were too many people around. Alice understood and sat beside him, slipping her hand through the crook of his arm, openly partisan.

Mrs. Arles's usual restraint had crumpled a little, and a frown ruffled her forehead.

"Do you have a look at Mr. Corwin, Joel," she said at once. "He's been moaning, and it may be serious. This is a dreadful thing. My brother is becoming too unreliable to have around."

Mrs. Arles's wheelchair had been placed halfway down the room, away from Tim, with whom she was so clearly angry. Beyond her, on another sofa, Farley Corwin lay outstretched, his eyes closed and blood still seeping from a nasty forehead cut. Peony knelt on the carpet beside him, frightened and fluttery.

At once Joel pulled over a chair and began his examination. "Do you know exactly what happened?" he asked Mrs. Arles.

"I have no idea," she said indignantly. "There was a terrible crash on the back stairs, and Dillow went out to find Mr. Corwin lying on the second-floor landing. He'd struck his head on the sharp edge of the newel post and was unconscious. *She*"—a glance toward Peony—"said that Timothy threw her husband down the stairs."

Peony pulled herself together. "I saw what happened. Farley went up to visit Tim. I went with him, and Farley was only doing magic tricks to entertain the old man. Then that —that monster picked him up and dropped him down the stairs! Farley might have been killed. It's a good thing he used to do tumbling in a circus when he was a boy, so he knew how to fall. But then that post at the bottom knocked him out."

Alice jumped up and faced Mrs. Arles. "Sometimes Peony makes up stores! Let me see if *I* can find out."

"That's a good idea," Joel agreed quietly. "Go ahead, Alice."

Mrs. Arles smoothed the cloth of her gold robe over her knees. It was as if the gesture smoothed out her face at the same time, and she made no objection.

I left the doorway and came to where I could watch Tim more closely. Alice stood in front of him and moved her lips, forming her words carefully. Apparently Uncle Tim could speechread fairly well, and he watched her.

"Tell us what happened, Uncle Tim. Why did you get mad at old Farley?"

He began to speak and the sound was rather like that my mother made when she talked—not entirely like the voices of hearing people. The story came out hesitantly, though I expected that the pauses were due to his lonely existence as much as to deafness itself. Nevertheless, he painted a clear and, to me, convincing verbal picture.

Apparently Farley had been intent on teasing the old man, under the guise of entertaining him. He had gone into Tim's room and had started handling objects—making them "disappear."

Alice looked around at us. "Uncle Tim didn't understand they were only tricks, and it looked like some things Uncle Tim cares about were being damaged. Uncle Tim told Farley to stop, but he went right on. So after a while Uncle Tim got very mad and he picked him up and dropped him on the stairs."

"Outrageous!" Mrs. Arles said, and she wasn't criticizing Farley.

Alice whirled on her. "He didn't *throw* him. And it wasn't

91

all that far to the landing. If he hadn't bumped his head, he'd have been all right."

Joel spoke to Dillow, who was still hovering. "Will you call Kirk in to help me? We'll get Corwin out to the car, and Kirk can drive us to the hospital. Don't worry, Corinthea. It will be all right. We'll just get an X ray and make sure."

Mrs. Arles nodded and spoke to me. "Will you help me back to my room, please, Jenny?"

For once Crampton wasn't hovering and I wondered where she was.

Kirk came in quickly, and Farley was carried out to the car. Peony went with them, and Alice ran outside to watch. I wheeled Mrs. Arles's chair to the door, and when I looked back, Uncle Tim sat in the same place, not watching us now, shut again into his silent world. I wanted to reassure him in some way, but he didn't know me, and this wasn't the time, so I maneuvered the wheelchair back to the library. Crampton came running down from the second floor and she and Dillow followed me. I had the feeling that neither one of them trusted the other. Once Mrs. Arles had been placed where she could look into the garden, she dismissed both of them with a wave of her hand.

"Sit down, Jenny," she told me curtly. "What has happened is upsetting, but not important—except that I must do something soon about Timothy."

This was not the moment to argue with her, and I sat down and waited for her to tell me what she considered was important.

"I want to know everything that happened at Letha's house. So begin at the beginning."

I described the visit briefly, trying not to dramatize. Though, when I spoke of Letha Radburn, that was difficult to avoid.

"She believes that Alice is Debbie," I finished. "She seemed absolutely convinced, but I don't know how to judge what she does."

"You must never forget that Letha's an actress, and you were her audience. She doesn't often have an audience to play to these days. At least not one that's fresh and new. And I'm sure she convinces herself first of all. But you mustn't be taken in. Did Kirk deliver the package I sent?"

"Yes. He waited until we were leaving, just as you instructed him to do. Then he gave it to her with the note from you."

I paused, thinking of the surprise Joel had contributed to the situation.

"Then what? Go on!"

I described how Letha had opened the package and seemed pleased over the return of the jade carving, even though Corinthea had waited so long.

"That was when Dr. Radburn told his mother that your grandson had never stolen it in the first place. Joel gave it to him in some sort of boyish gesture. Afterward, he was afraid to admit to what he'd done because of the thrashing his father would have given him. Edward let him get away with it, and never told you the truth about what happened."

Mrs. Arles sat quietly, her hands clasped in her lap, her eyes closed. When she spoke there was a tremor in her voice.

"For all these years I've believed him a thief! I blamed him—I sent him away to his eventual death. I can't understand why Joel never told *me* the truth, when he knew his mother blamed Edward."

I wondered about the other missing objects Letha had mentioned that Mrs. Arles now seemed to be ignoring.

"Perhaps the incident never seemed as important to Dr. Radburn as it was to you. Especially since both boys were so young."

"It was important to Edward. He was angry and upset, but I thought he was sulking. I'd defended him to Letha, and he could have told me the truth. There's so much I wish I could undo."

93

I thought of Kirk and the letter from Edward that he held, but I still needed to know more about possible ramifications before I said anything. And I wouldn't talk now with Dillow and Crampton probably listening.

Mrs. Arles changed the subject abruptly. "Apparently Letha hasn't convinced you that Alice is your child?"

"I'd like to be convinced. There are small things that might add up, but they're not strong enough to count on—not yet."

Mrs. Arles's sigh seemed one of relief, and I knew how much this woman wanted Alice to be her great-grandchild.

"I do know she needs affection," I said. "Some interest in *her*. I don't think she has much of that in her life."

"Nonsense! Peony is obviously devoted to her. I can give the girl a great deal more than sentimentality, however. She can grow up to be a woman of importance in this city. A good education will change her and polish off those abrasive edges. She can make a fine marriage and have a satisfying life."

There was no point in discussing "sentiment" with Mrs. Arles. She had her own brand of deep feeling, but I suspected that the emotion she enjoyed most was anger. It flashed at times in her eyes, even though it never added a line to her face. She belonged to a generation that didn't take to examining or analyzing emotion, and I found myself wondering what her own growing-up years had been like with her parents. And, later, her life with her husband and son? I'd seen no family pictures around the house.

"In any case," she went on, "if you can find no real proof to give me in another day or so, I shall accept the Corwins' claim and buy them off."

I spoke quietly in the face of her high-handedness. "Will you send Mrs. Corwin away? She appears to be the only one to whom Alice may have an attachment."

That, I thought, was another cruel aspect—when a stolen child was so young. Forced separation broke old ties, and even the memory of love faded. No matter how real it had been, it would be replaced by a new relationship, and if her present ties to Peony ran deep—as they might, even though Alice might be critical of her—that could be wounding for her to accept. Another separation. Much as it hurt me to believe this, I knew the wound would go deeper when the child was older.

Mrs. Arles spoke curtly. "Of course I will send the woman away. Farley will take his dreadful wife off gladly, once he has my sizable allowance in his hands. I plan to spread it over the years in a trust, so it can't be squandered. There will be a clause that will prevent them from ever coming back to make further claims. If they cause any trouble in the future, the trust will be terminated and they'll get nothing more. My attorneys have worked it out to the last detail. I want the child completely in my hands. That's one reason why *you* must be eliminated."

Eliminated? A harsh word. Mrs. Arles had no idea what Alice was like, and she'd learned very little from past experience. She might even have another rebellious Edward on her hands, though I already suspected that Alice could be a lot stronger than Mrs. Arles's grandson had been.

She heard something and looked toward the door. Crampton had returned to her shadowy corner but Dillow was still in the doorway and took a few steps into the room. Strangely, Mrs. Arles seemed uncomfortable under his suddenly direct look. Then she roused herself and stared him down, recovering her own position as mistress.

*"You* know what I intend, Elbert," she said.

It was the only time I'd heard her use Dillow's first name, and it seemed to carry a special emphasis.

"Perhaps I should offer my resignation, Mrs. Arles." He had stiffened visibly.

"Don't be ridiculous! Just remember the rules I've set down. We'll discuss this later. You wanted something now?"

"The child wishes to come in," he said, and stepped aside.

---

Dillow had apparently kept the little girl from listening and she edged her way in guilelessly. Mrs. Arles regarded her with more interest than usual.

"Come in, Alice, and tell me about your visit to Mrs. Radburn's."

Alice approached with her usual defensive air, as though she expected contradiction to whatever she said. "Mrs. Radburn's spooky, but I liked her. I like her name too— Letha." Alice gave the name a whispery sound, her eyes wide.

"Never mind performing," Mrs. Arles said. "Why did you like her?"

"She talks to me like I'm real. And she gave me something nice." Alice turned to me. "Do you have it in your bag?"

I opened my handbag and found the raven's feather first. Tucked under it was the fold of tissue that held the lotus pin. Alice accepted it from me, opening the paper eagerly.

"Look! Isn't it beautiful? I never had anything so nice before. Mrs. Radburn said I should show it to you." Alice went over to the wheelchair and held out the delicately carved bit of coral.

Mrs. Arles took it from her in astonishment. "Why—this is something Lewis Radburn gave me years ago. He brought it from India especially for me. I thought I'd lost it. I always felt sad when it disappeared because I treasured this little pin. I have no idea how Letha came to have it, but it belongs to me. She knew that very well, Alice, when she told you to show it to me."

Alice turned into a thundercloud in an instant, and if Mrs. Arles hadn't held the lotus pin out of her reach, she would have snatched it back.

"Dr. Joel's mother gave it to me!" she cried. "She said it was something to remind me of the time I visited her house. If you steal it from me, I'll come into your room and take it back. It's mine!"

---

96

For a moment Mrs. Arles held the lotus pin out of Alice's reach. Then she gave in suddenly, surprisingly.

"Stop that, Alice, and stand still. Letha gave you what didn't belong to her, but I will give you what belongs to me. Here, I'll pin it on your collar."

Having won so unexpectedly, Alice stood still and allowed the coral lotus to be pinned to her denim jacket.

"Now go along, both of you," Mrs. Arles said. "I'm very tired. Crampton, please bring me my tea."

Crampton went off to the kitchen at once. Since I had nothing to do for another hour or so until I was to meet Kirk, I stayed with Alice.

"Do you suppose Uncle Tim is still downstairs?" I wondered.

We looked into the big parlor, but it was empty, and Alice started toward the back stairs. "He's probably gone up to his rooms. But he said it was all right to bring you to meet him."

On the third floor Alice led the way to the rear, where a door stood open. "Wait here," she directed, and went in ahead of me.

The small sitting room was plain in its furnishings, and I suspected that these pieces were mostly castoffs collected over the years from the house below. The well-stocked bookshelves, however, looked handsome and well crafted. And books had undoubtedly been the old man's life. My father and mother at least had each other. On my right a door opened into a bedroom, while straight ahead, with sunlight pouring in, was a room with a workbench strewn with pieces of wood, carving tools, and small bottles of color.

Uncle Tim stood at a rear window, with his back to us, gazing out at the sky. Alice went to him and waited for him to notice her. I liked her sensitivity. A touch, when you didn't know anyone was near, could be startling. He saw her and, when she gestured, looked at me.

"It's all right to come in," Alice told me.

I went to where I could face him directly and held out my

97

hand. "Hello, Mr. Radburn. I am Jenny Thorne." I spoke naturally, knowing that too great an *effort* at enunciation might put him off. I still had no idea how proficient he was at speechreading. There were so many misconceptions about this skill, and it was never the full answer to hearing problems. Names were always difficult, but Alice had put mine down on paper for him earlier.

"You can call him Uncle Tim," she told me. "He likes that best."

The old man took my hand in his big, calloused one, and said, "Welcome, Jenny Thorne," a bit shyly.

"May I look around?" I gestured to the room, since body language always helped, and some signs were universal. One thing the deaf person didn't have as a guide was the tone of voice. The hearing relied on this without even thinking about it. So body movements had to substitute for expressive sound.

He understood and nodded.

The workroom was larger than the other rooms, and his life was here, even more than in the books. Shelves along one wall held rows of carvings—all of them miniature totem poles, a few inches tall, and colorfully painted. He didn't seem to have carved anything else—just totem poles. I went to look more closely.

"May I touch?" I asked.

Alice had her own sign language, and she interpreted, in case he didn't understand, raising her eyebrows in a question and touching one of the carvings. The old man inclined his head and smiled at me uncertainly. He didn't in the least resemble the stolid man who had vented sudden anger on Farley Corwin.

I could understand what a godsend Alice must have been to Uncle Tim. His sister probably didn't bother to form words clearly when she spoke to him, and she often moved her hands meaninglessly. For Tim, Alice was a little *accepting* human being who cared about understanding what he was thinking and feeling. And that, perhaps, was something she had been given by me and my parents by the time she was three! Tim's "shell" had been conditioned by those around him, and by his fear of that "bad place" where he had been held for a time. Who knew how strong that fear might be, so that he'd never dared to break out for himself?

I smiled back and picked up one of the little figures. I had often seen photographs of big totem poles of the Northwest, and I knew something about carving—since it was one of my father's hobbies, when he wasn't working in gardens. Tim's workmanship was beautiful, and far more skilled than my father's. The figures, with their bright paint and strange human, bird, and animal faces, were small works of art. Each carving was subtly different from the others in various small ways.

"He doesn't copy from the big poles," Alice explained. "He doesn't just take other people's ideas—he likes to make up his own. The Indians who carve the real totem poles in Thunderbird Park taught Uncle Tim how. They like what he does and they like *him*. They're his friends. It doesn't matter to them if he can't hear, or if he doesn't talk like other people. Sometimes I go with him when he visits the park."

"Good for you!" I told her. I wanted to compliment Tim on his artistry, but he had walked over to the window and had his back to us. I suspected that he still had the matter of Farley Corwin to think about. "Does Tim have other friends who come to see him—friends he can visit?" I asked Alice.

"*She* won't let him have friends. Not old Corinthea! Though she doesn't mind about the Indians. I suppose she thinks they don't count, and they don't want to come here."

Familiar indignation rose in me again. I knew what the attitudes of the hearing could be. My father had suffered over this when he was young. And I had seen deaf children come into my classes frightened and withdrawn, because those near them were ashamed of their deafness and embarrassed by it. Some parents hated sign language because it

99

made a child "different"—conspicuous in the "wrong" way. Only recently a mother had told me that she just wanted her daughter to "lipread," so she would be like everybody else. But for a child who was born deaf, this was a difficult skill to acquire, and such children needed to be introduced to every possible way in which they could communicate.

"That's a raven at the top of that totem you're holding," Alice said. "Uncle Tim's told me stories about ravens." She nudged him and tapped the totem, so he would know what we were talking about.

"I saw a raven this morning," I told him. I turned the small totem so I could admire the careful patterning. "Mrs. Radburn gave me a feather today. Joel's mother." I took it from my bag and held it out to Tim. "Tell me about ravens," I said.

He took the big feather, admiring its natural perfection. Then he motioned me into a chair and seated himself on a high stool. Alice, knowing a story was coming, sat on the floor, cross-legged, ready to listen. She was far happier up here in Tim's workroom than I'd seen her anywhere else.

Just as I had expected, there was nothing wrong with Tim's speech, since he had been able to hear as a child and had learned to talk and read and write like everyone else. There was nothing wrong with his intelligence either.

"Once a long time ago—so the Indians say," he began, "there were some fishermen who were driving the birds away, so they couldn't take the fish the men thought belonged to them. The raven told the fishermen that he would steal the moon if they didn't stop what they were doing to the birds. The fishermen just laughed at him. So the raven took the moon in his beak and flew away with it. The men, who fished by moonlight, couldn't catch any more fish, and they had to make a pact with the raven to bring back the moon. They even promised to put him on their totem poles if he brought the moon back, and after that, whenever the men saw a raven they would throw it a fish. And they put ravens on their totem poles in a place of honor."

"That's a wonderful story," I told the old man, and he looked pleased as he gave back the feather.

As I held it, studying it once more, the same hint of memory touched me that I'd felt when I first took the feather from Letha, though the thought was still elusive.

"Uncle Tim tells good stories!" Alice's face had lighted and the sulky, resentful child was gone. This was the way Debbie would have been. I *knew* that. She'd have had an instinct for dealing with the deaf. I longed to touch her, but as Joel Radburn had pointed out, she already had a mother.

"Can we show Uncle Tim some deaf signs?" Alice asked me.

He was watching attentively now, and I made the sign for greeting, and spelled out T-I-M on my fingers. Alice imitated me and then handed me a pad and pencil, so I could write down for Tim what I'd done.

Hesitantly, Tim tried the sign himself, and I spelled "Alice" for him as well.

"Did you talk to the old—to Corinthea—about sending Tim to school to learn things that would help him?" she asked. "Maybe I could go too."

"There hasn't been a good time for that," I told her.

Alice scowled. "She's mad at him now, and she won't ever listen. She's a stupid old lady."

"I don't think she's stupid. She just doesn't understand."

"But he's her brother—she ought to understand."

I had no answer for that. Sometimes families were the worst obstacles of all when they tried to pretend that deafness didn't exist. There could be a strange sort of denial growing out of mistaken pride. I suspected that Mrs. Arles would like to pretend that her brother didn't exist.

Alice went on. "Once Uncle Tim told me there was a big fight between his sister and my father, before he went away. Afterward, she sent Uncle Tim off to a place where they

101

keep people who are mixed up in their heads. Edward—I guess he's my father—never came back because he was so mad at his grandmother. Though he went to see Uncle Tim first and told him he was leaving."

"But Mrs. Arles did take her brother back."

"I think it was only because the doctors said there wasn't anything wrong with his head. Dr. Joel told me some of this when I asked him. Not being able to hear doesn't make him crazy. But he thinks his sister would still like to be rid of him, so he has to be careful. Today he forgot about that with old Farley, and I'm glad."

Tim couldn't follow what we were saying now, but there were things I wanted to know, and the picture of Corinthea Arles that emerged seem increasingly unappealing.

I set the small totem back in its place on the shelf and put the feather away. Then I turned to Tim. "Do you sell these?"

He shook his head and Alice answered.

"He doesn't want to compete with the Indians, who need the money. His friends have tourist totems that are very fine —bigger than these. Maybe a foot or two high. They only work on the real big totem poles when they have a special order for a museum or a park or something. Besides, he says his sister wouldn't let him sell them anyway."

"I think they're beautiful," I said. "I'd like to own one myself. I'll tell him that in sign language."

Ameslan signs can be descriptive. I touched the totem I'd put back, and signed with my hand and my facial expression. Uncle Tim smiled his understanding and pleasure, and I showed him how to make the sign for "beautiful"—almost but not quite touching my chin and my forehead and circling my face. This is a gesture that seems to uncover the face—as though a veil were gently pulled away.

He made the same sign eagerly, pointing to me. Uncle Tim would be a quick learner if he ever got a chance. But unless there were those around who understood, it would do him little good.

———

Alice imitated my movements, picking up the signs quickly, so that I wondered if her hands remembered. As he watched her, the old man's attention was caught by the lotus pin on her collar. He touched it and asked her where it came from.

She explained with words, and when he didn't seem satisfied, she wrote on his pad, telling him that Letha Radburn had given her the pin, and that Mrs. Arles had wanted to take it from her—but then had given it back.

This seemed to upset Tim. Quite suddenly, he pushed Alice toward the door, shaking his head as if something worried him—perhaps even frightened him. His excitement and concern were troubling, but he clearly didn't want to explain.

All he wanted now was for us to go, but before we left I stopped in front of him and made the sign for "thank you," putting my fingers to smiling lips, and then extending the hand toward him, palm up. He didn't need words to know what I meant. For a moment he stared at me as though he were confused—perhaps torn between wanting me to leave and wanting to respond.

"It's all right," I said, and made the sign. He was staring at the pin again, and Alice pulled me away.

As we left, Tim slammed the door behind us—probably intentional, since he would remember such a sound.

"Why was he so upset?" I asked Alice as we started downstairs.

"I don't know. Maybe he remembers something about the pin. I'll find out sometime when he's not so excited."

I thanked her for taking me to see Tim, but she was no longer paying attention. As we reached the foot of the stairs, she seemed to be listening for something.

"What is it?" I asked.

She remembered in relief. "Farley's gone! That makes everything better."

"Does he frighten you?"

Her eyes widened and for just a moment she let her guard down. "Sometimes he does." Then she ran off along the hall, as though she'd let me see too much.

In that moment I hated Farley Corwin more than I'd ever hated anyone. I didn't want to be what Joel called "civilized."

Now, however, it was time to go out to the garden to find Kirk, and as I turned down the hall toward the back door, Dillow came from Mrs. Arles's room.

"If you please, Mrs. Thorne, Mrs. Arles would like you to join her for supper this evening. At six o'clock."

"I'll be there," I told him. "Have you heard anything from the hospital?"

"Kirk brought Mr. Corwin back, Mrs. Thorne. He seems to be all right."

Every inch of him seemed to show disapproval of Farley Corwin.

I thanked him and went out the back door on my way to the lower garden. This time I would not let Kirk McKaye off so easily. Whatever might connect Edward to Alice—or not connect her—was important to me now.

# 7

No one seemed to be around when I left the house and hurried down the curving stone steps. It felt good to escape the oppressive atmosphere of oak and stained glass.

As I neared the lower level I heard voices and slowed my approach. First Kirk, speaking softly, then Peony Corwin answering, her tones rising shrilly. I stood still, listening.

"You can't prove anything!" Peony cried. "I don't believe what you say! It's all lies!"

This might be the moment to confront her, while she was already off guard, and I stepped out upon the cedar rounds, moving into sight of the two on the bench. Kirk looked around first, his eyes dark with an anger that wasn't directed at me. My presence seemed to alarm Peony all the more. She jumped to her feet and rushed off frantically, giving me a wide berth, as though I might try to stop her.

"Bad timing," Kirk said when she was out of sight.

"This is when I was supposed to come," I told him. "And, by the way you look, maybe it was good timing. Why are you so angry with *her?*"

He stood up, making an effort to relax. "I suppose it's foolish to let her get under my skin. She's a born victim—too easily manipulated. Though sometimes victims can be pushed too far."

"Does she know that you were Edward's friend?"

"She knows," he said shortly. "That's why she's scared. She knows I don't mean Corwin any good."

He stretched long arms over his head, as I'd seen him do before. His hands seemed to welcome sunlight through the very palms—as though it might wash out the darkness and anger I had sensed in him. When he let his arms drop, some of that tension was released, and I relaxed a little too.

"Let's get away where we can talk," he said. "There are too many listening spots around here. You're full of questions —which I probably won't answer—but at least you can try." He started toward the far end of the garden and I followed, as he took for granted that I would.

The rear gate opened on a side street, where Kirk's Volkswagen was parked. I got in beside him and he turned the car downhill toward the center of Victoria. In contrast to Joel Radburn, who always seemed natural and at ease, this man was a volcano, with fires far from banked. Somehow he repelled and attracted me at the same time. "Truth" and "confidence" were not words I'd use about Kirk McKaye, and it was the attraction that worried me most.

The act of driving seemed to quiet him a little, and he didn't speak again until he found a place to park at curbside and we got out.

"Let's walk for a while," he said. "That was pretty bad back there. I didn't mean to scare her and put them on guard."

"Because of the letter from Edward?"

We were near the waterfront, and he motioned toward a steep flight of steps. "Let's go down to the lower level."

We descended to a wide cement walk which ran below the causeway that carried traffic across this inner end of the harbor. On our right, small boats were clustered, with white hulls and masts bobbing gently, both Canadian and American flags in evidence. Across the right angle of the harbor a big white ferry had been docked, waiting for passengers to Seattle or Port Angeles.

From down here the road and noisy traffic on the upper causeway were both invisible. Ahead, above the embankment, rose the great brown edifice of the Empress Hotel, dwarfing everything else nearby, the red and white Maple Leaf flying from its standard. Still farther ahead, across the right angle of water, stretched the Parliament Buildings with their green domes, and again a tall pole that flew the Canadian flag. On top of the main copper-covered dome stood a gilded statue of Captain Vancouver. Just above the wide walk we followed, the words WELCOME TO VICTORIA had been planted in yellow flowers against a steep bank of velvety grass. Gulls swooped and soared overhead, their cries raucous as they flew inland among the buildings.

Since only a few strollers followed this lower level at the moment, I had little sense of being in the heart of a city. Low, rounded lamps a foot or two high, looking like blue mushrooms, rimmed the edge of the water, connected by chains painted the same cadet blue. At intervals tall blue lampposts topped with huge white globes displayed flower baskets hung from their horizontal arms. Those flower-basket lampposts were a special Victoria signature.

"Let's sit down," Kirk said, and led the way to a blue bench against the cement wall of the causeway. This special blue was seen everywhere, and it added to my pleasure in the scene.

By this time Kirk's anger had drained away, though it had left a somber residue.

"You want to know about Edward's letter," he said. "But why should you care, if you're going home in a few days? It has nothing to do with you."

I told him why. "After you left Alice and me in the garden this morning, something strange happened. She's a solemn child and she doesn't laugh very often. But what you said about calling Mrs. Arles Corinthea to her face struck her as funny. And when she smiled, I saw Debbie. This is what Mrs. Arles caught too in the picture that brought me here. She sensed the likeness so strongly that she had to get in touch with me. And now I've seen it too. The resemblance I saw in just that instant was so clear—between Alice at ten and Debbie when she was three—that for a few moments I was *sure.*"

"And you aren't now?"

"I don't know. It was like a lightning flash—gone in seconds. I haven't found anything that strong again, and yet there are touches that remind me of Debbie. Though nothing that gives me the proof Mrs. Arles must have. Just the same, I'm not ready to give up and go away. Not yet."

"What happened when Dr. Radburn took you in to see his mother?"

"Alice calls Mrs. Radburn spooky, and perhaps she is a little. She told me immediately that Alice *is* my daughter. But that's hardly proof, either, and it doesn't impress Mrs. Arles."

"If this should be true, then the Corwins . . . ?"

"Kidnapped my little girl. That's why I want to know more about your letter from Edward Arles. He might have said something—anything that could help me to decide, one way or the other."

"His letter was short and it said very little. It was the enclosure of a journal he kept that matters."

"A journal? Then there must be answers!"

"Not clear enough answers—no. Not about what you want to know."

"Will you let me see it? Did he write about Farley?"

"I don't want to show it to anyone yet, and I don't think it would really help you. But yes—he wrote about Farley Corwin."

"Why can't you tell me?"

Kirk stared fixedly at the water, at the bobbing masts of small boats. "I don't think you'd want to know. If you are to stay in the house for now, it's better if you don't know too much. It might even be safer."

I couldn't accept that. "Don't treat me like a child who has to be protected. I've been on my own for years."

For the first time since I'd come out with him, he looked straight at me—seeing *me*. The dark blue of his eyes—that ocean color—seemed clear and deep. As though I could look down and down, far into this man—if I wanted to. I didn't dare, and I looked quickly away. I couldn't remember when a man had made me so aware of him—not for a very long time. I'd been too busy trying to shut out grief to let life touch me. But why this man, now—what was it about him that had this unwelcome effect?

"I'm sorry," he said quietly. "I'm sure you left childhood behind long ago. Alice doesn't know you lost your daughter, but she knows that both your parents are deaf—she heard that from you, and told me. So I suspect that you took on responsibility pretty young. I don't think you'd fall apart over what Edward has written."

"That's right—I don't fall apart. And I need to know all I can about these Corwins."

"All right. Edward was afraid that some accident was going to happen to him. Some *planned* accident that might cost him his life. He hinted that Farley Corwin might be behind anything that happened."

"You're talking about *murder?*"

"Edward didn't trust Farley—or Peony either, even though he was married to her. I suspect she's too spineless to be really vicious, unless, as I say, she's pushed too far."

"Did you tell her what was in the journal? Is that why she was upset and frightened just now?"

He didn't answer, and I knew he had told me as much as he meant to.

"Have you come here to prove something against Farley?" I asked.

"I don't think much proof can surface now. But there's another road I can follow."

"The road you've started down by scaring Peony? Won't

she go right to Farley with whatever you said to her—and put him on guard?"

His smile had a wry twist. "You know something—I don't believe she will. But she'll do a little shivering on her own for a while."

"What if she persuades him to leave? Then they'll take Alice with them, and I'll never know."

"Whether Alice is Peony and Edward's daughter or not, there's too much at stake for them to run away easily. Corwin has gambled on this, and he'll risk it that there is nothing I can prove. If I go to Mrs. Arles she'll be all the more eager to take Alice herself. But I want more certainty than that, and I'm not ready yet to move."

"What if they really are kidnappers?"

"Then they might just leave her and run. That is, if they find out who you are and think *you* have something on them. Which, in a way, would give you your proof."

I didn't like any of this. What I wanted—the impossible thing I wanted—was an admission, even a confession, from Peony Corwin. That would be the only real proof, and if it came at all, it would be from her—not Farley.

"Listen to me, Jenny—" He spoke more gently, and the lower vibrancy in his voice did something strange to me, as though he'd touched me, quieting and soothing my taut nerves. Even though what he said carried no reassurance. "I don't think you should count on anything as far as Alice is concerned. Don't become too attached to her just because you want this so much. I'm afraid that I don't really believe Alice is your child."

I didn't want him to be sorry for me. I didn't want this kindness from him. "Do *you* want her to be Edward's child?"

There seemed a new sadness in him. "What I want isn't important to you. We're on different roads."

"There's more in the journal, isn't there? Something that's convinced you?"

He didn't answer but put a hand on my arm, nodding toward the walk along the water. I saw that two men were strolling below our bench. One was Timothy Radburn, his mane of gray hair wildly on end in the wind, and his shoulders slightly bent, as though he tried to bring himself down to ordinary size. The man who walked beside him was Joel Radburn.

"They'd better not see us together," Kirk said. "I'm still the chauffeur, and I need more time before they fire me. Shall I take you home now, Jenny?"

I wanted to go with him, and I didn't. There was an undercurrent of excitement that seemed to cling to Kirk McKaye —something that might surface to my peril. Something I wasn't ready for.

"I think I'll join them," I decided. "Dr. Radburn will take me back to the house."

Kirk accepted this easily. "Okay. I'll see you later," he said; and went off toward where we'd left his car. I stared after him for a moment, thinking what a strange, secretive man he was. A man who was possibly driven by thoughts of revenge because of what had happened to his friend? Yet there seemed some deeper motivation that I didn't understand. Too many years had gone by since Edward's death— so what had he written in his journal that had brought anger against Farley Corwin to the surface in his friend?

I shook off my disturbing thoughts and hurried after the two men. Joel heard me coming and looked around.

"Hello, Jenny. Uncle Tim, this is Jenny Thorne. You've seen her at the house."

Tim watched his lips and then glanced at me, not welcoming my presence. I made the sign for greeting, but he didn't respond. That lotus pin really had upset him, and I wished I knew why.

"What are you doing here?" Joel asked.

"I thought I'd explore."

"A good idea. We're going over to Thunderbird Park, if

you'd like to come with us. When I went to see Uncle Tim after we brought Corwin home and I'd reported to Corinthea, he seemed upset. So I offered to take him for a drive. My car's still at home and I took the Mercedes."

"How is Mr. Corwin?"

"Concussion. Nothing serious, I think, though he'll carry a few bruises until he heals. His temper's damaged and I don't trust him not to be nasty again to Uncle Tim. I wish Corinthea would get rid of those two. What about the little girl, Jenny? Are you any closer to a decision?"

I'd held back from telling either Joel or his mother what had happened in the garden, since I hadn't wanted to influence Letha's "impression" one way or the other. But now I related the experience again.

"Trust your instincts," Joel said. "That's what my mother always advises. Go deep inside yourself and see what you can find."

I only wished I knew how to do that.

We had come to a flight of steps that led to the street above, and as we started up toward the statue of Captain Cook that overlooked the area, gulls swooped overhead, and I was glad I could hear their squawking, aware that Tim couldn't. I remembered how difficult it had been for me as a little girl to realize that there were all sorts of wonderful sounds my parents couldn't hear. Not the sound of rain, or even thunder; not someone singing a catchy tune; not a child who cried—me. It had never done me much good to scream and complain, unless my tantrums were visible. Once when I was older I'd put plugs in my ears to help me understand what it was like to be deaf. But I could always hear around the plugs, so the experiment didn't work.

I wanted to include Tim in this conversation—not that it would be easy for him to speechread as we walked—but something in his expression indicated that he was preoccupied with whatever was troubling him.

I picked up Joel's last words.

———

112

"I don't know how to trust my instincts. I don't know what my instincts are. They get all mixed up with what I want. Besides, even if I were sure, how could I claim Alice? There's no way to take her out of Peony's possession."

"Only if Corinthea should decide to buy off the Corwins. But of course in that case Corinthea herself would claim Alice as her great-granddaughter, and that would be the end of it for you."

On the street level we stopped to watch the One-man Band playing near the top of the steps. He was a bearded, affable fellow—one of Victoria's engaging landmarks—and at the moment he had paused to talk to the group gathered around him. A canopy hung with tuneful bells shielded him from the sun, and horns, tambourines, and a mouth organ fixed handily at a level where he could play it, all kept him busy. His wheeled cart used every inch of interior space, and in a moment the music started up again. He proved to be a skilled performer. "The World Is Waiting for the Sunrise"— an old tune composed by a Canadian—filled the air.

But Tim had seen all this before, and he couldn't hear it anyway, so he wanted to go on. As we paused to cross through busy traffic, Joel asked me a question.

"How do you really feel about Alice?"

"I'm drawn to her," I admitted, "and it upsets me to see how she's been treated. But I would feel that way about any child in her circumstances. Do *you* think she's Mrs. Arles's great-granddaughter?"

"I don't know. There are holes in the Corwins' story, and I'm sure they're capable of an elaborate hoax. That's the way Farley's mind seems to work, and Peony follows him docilely, though with some resentment, I think. I hate to see Corinthea go through with this, but she's a strong-minded lady. She wants the child to be her own blood, and it's to her credit that she even gave you a chance."

"I know. But what am *I* to do?"

"You might try my mother's way." He took my arm and

Tim's as we crossed with the light. "It might give you a new lead of some kind. Do you want me to set something up?"

"If you like. What can I lose?" I began to look around, since this was the first time I'd seen downtown Victoria by daylight. "Where did you say we're going?"

"Thunderbird Park. It's right over there, behind the Provincial Museum. Tim likes to come here whenever he can."

The museum was large, modern, and impressive, decorated with vertical white lines and a diamond design. Beside it, Thunderbird Park seemed tiny—only a small square of grass set down in the midst of the busy city. Its tall totem poles and individual carved figures were set about at random. On some poles the paint was still bright and colorful, while others had weathered to the gray-brown of cedar.

As we reached the park, Joel explained that most of these totem poles were replicas of the old original poles that were beginning to rot away.

"The Provincial Museum saved the old poles to be stored indoors safely, and brought in a chief carver for the program to be instituted. Mungo Martin was a Kwakiutl chief, and he knew the old ways of Indian life."

Straight ahead, as we approached, with the museum dwarfing it, stood a low house whose roof sloped gently to either side from a center ridgepole. All across the white front a huge face had been painted. Animal or human—I wasn't sure which. A wide green panel held two eyes, very black, with white around them. Dark red marked the nostrils and outlined a wide mouth stretching the width of the building and displaying two rows of big white teeth in a grin that seemed ferocious. Animal, surely.

Tim muttered something I couldn't catch, and when I looked at him questioningly, he repeated the word: "Wa'waditla."

Joel explained. "If Tim wasn't upset today, I'm sure he would tell you all about Wa'waditla. I've learned most of what I know about Indian mythology from him. Mungo Mar-

114

tin built this house and carved some of the poles. Wa'waditla was the name he gave the house, and it means, 'He orders them to come inside.' That's a phrase that speaks of power and command. Indian community houses were built like this."

Set in front of the house was a very tall totem pole and I looked up at the bird figure that topped it with spreading, intricately carved wings. Tim spoke again, giving the figure a name: "Tsoona."

"Tsoona was the thunderbird who became a man," Joel said. "It's the crest of that particular Indian family. Mungo Martin celebrated four tribes on this pole by using the heraldic symbol for each one. There at the bottom is the wild giantess holding her child."

The giantess wore a fierce expression, her lips rounded as though she blew out a strong gale. Hands clasped the child, who resembled her on a smaller scale, though the child looked fearful, rather than fierce. Between the thunderbird at the top and the child at the bottom were other strangely carved faces. Strange, at least, to me. All the poles faced toward the street, watching the city.

"Why is it called a thunderbird?" I asked.

"Because when it flies its wings make the sound of thunder. It's a mythical figure that appears often in Indian tales." Joel glanced at me curiously. "What do you feel about these faces?"

I considered that. "Only that they're weird, unfamiliar. They make me a little uneasy because I don't understand what they mean. I don't think I'd want to be here with them at night in the dark. There's a sort of power . . . as though they belong to ancient ways and times. Times before the white man ever came. Perhaps more magical times than ours."

Joel was watching me with new interest. "I'm glad you can feel that, Jenny. There are some who say the totems whisper to each other. They have tales to tell, and they know how puny we are beside them. It's not that those days were so magical but that the magic has gone underground and out of ordinary, skeptical view."

"Or perhaps it's just hidden itself in figures like this," I said. "If I stood here alone and stared into those eyes long enough, perhaps something strange would flow out and touch me."

"Would you want that?"

"I don't know. I've never had a feeling quite like this before. Perhaps it started the moment I got off the plane on this island. The feeling of something mysterious in the air."

Joel smiled. His nature was at the opposite extreme from Kirk's, I thought—far more understanding and sympathetic. Perhaps because he wasn't lost in some dark dream of vengeance, as Kirk might be.

"My mother would approve of your feeling this way, Jenny," Joel said. "She'd say you were getting in touch."

"With what? Something inside me?"

"Yes, and perhaps something outside—who knows?"

Tim had wandered away, at home in this little park with its sparse forest of totem poles.

"Let's go over to the workshop," Joel said.

We followed the old man to the open workroom, where passersby could look in and watch the carving in progress. At the moment no one was there, but a huge cedar trunk lay full length on the floor of the shed. With its bark stripped away and forms beginning to take rough shape in the wood, it had begun to emerge as a totem pole. Divisions had been cut, and in one section a beaked nose showed beneath beetling brows and round eyes. Tim studied the carving on the log with interest and understanding.

"Eleanor Neal was one of the great Indian carvers," Joel said. "Sometimes she'd autograph cedar pole chips for those who came to watch her work. Charlie James, Eleanor Neal, and Mungo Martin were the great recent carvers. They're gone now, but their descendants continue to keep the old art alive. Poles made here in Victoria stand all over British Columbia, and in museums around the world as well."

The big shed showed evidence of daily work, with benches and tools and a floor that was accustomed to wood chips and sawdust. Tim touched Joel on the arm.

"Come over here," he said, and led the way to a bench in the park. We sat down with the traffic of the city flowing past as time neared the rush hour. The sidewalks were already thronged with office workers pouring out of their buildings.

Tim paid attention to none of this, and he began to talk to Joel earnestly. "Your mother gave Alice a pin your father brought from India. Gold and coral—like a lotus flower. Where did your mother get the pin?"

Joel shook his head, and Tim went on. "You were at school when Edward went away. There was a big fight with my sister, and she told him to go. So I gave him money. Corinthea doesn't know. Edward said never to tell her because she would send me back to that place where I went for a while. That bad place."

"*You* gave him the money?" Joel repeated in surprise, and Tim explained further.

"I told Edward I had enough money to spare. But I got it by taking some of those things in the house and pawning them. One of my Indian friends helped me. All those valuable things belong to me too, though Corinthea never admits that. Our parents left everything to both of us equally— but there was nothing I could claim, if I wanted to stay here. Though it's my home too. The only thing I really stole to get money for Edward was the lotus pin. I knew my sister cared about the pin, and I wanted to hurt her. Now it's come back. Why?"

Again Joel shook his head and spoke carefully so the old man could read his lips. "I don't know. I will ask my mother."

Tim looked gloomy and Joel patted his arm. "It's all right. You had to help Edward. I understand."

117

I touched Tim so he would turn to me. Then I made the sign for "all right" with the side of one hand sliding out across the palm of the other in a gesture of reassurance. This time he responded by smiling and repeating the sign toward me.

"Poor old Edward," Joel said. "He got blamed for everything. I've heard the story of how he stole all those things from the house and pawned them, so he could have money to get away. Of course he probably didn't care by that time if he was blamed, and he must have wanted first of all to protect Uncle Tim. Of course this was another black mark against him with his grandmother. Yet if Tim tried to clear Edward's name now, she would only transfer her anger to him. I don't think she's capable of forgiveness."

"Sometimes I almost feel sorry for her," I said. "She has so much, but she's cut herself off. She's so unlike your mother."

"You're right, Jenny. I'm glad my father saw that, or I wouldn't be here now. Well, we'd better start back—it's getting late."

I looked at my watch, remembering that I was supposed to have supper with Mrs. Arles tonight. As we left the park and walked toward the Inner Harbor, I could see the tall, graceful Carillon Tower down the street, standing against the sky. Its bells were played only for special occasions, Joel told me.

Sunset colors of gold and magenta and pale green stained the water and tinted the buildings of Esquimalt on the peninsula that was part of suburban Victoria.

As we drove toward Radburn House, Joel pointed out the great structure of Craigdarroch Castle high on a hill overlooking the city. Robert Dunsmuir, who came to Vancouver Island from Scotland in the mid-1800s, had built the enormous house, expecting to live there. He had died too soon, but his wife had moved into it and raised their family in its many rooms. It was now a museum, Joel told me, and one of the places he would take me to see before I left Victoria.

I still wasn't ready for sightseeing, though I was glad to have had this interval away from Radburn House, and especially glad that I hadn't gone back with Kirk.

In a sense, he affected me in almost the same way as the totem poles—so that I felt uneasy in the presence of something secretive and much too mysterious. Kirk's meeting with Peony seemed especially disturbing, and my time with him had illumined very little.

# 8

When we reached the house, Kirk was summoned to drive Joel home, and Tim scooted upstairs as though he didn't want to be left alone with me.

Dillow met me at the door and he seemed able to exude disapproval without changing his expression or his manner.

"Good evening, madam," he greeted me. "I am sorry, but Mrs. Arles expected you by six o'clock. It's twenty minutes after, and she prefers to dine early at present. So she has asked me to explain that she has invited Mrs. Corwin to join her this evening, instead. Perhaps you would like your meal in the dining room, Mrs. Thorne?"

Mrs. Arles's action seemed as rude as my being late. I wondered if it meant that she had made up her mind about Alice. In which case, she would more likely have business with Farley, so her choice of a supper guest seemed strange.

"Of course," I agreed. "I'll go upstairs for a moment and be down right away."

Dillow hovered watchfully, and I wondered about the real man behind the skilled butler who managed this house. Thanks to Kirk, I knew a secret about him that might outrage his employer if she knew. There could be depths in Elbert Dillow that might be interesting to probe, since I had already seen him stand up to Corinthea Arles.

On the stairs, I paused with my hand on the banister,

looking down at him. "Dillow, were you here when Edward Arles was growing up?"

For once, his bright dark eyes met mine. "Yes, madam. I came here when Edward Arles was a small boy."

"Then you were here when he left?"

"Yes, madam." He began to edge away from me down the hall. And I asked another question quickly.

"Do *you* think Alice is Peony Corwin's child?"

Only his blink showed that I'd surprised him, and he spoke quietly. "I believe she is, Mrs. Thorne," he said, and hurried away.

I went upstairs feeling depressed. Dillow could be reflecting Mrs. Arles's decision to accept Alice. So what was left for me here? Except for the child herself, my growing questions about her, and my feeling toward her that had warmed during the day. Yet I had nothing to offer, no claim I could make that would stand up legally.

As I started along the upper hall, Crampton startled me by darting out of the same room I'd seen her come from once before. By this time I knew it was the Corwins' room. We stared at each other for a moment, and then she scuttled away on small feet that didn't match her body. When I entered my room, Alice was once more waiting for me. A faint scent of violet perfume drifted in Crampton's wake, and Alice sniffed.

"She steals old Corinthea's perfume," Alice said.

This time she'd left the door open and wasn't hiding. She looked small and perky sitting in a big chair and she held one of Uncle Tim's small totem pole carvings in her hand.

"You were gone a long time," she accused.

"I didn't know you'd miss me. I went exploring downtown, and I met Dr. Joel and Uncle Tim, and they showed me Thunderbird Park."

"I wish I'd come with you, but I was watching my mother. Sometimes I do that, though she doesn't know. She's been acting funny all day. I think Farley's scaring her again. He's pretty mad at Uncle Tim. Look—" She brought the small carving to me. "Uncle Tim sent you this. He can't sell them but sometimes he gives one to somebody he likes. I have a totem he made specially for me. He wants to learn more of those signs you know. We can both do the ones you showed us today. He picked this out for you."

The carving was about six inches high and beautifully executed. Each human and animal face had its own individuality, and, as Alice had explained, the old man didn't copy from the art of the Indians. A raven stood at the top, but it was less stylized than those I'd seen in Thunderbird Park. Down the pole beneath the raven were children's faces, one of them a likeness of Alice.

"He's done *you!*" I cried. "I like this very much. Tomorrow I'll go upstairs and thank him."

Alice was pleased that I'd recognized the tiny face, and she smiled—that same smile that caught at my memory so poignantly.

"He made that a few weeks ago, and it's a family pole. My father's face is there too, and so is my mother's. But he didn't put in his sister, and he never does his own face. Of course, he exaggerates a little. He says it's like doing a caricature."

I examined the carvings more carefully and recognized a younger, prettier Peony. The face that was Edward's was young too, and thinly handsome, rather a delicate face— very boyish. This must be the way Tim remembered him.

"How could he know how Peony looked when she was younger?" I asked.

"I don't know. Anyway, I've got to go now. Uncle Tim said I could eat upstairs with him tonight. He has a little kitchen and he's a very good cook."

"Thank you for bringing this to me, Alice. It's been an exciting day, hasn't it?"

She fingered the coral pin on her collar. "Yes! I like exciting days. Mostly nothing happens around here."

She ran off and I set the small totem on the dressing table, where its reflection looked back from the glass. Now that I was alone, I took the raven's feather from my bag and sat down to study it. An "omen," Letha had said. But of what—for what?

Suddenly a long-ago scene was sharp in my mind as I remembered a time when I was little—perhaps younger than Alice—and I'd been out in the backyard with my mother. I'd found a robin's feather and brought it to show her. It was early evening, and a full moon was rising. A question I'd never asked before came into my mind, and I spoke the words aloud, facing her. Since she could speech-read well, she'd always encouraged me in verbal skills. The question I asked was whether she would ever be able to hear again. She smiled wistfully and held the robin's feather up against the moon. Her chances of ever hearing my voice, she told me in her clear speech, were as remote as hearing a feather drop on the moon.

But as she gave the feather back to me, she'd said it was always best to believe and hope, and that a feather was for luck.

Now I transposed the meaning of her words. Was my chance of recovering my child as remote as the sound of a feather dropped on the moon? Yet I had been brought *here*, of all places on earth, so what if this feather was more promise than warning? My lucky feather! I put it carefully beside the totem on my dressing table.

When I was ready, I went downstairs to the dining room and found that Farley Corwin was still at the table. So Crampton had known his room would be empty. His head had been bandaged, and he looked paler than usual, his crest of black hair a contrast to his white face. He didn't look well, and he certainly looked disgruntled. However, he rose as I came into the room, and the intensity of his look had the usual disquieting effect on me.

"So we have a tête-à-tête tonight," he said, turning on his

easy charm. "We've been deserted, it seems. May I serve you from the buffet?"

I shook my head, helping myself to filet of sole, creamed potatoes, and broccoli. It seemed a long time since lunch in Oak Bay, and I found I was hungry in spite of Farley's company.

"Are you staying on for a few more days?" he asked as I sat down and began to butter a hot roll.

"I'm not sure." Perhaps this was the time, when Peony wasn't present, to get everything into the open. There seemed no point in delaying any longer. Particularly not if Mrs. Arles had gone over to their side.

"Tell me," I said, "—you travel a lot—have you ever been in Connecticut? Near the town of Guilford?"

This didn't seem to shake him in the least, though his smile was hardly friendly. "You mean the town you've come from, Mrs. Thorne? The town from which your little girl was kidnapped?"

The surprise element had been turned on me. "How did you know about that?"

"Answers have a way of surfacing. Mrs. Arles had a little talk with us today while you were out. Of course my wife and I were astonished that you should think for a moment that we might have committed so terrible an act."

He looked rather like a smiling tiger, I thought grimly, and trusted nothing he said. This was exactly the sort of bluff he would have to play out if he and Peony were to push their claim to Alice. But it upset me all the more to have Mrs. Arles talk to them without warning me first.

"You're not eating," he said. "You look upset, Mrs. Thorne. Surely you don't think Alice could be anyone's child but Peony's and Edward Arles's?"

I wondered if Peony had told him about her meeting with Kirk in the garden. Kirk had felt she wouldn't, and he seemed to have no suspicion that something might be closing in on him from another quarter.

"Tell me about Brazil," I said. "About the expedition you were on with Frank Karsten. Why would *you* go on such a trip?"

This didn't throw him either. He answered glibly enough.

"I knew Peony well by that time, since she'd worked with me. She wasn't at all suited to such a trip. Edward Arles seemed a careless, self-centered young man, and I don't mind telling you I was appalled when she married him. He was totally wrong for her, though she was foolishly infatuated. Of course I cared about her a great deal by that time. Edward was rich—or at least he would be when he inherited from his grandmother."

Farley actually sounded sad and regretful—the practical illusionist in everything he said and did, misdirecting his audience. His long, graceful fingers flicked the air as though about to bring something gossamer and unexpected into being. A silk kerchief out of nothing wouldn't have surprised me. But he wasn't engaged in that sort of legerdemain at the moment.

"It was an inspiration for me to sign on as cook. Not the first time I've cooked for a living. I'm pretty good at it, and that sort of camp fare wasn't fancy. I suppose Edward was a bit jealous, having me turn up. No matter—I was there when she needed me. And a good thing, as it developed."

I thought of what Kirk had said about Edward's journal and the "planned accident" he thought might happen to him.

"How did Edward die?" I asked bluntly.

Farley answered without hesitation—as of course he would. "No one really knows how it happened. One of the natives who'd gone along on the trip was with him on the river—and he died too. Something happened to their boat, apparently. Peony had only been married two months, and she was already pregnant. I managed to get her back to a more civilized place."

Kirk hadn't told me whether Edward's journal had mentioned his wife's pregnancy. If it had, that was something I wasn't ready to face.

Farley went on. "After Edward's remains were found, Peony and I sent his things to his grandmother and wrote to her about the coming baby. But Mrs. Arles would never see her." He shook his head in what seemed to be sad bewilderment. "Mrs. Arles showed no interest in Edward's child at that time. I had several engagements in small places over there where magic has a great appeal. So Peony's baby was born in a river town in Brazil. By that time, Peony had nowhere to turn, and she married me. I think it was me she looked to all along anyway."

The story came out in quiet, reasonable words—the illusion of truth quite perfect, so that the listener was supposed to be distracted by the irrelevant, while the magician concealed what was never meant to be seen. I was not as gullible, however, as he would have liked.

"Was there really a baby?" I asked.

His surprise seemed genuine. "Of course. My wife has all the papers to prove it. Though, of course, it was years before Mrs. Arles agreed to see her great-grandchild."

All this had the ring of truth and Farley regarded me almost kindly. "I'm sorry, Mrs. Thorne, I don't think Mrs. Arles should have brought you here and raised your hopes so senselessly. I know she dislikes me, and she thinks Peony wasn't good enough for *her* grandson. But the fact remains that Alice is Edward's child, and that's all that counts. You might as well go home, Jenny Thorne."

I had nothing to offer against his words. Only my own rising conviction stood against his lies.

Unable to sit at the table with him for another moment, I jumped up and went to a tall window, where draperies had been closed against the darkness outside. I stepped between folds of heavy brocade, as though I could shut myself away from Farley's insidious arguments and listen only to my inner voice, which rose in strong protest. *Only my instincts*

126

*matter,* I told myself. If I gave up now, I would never know whether Farley and Peony had built up a monstrous masquerade, in which Debbie and I were victims—a masquerade that was even now engulfing Corinthea Arles.

I was still at the window, half hidden by long draperies, when Peony rushed into the room. She didn't see me as she ran to hug Farley, and I turned quietly to watch them both.

"It's going to be all right!" she cried. "She means to accept Alice as her great-granddaughter. Now my little girl will have everything I've never been able to give her!"

My hand caught at a brocade fold. I knew I'd heard a loving mother speaking—not an evil kidnapper. Farley held Peony, quieting her, aware of my listening presence.

"I'm pleased with you," he told her. "I'm glad Mrs. Arles has had the good sense to accept the truth. But, Peony, honey, this is difficult for Mrs. Thorne, who has just been having dinner with me. Apparently she came here believing that Alice was the child *she* lost long ago."

He turned his wife so that she saw me at the window, and I caught her look of alarm, not hidden quickly enough. She was the one who might betray everything.

He gave her a little shake that could have been a warning. "What else did Mrs. Arles say? How long will the arrangements take before you can leave Alice with her and we can go away?"

Peony stiffened in his arms, and now she withdrew herself, clearly frightened, but ready for once to stand her ground.

"I'm sorry, Farley. Mrs. Arles wants *me* to stay. Alice needs her mother here, and Mrs. Arles realizes that. But she doesn't want you to remain here. Not now."

It was as though the rabbit had suddenly faced up to the magician. Farley Corwin, however, was still playing to an audience—me.

"We'll work this out, honey. When Mrs. Arles is ready to talk to me about the details, all this can be settled."

127

"I *never* wanted to leave Alice," Peony said breathlessly. "That was your idea. But of course you can come to visit us any time. You know that."

"Of course," Farley said smoothly, though I sensed anger rising in him—as Peony must have sensed it too—and I wondered if she could possibly hold to her stand against what he wanted. Though now she would have Corinthea Arles's support to help stiffen her resolve. A strong love for Alice came through, and there were two mothers in that room—with no biblical judge to make a decision.

I couldn't endure any more of this, and I hurried out of the room, moving so quickly that I almost ran into Dillow, just outside the door. He seemed embarrassed to be caught eavesdropping, and I supposed he was there to report everything back to Mrs. Arles.

"Is there a telephone I can use privately?" I asked him.

He said, "There's one in the parlor, madam."

I went quickly into the front room. The dining room opened from it, some distance away, so there wouldn't be that much privacy. I didn't care. The Corwins wouldn't know what I was talking about anyway.

I sat down at the small table and opened the phone book. It took only a moment to find and dial Joel Radburn's number. The ringing went on and on, with no answer, so I looked up his mother's number in Oak Bay. This time Letha's maid, Iris, answered, and I asked for Mrs. Radburn. Letha's warm voice came on almost immediately.

"Oh—Jenny! How nice to hear from you. Have you been thinking about what I offered to do with Alice?"

"Yes, I have. How shall we arrange it?"

She considered for a moment. "I'd rather not do this here where there are too many vibrations connected with the past. Let me pick you and Alice up tomorrow morning, and I'll take you to Joel's apartment. He'll be out at that hour, and it will be a quiet, responsive place."

I wasn't sure that I would be allowed to take Alice anywhere, and I hesitated. In her quiet way Letha seemed to sense my doubt.

"Don't worry. We'll work it out. I want to see Corinthea anyway, and if I come to thank her for sending back the jade carving, she can't very well refuse me. Did anything happen concerning the lotus pin I gave Alice?"

I was aware of a listening audience in the dining room behind me, and I answered carefully. "I can tell you when I see you. I'll be ready when you come. And thank you."

Dillow had disappeared when I returned to the hall. I went up to my room, feeling restless and thoroughly unsettled. How could I hold to that instinct Joel had told me to believe in, however strongly it might rise? All the circumstances seemed to be gathering against me. My last hope was Letha Radburn, who had some gift I didn't understand, but which I knew I wanted to take a chance on.

In my room, still thinking of Letha, I picked up the raven feather I'd left on the dressing table, wondering what to do with it. It was too big to carry around and would only be damaged in my bag. What had she said—that it was supposed to protect me? From what? No one feared *me*—not even Farley or Peony Corwin. All the odds were on their side when it came to Alice, to say nothing of immediate possession.

I went out on the small porch that fronted my room, still carrying the feather. When I leaned against the wooden railing it felt rickety, and I didn't touch it again. A breeze blew fresh and cool on my face, reviving me a little. Stars seemed bright and very close, and the moon had risen, nearly full. Wherever there was water, its surface danced with light sequins, and everywhere trees stood black against the luminous sky, murmuring in the wind.

I thought of those tall totem poles in Thunderbird Park, and of what Joel had said about their whispering to each other, perhaps telling ancient stories meant only for themselves. Sometimes, in this far outpost of the continent—or

129

perhaps this was where the continent began—magic seemed possible, even likely. Letha's magic, not Farley's.

Remembering that time in the backyard at home with my mother, I held the raven's feather up against the moon. The feather was so big, and the moon so faraway small, that its orb was hidden, only a faint shimmer gleaming behind the comb.

For some reason, the thought of Kirk McKaye was suddenly strong in my mind. I couldn't see Mrs. Arles's garden from the front of the house, but I wondered if Kirk ever came to sit there in the dark, thinking his own secret thoughts. Letha might not be my only chance for defeating the Corwins. If Kirk held something over them through Edward's journal, perhaps there was still hope.

Something stirred below me on the drive that led downhill away from the house, and in the moonlight I could make out a man. For a second I thought it might be Kirk, and then two other figures joined the first, and the three stood talking together. The first man was Farley Corwin, the woman was Peony. The second man was Elbert Dillow. This made me curious. The three seemed engaged in a private, perhaps secret, conversation. Dillow had always seemed to dislike them both, his manner stiff and disapproving of the Corwins. It was strange that he would meet them away from the house—so Mrs. Arles wouldn't know?

As I watched, the three began to walk together down the drive, quickly out of sight around a curve. I returned to my room, filled with even more distrust. If Dillow was involved with those two, then his supposed loyalty to Mrs. Arles might be in question. I recalled again the small altercation I'd sensed between Dillow and Mrs. Arles when he had served us supper last night. If only there were something I could *do* —some way in which I could fight back. Perhaps even use this new discovery of a possible conspiracy. Nothing suggested itself, but at least I would now watch Dillow more closely.

————

The book by Frank Karsten that I'd picked up in Mrs. Arles's room still lay on a table. It was early, so I would read for a while before getting ready for bed. The big chair where Alice had sat invited me and I turned on a lamp and settled down to page through the book. Mostly I skimmed, reading here and there, watching for mention of names I might recognize.

Preparations for the trip were described in more detail than interested me, but Karsten was not writing a dry record, and his narrative dealt entertainingly with people and incidents. When the word "magician" leaped out at me, I began to read more carefully. Karsten told about a Farley Corwin who had signed on as assistant to the expedition's cook. Apparently Karsten had noticed the man unfavorably. On the other hand, he wrote of Edward Arles with liking and respect. Before he joined the expedition, Arles had taken time to do research on the plants that interested Frank Karsten. He had seemed ready to endure the hardships of such a trip because the goal was to discover new herbs and plants that would be useful in medicine. Edward began to emerge as less of a black sheep than he'd been painted.

However, Karsten mentioned regretfully that Arles had brought his new young wife along, in spite of advice against doing so. Nellie Arles was not the type of young woman to deal with this sort of rugged life, but because Karsten had wanted Edward, he had allowed his wife to come along.

*Nellie?* I wondered, and read on.

His new wife seemed to cling to Edward, and he was obviously concerned about her. So, against his better judgment, Karsten put up with her—to his later regret.

The description of Edward's wife resembled Peony, so I supposed that was the fanciful name that had been chosen for her stage work with Farley Corwin.

What Karsten disliked most was the trickery involved when Farley quietly signed on by selling himself with the temperamental cook. Karsten seemed well aware of Farley's interest in Nellie Arles, and the almost hypnotic control he had over her at times. He wondered if one of the reasons Nellie clung to Edward was to escape from Farley. But these were matters an expedition leader had no time to trouble himself about, unless they interfered with work. Eventually, he seemed to put Corwin down as an older father figure for Nellie, and hoped that no triangle would develop. Time was running out, as there had been delays, and it was only the work that mattered.

The book was based on a diary Karsten had kept, and a graphic sense of jungle and river came through in his words. I found myself caught and transported into a world almost totally green—varying shades of green, interrupted by splashes of floral color.

Orchids grew everywhere, sustaining themselves on air, with very little sun filtering through the leathery leaves of the jungle. Flame vines, crimson passion flowers, and frangipani—all a wild delight to the eye—grew everywhere. Karsten recorded the very smell of the jungle—a mingling of flower scents, rotting wood, and rampant vegetation. There was the smell of the river as well, sometimes strangely fetid, even though it was flowing water.

Few animals were seen, most of them shy and hidden, so that perhaps only eyes watched from the vegetation along the banks as the boats slipped past. Sometimes the water smoked with low mists, and there was heat night and day—and mosquitoes.

I thought of Alice relating her "memories" of river and jungle—stories told her by Nellie-Peony, and not really her own recollections—though they certainly recalled Peony's own hatred of the place.

All this, however, had nothing to do with what I wanted to know, and I began to turn pages rapidly, seeking for more. The day-to-day recording, quoted from his journal, didn't mention Edward, his wife, or Farley Corwin for some time.

If anything was happening, Karsten must have closed his eyes and attended only to the need to concentrate on his work. Or else, if there were other notes, he hadn't transferred them for publication. No more was said—until tragedy struck.

Now I began to read every word. Camp had been set up in a suitable spot, wresting a space of land from the jungle so they could gather the specimens Karsten wanted. Then Edward Arles, on a trip back along the river—his purpose unexplained—was drowned. Maddeningly, Karsten went into no detail. His sense of shock and grief came through, and I had the feeling that he'd begun to regard Edward Arles as he might a son—so he couldn't bear to write about what had happened. If there was treachery—that "planned accident" —he seemed to know nothing of it. So perhaps it had been all too successful. A grave in the jungle was the last resting place for Edward Arles.

However, Karsten did write that Nellie had gone to pieces and become seriously ill. He mentioned that she was pregnant and desperate over the loss of her husband. Clearly, she couldn't stay on without danger to her and the baby. It had been Farley Corwin who volunteered to take her back to civilization. Karsten had given him a native bearer who knew the river, even though this left the expedition shorthanded. Karsten's relief to be rid of them came through clearly. There seemed no suspicion that they'd had any hand in Edward's death. But then—Karsten wouldn't have written that for publication.

What had happened on the rest of the expedition didn't interest me, and I skimmed pages to the last chapters, when Karsten returned to the town from which he'd left months before. Here he was able to get word of Nellie Arles and Farley Corwin. They had managed to return safely. The baby had been born—*a little girl named Alice*—and they had moved on to larger towns where Farley could use his

133

magician's craft to earn them a living. So Edward's baby really had been born in the jungle.

Tonight I'd even glimpsed Peony as a mother, willing to stand up against Farley in order to stay with her child. So where did that leave me? What was my so-called instinct except a strong wish for Alice to be my Debbie? Nevertheless, logic had nothing to do with the way I felt. Farley could very well be a villain, as I imagined, and whatever slim thread remained for me to take hold of, I intended to grasp it and try to find an answer. Karsten's book told me that a girl baby named Alice had been born to Peony. But how did I know the child had lived and grown up to be *this* Alice? There was still the possibility of fraud.

# 9

Before I went to bed I looked for something I hadn't taken from my suitcase. At home I had packed Debbie's favorite toy at the last minute, thinking that it might be a link with the child I hadn't yet seen. Might it still be?

I sat for a little while with the cloth puppet in my hands. It was a frog like Kermit—greener than green, with long dangly legs, and a red throat when its mouth was open. The head was a mitt I used to slip over my right hand when I told frog stories to Debbie, making the creature talk. She had loved the puppet devotedly, and this had been the toy she chose to sleep with at night. She had even named it. Of all names, she'd picked Amarillo—after she'd heard a news broadcast that mentioned the Texas city. She'd always loved words with *l*'s in them, and the frog became Amarillo permanently. Just as the lamented turtle had been named Shelly because its shell had so intrigued her. That name too had syllables to roll melodiously.

The frog looked up at me from my hand, eyes bulging. "Is Alice our Debbie?" I asked. Amarillo merely squished up his face in the way Debbie had loved. He wasn't of much help, and he didn't talk back to me at all.

I put him away and got into bed.

Sleep came easily for once—several hours of deep, restful sleep, before I began to dream. Something was making a

135

whistling sound in my room—a persistent sound that came at intervals and wouldn't let me go back to sleep. A penetrating sound—not in my dream. I sat up in bed, and the whistle was repeated.

Still groggy with sleep, I got out of bed, trying to locate the source of the mysterious whistle. Yes—it was coming from behind the desk. I managed to angle the piece of furniture out from the wall and discovered the curious contraption hidden behind it. This looked like a variety of telephone and would date back to early in the century when this house was built. A speaking tube emerged slightly from the wall, with an ear cup and connecting tube hung upon an attached fork. This must be an old tube system that was used to connect rooms of the house. The whistling would be managed by someone at the other end blowing into the tube connected with this room.

It whistled again and I put the cup to my ear.

A voice spoke faintly. "Listen to me, Jennifer Blake. Your child died a long time ago. You *know* the truth. Accept it and go away—while you still can."

If I hadn't been wide awake by this time, aware of my bare feet and thin nightgown in the cool room, I might have thought it a dream voice—a nightmare voice, totally unreal.

"Jenny!" The tube spoke again in my ear. "You *are* awake and you hear me. Your daughter is dead. Alice is *not* your child. Go away before something terrible happens."

I hung up the tube quietly and stood staring at the wall. Nothing whistled again. The voice had used my real name— Jennifer *Blake.* The mechanical imperfection of this early system had disguised the sound, and I couldn't tell whether a man or a woman had spoken to me. Yet by the time I searched out the source of this communication, probably no one would be there.

Nevertheless, I put on my robe and slippers and opened the door to look into the hall. A dim night light burned near the stairs and shadows grew thick at this end. At first I saw nothing and I walked a little way down the hall before I stumbled over outstretched legs. A woman sat on a bench against the wall with a pillow supporting her head. When I bumped her legs she came awake with a snort of alarm. It was Crampton.

"Did you hear the whistle?" I asked.

She stared up at me in confusion, and I grasped her arm, helping her to her feet. She wore a woolly brown robe, and her gray hair was pinned up with incongruous rag curlers. She leaned on me heavily for a moment, as she swam back from sleep.

"What whistle?" she demanded. "What has happened?"

I hushed her. "Don't wake the house. There's a speaking tube in my room. It whistled and woke me up."

"The speaking tubes," she muttered. "They're still all over the house, though nobody uses them any more. There's a board in the butler's pantry with some connections to several rooms. Anybody could use them."

Someone had tried to frighten me. Someone with a great deal at stake, whose cause might not be altogether certain?

"What are you doing here at this hour of the morning?" I whispered.

"Humph!" It was a sound of impatience—with herself. "I wouldn't have been much good if anyone had come to your room, would I? I meant to stay awake."

"You were guarding *my* room? Why?"

She shook her head as though tossing away cobwebs. "Nobody cares about Mrs. Arles the way I do. Certainly not Dillow. She's old and sick, and too easy to fool. That's what they're all trying to do—trick her, fool her. It's all money and revenge and wickedness! But I care about *her*. She was good to me when I needed help, and I'm the only one who's trying to protect her."

"But you've left her unguarded downstairs."

"I gave her a sleeping pill—and *she* isn't in danger."

"But you think I am?"

———

137

"You could be if they get too nervous about you."

"Do you think Alice is my child?"

"I don't know anything about that. I just don't think Alice is Edward Arles's child. Those Corwins are up to something. And maybe Dillow too. I don't trust him. But I don't give up easily, and I'll find a way. I'll keep watching and looking. But you'd better go back to bed now, Mrs. Thorne. Whoever it was will probably leave you alone for the rest of the night. I didn't get to tell you that you should lock your door. I found a key for it today—here it is."

I took the key and thanked her.

"It's not for you," she told me darkly. "If you try to hurt her, I'll be against you too."

"I don't want to hurt anyone," I said. "I only want to recover my daughter."

She went off toward the stairs, her big body moving lightly, silently.

In my room I turned the key in its lock, and it made a comforting rasp. Strange that I found an ally in Crampton. And somehow reassuring. *She* wouldn't be given to vapors, and she didn't believe Alice was Edward Arles's daughter. I wanted to know more about her reasons, but that would have to wait.

When the lights were off, I got into bed again, though I didn't fall asleep until it was almost daylight.

The next morning I was up early in spite of losing sleep, and I breakfasted alone. Dillow looked a little smug this morning, as though he knew something I didn't.

But I might know a few things he wasn't aware of, and I didn't mention that Letha Radburn would appear around nine o'clock.

Since Mrs. Arles didn't summon me, I stayed away from her room, and I avoided the garden, not wanting to see Kirk McKaye right now. One thin hope I clung to was Joel's amused conviction that his mother had some sort of extra sense he couldn't explain, but which he respected.

Alice came into the dining room while I was finishing coffee and toast, and I thought she too looked smug and pleased with herself.

"Corinthea's made up her mind," she announced. "I guess I really am going to be her great-granddaughter. She told me last night that she believes Edward was my father—so I'll be rid of old Farley. And I guess someday I'll be rich."

"I thought you didn't like Mrs. Arles," I said.

"I don't much. But maybe she'll be different now, if she's sure I'm Edward's kid. Of course I was sure of *me* all along. I'm here and I'm alive. So I don't know what's been wrong with *her*."

"What about your—mother?" It was hard to use that word for Peony.

"She's going to stay here, I guess. Unless old Farley makes her go with him." For the first time Alice looked troubled, and pain stabbed again. A child transplanted learned to love away from her true parents, given half a chance. So let Joel's mother advise me about this!

I stayed at the table until Alice was through with a good-sized breakfast. Watching her, I wondered if there had been times when she'd gone hungry in the past, what with Farley's off-and-on employment. She seemed to eat each meal as though she never expected to see food again. Though where it went on her thin frame I didn't know.

When she'd finished her last bite of ham and forkful of scrambled eggs, I said, "Will you come upstairs to my room for a moment, Alice? There's something I'd like to show you."

She had nothing better to do and came with me readily. Dillow watched us go off together, and I sensed disapproval. He didn't want *me* tampering with Alice, and I wondered if it had been his voice on that connection last night. Alice

———

139

made a face behind his back and scooted upstairs ahead of me.

When I'd closed the door of my room and asked her to sit down, I took Amarillo from under a pillow and held him out to her, green legs dangling, red mouth open.

"Do you remember this?" I asked.

She looked at the frog with interest but no particular recognition, and watched as I slipped my hand into the mitt that formed its head. She paid no attention to my strange question but laughed when I made the frog do his various faces.

"Where did you get that?" she asked. "He's real funny."

I sat down opposite her. "I had a little girl once. She was just your age, Alice. This was her favorite toy, and I used to make it tell her stories and talk to her. She liked to make it talk back, and she even slept with this very frog at night."

Alice played with the puppet for a few moments and seemed entertained. But whether any memory returned to her I couldn't tell.

"If you were going to name him, what name would you pick?" I asked.

"I don't know. Maybe Froggy would do. How does he work?"

I slipped the mitt over her hand—a larger hand than Debbie's had been but still small, with the bones barely covered. She immediately squeezed the face into contortions—what Debbie had called "squishing"—and seemed pleased with him for a few moments. Then she grew bored and returned him to me.

"Is that all you wanted to show me?"

"Don't you like puppets and making up stories?"

"I don't know. I guess I never tried that. Maybe if I had a puppet—"

It was a hint, but I couldn't give Debbie's frog away to this changeling.

———

140

Alice returned to my earlier words. "You said you had a little girl—once. What happened to her?"

"She was taken away from me."

"You mean stolen? Didn't you ever get her back?"

"No," I said, watching her tensely.

Alice stared at me, and now there seemed a new uncertainty in her. Almost as though my words had frightened her in some way.

"That's awful!" she said. "Awful for your little girl. It would be scary to be taken away from her mom."

"Yes, it would," I agreed. "It was awful for me too—as Debbie's mother."

"Was that her name—Debbie? It's a pretty name."

"I like it. It's shortened from an old-fashioned name, Deborah. But she couldn't manage to say that because she was only three. So we called her what she called herself—Debbie."

"Debbie." She repeated the name as though testing it. "I wish *I* was called Debbie. I never liked Alice. It always sounds like—like somebody else."

I hardly dared to breathe. "What do you mean?"

She shook her head and got up to wander around the room. "I don't know. Sometimes I don't feel real. I was only saying that about knowing I'm *me*. Sometimes it's like being Alice in Wonderland." She picked up the puppet from the couch where I'd dropped it. "What did your little girl call her frog?"

I had already given away the name Debbie, and I didn't want to mention Amarillo. I wanted her to tell me that.

"It's a secret, and secrets mustn't be told."

"I don't like secrets," Alice said.

"I don't believe that. You like mystery stories, and you like to guess about things."

"Secrets in stories, maybe. But not when everybody around me keeps things from me. Farley and my mother always have secrets they won't tell me."

"Perhaps everyone has secrets—including you."

She thought about that. "Old Corinthea's full of secrets. Yesterday afternoon I snooped when she was sitting on the terrace out in back. She was reading a page that looked like it was torn out of a notebook. She even had on those glasses she doesn't like to wear, and she was holding a magnifying glass too. She looked real pleased about something."

I had no idea what this might mean, but it made me uncomfortable, since it might have something to do with Mrs. Arles's new decision to accept Alice.

"Dillow has a secret," Alice went on.

"I expect he has a lot of secrets. Do you know any about him?"

"He doesn't like me when I tease him, but sometimes he looks at me as though he was trying to make himself like me."

I smiled. "Perhaps he's thinking about your becoming Mrs. Arles's heir. If that happened, he might work for you someday, if he's still here when you grow up."

"No, he wouldn't. I'd fire him right away."

"Well, don't plan on it too soon," I said dryly. "What if it should turn out that you're not Mrs. Arles's great-grand-daughter after all? Would you mind very much?"

"I've thought about that. But then who would I be? That's scary to think about too. I mean, wouldn't Peony be my mother?"

I didn't know where to go with that.

Alice had begun wandering about the room, and she found the totem pole she had brought me from Uncle Tim.

"I'm glad he gave you that. It means he likes you, so maybe you'll stay and we can learn more of those signs you do."

"Would you like that, Alice?"

She shrugged. "Maybe. It's not so boring with you here. Things happen that I don't expect. Like going to Oak Bay yesterday."

"We may go somewhere today, too. Mrs. Radburn is coming to see Mrs. Arles this morning—in just a little while. She wants to take you and me out for a drive. So why don't you go and change your clothes now, so you'll be ready?"

Alice looked doubtful. "But Mrs. Radburn and old Corinthea are enemies. Ma told me that. So how come she's going to visit my great-grandmother?"

I wondered how Peony had known. But of course Edward had probably told her long ago.

"Mrs. Radburn has a plan, Alice. Something that might be interesting for us to do. It's not exactly a secret, but I don't know all the details yet. Let's take the frog along, shall we?"

"Okay," Alice picked up the puppet, and just as she reached the door, Dillow knocked.

When I opened it, he looked from Alice to me suspiciously, and then focused on the frog.

"What's that?" he asked.

Alice slipped the mitt over her hand and poked the frog face at him, creasing it to a silly grin. Dillow drew back indignantly and spoke to me.

"Mrs. Arles would like to see you downstairs, madam. As soon as possible."

"I'll go right now." I winked at Alice. "See you later. Bring the frog."

She grinned back, enjoying the secret of Letha's coming. Before I went out the door, I picked up the Karsten book, and then, on impulse, the feather that lay beside the little totem pole. When I'd put the feather in my handbag, I spoke to Dillow as we went down the hall.

"Around three this morning someone whistled into that old speaking tube in my room. Do you know anything about that?"

Since Dillow seldom showed any emotion other than disapproval, I couldn't tell if I'd surprised him.

"Perhaps it was a dream, madam."

"No, Dillow. I got out of bed and found that contraption

143

behind the desk. When I listened with the earpiece a voice told me to go away. A *real* voice, warning me."

He shook his head as if he didn't believe a word I'd said. "Mrs. Arles is waiting," he reminded me.

It could have been Dillow, or Farley, or even Peony, I thought.

On the stairs red carpeting gleamed softly in spangles of light from stained glass, but the lower hall, as always, seemed deep in its paneled gloom.

At the far end, Corinthea Arles's door stood open, and Dillow slipped past to announce me. Once more Crampton sat in the shadows beyond the bed, and we didn't speak or look at each other. I was sure that she'd have told no one about our nocturnal adventure.

This morning Mrs. Arles's robe—all her gowns were cut in similar graceful lines—reminded me of the russet color of a forest floor in autumn, and she wore a teal-blue shawl around her shoulders, its pattern one of floating red maple leaves. As I came in and took the chair she designated, she watched me calmly. This time I knew what was coming, knew that all I could do at the moment was try to delay her decision.

"Good morning, Jenny," she greeted me, her voice lighter, more cheerful than when I'd been with her before. "I hope you slept well last night. Though I didn't. I was up on and off most of the night."

That hardly bore with Crampton's statement about a sleeping pill, and I wondered if Mrs. Arles's could possibly have been the voice on the tube.

"Crampton tried to give me a pill to make me sleep, but I fooled her," she went on, smiling a bit wickedly when Crampton's chair creaked beyond the bed. "I can think best in the late hours, and I knew I had to come to a decision."

I searched my mind futilely for some way to keep her from speaking out irrevocably, but there seemed no way to stop her.

---

144

"I'm sorry you've come all this way for nothing," she continued. "I should never have phoned you in the first place. But I have that sort of conscience. Once I saw Debbie's picture, I had to be sure. But of course you know all that. And of course you must realize by this time that Alice can't be your lost child. All the proof I've been given points to her being Edward's daughter, and I have decided to accept her as my great-granddaughter. I've already told Peony this."

I grasped at a straw. "Have you found out from Peony what really happened to your grandson?"

"I have never wanted to hear the unhappy details."

I held out Karsten's green-jacketed book. "I'd like to return this. There are passages you may want to read since they concern the woman Edward married. He seems to call her Nellie whenever he refers to Edward's wife."

"Of course. That's her real name. Peony is the ridiculous name she adopted for her work with Farley Corwin.

Mrs. Arles took the book from me and set it aside as though it didn't interest her. Perhaps that was just as well, since Nellie's pregnancy and the birth of her child were corroborated. But there was something more I could say.

"Frank Karsten felt there was bad blood between Corwin and Edward. What if something happened on that expedition—so that Edward's death wasn't an accident?"

Across the room Crampton stirred uneasily.

Mrs. Arles seemed to dismiss this, quite capable of shutting out anything she didn't want to accept. "Does Karsten hint at any such thing?"

I couldn't tell her who was hinting—not yet. "No, not exactly. But I couldn't help wondering."

I knew that sounded feeble, and she regarded me with a pitying look. "I'm sorry, Jenny, but I'm afraid you must stop hoping. It will only hurt you more in the long run. Nothing that happened on that expedition can matter to me now. Except that Nellie-Peony became pregnant. She has told me about the birth of her baby."

"A baby was born," I said quietly. "And she was named Alice. But what if that baby died? By that time perhaps Farley had married Peony, and what if he never gave up hope that you would recognize your great-granddaughter? Without a baby, his plot couldn't succeed. They didn't come near you for quite a while. Years."

"They wanted to, but I wouldn't let them."

"They might have been watching for a child they could substitute. Farley seems able to make Peony do anything he wants. I think—"

She interrupted me. "That's enough! This is all pure fabrication. You are making up what you would like to believe. But you've had your chance to be with Alice, Jenny, and you must surely recognize by now that she isn't your child."

Nothing I'd said had swayed her, but something in me still wouldn't give up. "There's a feeling I have—there are little touches now and then that I almost recognize. If I could have just a little more time—"

"Naturally you feel this. But it's only wishful thinking, Jenny. As for Farley's influence over Peony—it's about to come to an end. She has agreed to separate from him in order to remain with her child. I would never allow him to stay here, and I wanted to test her. Only a mother could feel as strongly as she does. Her willingness to stay convinces me more than anything else."

"An adoptive mother can love every bit as strongly as a natural mother."

"Even if the child were kidnapped? No, you're going down the wrong road. I do understand how you feel. I blame myself for rousing your hopes and then being forced to dash them. But this is the way it really is, Jenny. *You* don't want Alice, when she's not your child."

"What has convinced you?" I asked. "What made you suddenly sure?"

She considered my question for a moment and then came to a decision. She picked up an envelope from the table

146

beside her chair and handed it to me. "I suppose there's no reason why you shouldn't read this. It's a page torn from a notebook. This sheet was apparently overlooked among Edward's belongings that were returned to me after his death. Dillow was going through those articles again yesterday, and he found what must be a page torn from a record that Edward kept while he was on the Karsten expedition. You might as well read it. The handwriting is Edward's—I remember it very well."

I took the envelope and drew out the single sheet, knowing exactly how Dillow had happened to "find" it after all these years. This would be a page torn from the journal Kirk McKaye had mentioned to me. I unfolded the sheet and read the handwritten words. The brief passage made no mention of the "accident" Edward feared might happen, though there was a hint that he might not come through. In only a few lines he had written about the child Nellie was carrying.

> I don't know whether I will come through this adventure safely, but I hope my child will live. I hope Nellie will take the baby to my grandmother. I have told her that is what I want her to do—if anything happens to me.
>
> More than anything else I regret the lies and misunderstandings that parted me from my grandmother when I left Victoria. She was wrong and I was wrong. She condemned me for something I didn't do. I needed the money to get away, and Uncle Tim got it for me.
>
> If ever I come out of this safely, I'll take the baby home to my grandmother myself and tell her all of this. I'll stand up to her and protect Uncle Tim.

That was all, but it was enough. I could see how thoroughly such words would sway Corinthea Arles. Yet something in me remained unconvinced, though these words had probably swayed Kirk too, since he had wanted to put them

---

into her hands. I only wished there had been more here about Farley Corwin and his possible betrayal.

I put the page back in its envelope and returned it to her. "This doesn't change any of what I've said about Alice. Edward didn't live, and you still don't know that this child is your great-granddaughter."

"I know," Mrs. Arles said quietly, and I was startled to see tears in her eyes. "I am sure *now*. Edward has given her to me. Of course I shall have to have this out with Timothy and learn what role he played. He is to blame for whatever happened. I shall send him away to where he can do no more harm."

"That's not fair!" I cried. "I want to talk to you about Timothy. I've lived and worked with deaf people and—"

"You know nothing about anything," she said sharply. "I am really losing my patience with you."

Crampton coughed softly, and Mrs. Arles glanced in her direction. "The door chimes," Crampton said.

This would be Letha arriving, and I wondered what possible spell she could cast on Corinthea Arles in order to get Alice away in my company. From now on, undoubtedly, Mrs. Arles would never want me to be alone with Alice.

Dillow came down the hall, with Letha Radburn close behind. She was taking no chance of refusal. At the doorway she rushed past him into the room, afloat in color.

Today she was exotically dressed again, in a swirling lavender skirt appliquéd with sphinx heads. An amethyst necklace along with amber beads dangled against a pale pink blouse, tinkling musically as she moved. I wondered why on earth she'd gotten herself up in this gypsy fashion, when she must know it would offend Mrs. Arles. Only her makeup was subdued, and her rose-tinged lips smiled tremulously as she came into the room holding out both hands.

Mrs. Arles recoiled, reluctantly allowing her hands to be taken in Letha's warm clasp.

Letha seemed not to notice. "It was so good of you to send

the jade piece back, Corinthea. And good of you to write the note you did. I wanted to thank you myself. May I sit down for a moment?"

She took an opposite chair quickly, her entire performance probably intended to overwhelm and confuse—which was exactly what it was doing. There was no opportunity for Corinthea to freeze her out, or even to resist.

"I enjoyed meeting Mrs. Thorne yesterday," Letha ran on. "And Alice is a darling. A very bright child."

Mrs. Arles managed to speak for the first time. "A child who you don't believe is Edward's daughter."

"It will all sort itself out, I'm sure." Letha sounded breezily confident. "Just so there can now be peace and forgiveness between us two, my dear."

Nothing about Corinthea Arles suggested peace or forgiveness, and she had put on her most distant manner.

"There's another reason why I've come," Letha went on, ignoring the wall. "You know that I sometimes receive—shall we say—messages? You've never believed or approved, but whether you do or not isn't important. I really must tell you something—in fact, warn you."

She paused, and Mrs. Arles recovered herself a little. "I haven't the faintest idea what you're talking about, Letha. Do come to the point."

"I mean to," Letha spoke emphatically. "What I have to say concerns the man you've hired as chauffeur. The moment I saw him I knew something was wrong. Something that might affect you. These impressions I receive are often sound and true, as Joel will tell you. What do you know about this man, Corinthea?"

"All that's necessary to know is that he's a good driver. I've observed that. And Dillow never hired anyone without checking that person out carefully. I really haven't paid much attention to him, and I'm afraid I'm not as impressionable as you seem to be."

"Get rid of him, Corinthea. Get rid of him before he does

149

some irreparable damage. He's an angry man. I could feel it even more strongly when I passed him on the driveway just now."

"Really, Letha!"

Letha Radburn raised her hands in a dramatic gesture and let them fall. "Well, I've done what I can. If you won't listen—"

"I will listen when you have something besides these vague notions to give me."

"Would you allow me another chance to see him—observe him? Perhaps I can learn something more convincing."

"How would you manage that?"

Letha left her chair, beads and gold bracelets chiming, and walked to a window overlooking the garden. There she stood quietly, her forehead with its black wings of hair pressed against cool glass. I felt as though I were watching a play, except that it was a great deal more than that. Whatever evolved out of this odd confrontation could affect me, Alice, all of us.

When she turned around, however, Letha was smiling. "I had planned to invite Alice and your guest, Mrs. Thorne, to come for a drive with me this morning. Mrs. Thorne shouldn't leave Victoria without seeing the Butchart Gardens, and perhaps the little girl hasn't seen them either. I would enjoy taking them out there. So why don't I leave my car here for now and have your chauffeur drive us? This would give me a real opportunity to observe him and see if something more comes through to me. You remember, Corinthea, that Lewis always had a great respect for my gifts. And I know that you respected him."

For an instant Mrs. Arles's deep-set eyes blazed with a light I hadn't seen before. Letha was really pushing it.

"Lewis went off to India and turned addlepated," Mrs. Arles snapped.

Letha's smile, in contrast, was serene. "I believe he gained a wisdom that you never recognized, and I'm sorry about

150

that. Nevertheless, please allow me another chance with this man who drives your car, Corinthea. It really is important. It may even have some bearing on your relationship with the child."

Somehow, in her theatrical yet indirect weaving, Letha had managed to wear her adversary down. Corinthea closed her eyes, leaning her head against the chair rest, showing no further interest in Letha or me. "Oh, what does it matter?"

We had been dismissed to do whatever Letha pleased.

Letha said good-bye quickly, and the old woman barely formed the word in response. I followed Letha out and, as we went down the hall, I saw Alice sitting on a lower step of the stairs. She had put on her denim outfit and combed her too curly hair. Clasped in her hands was Amarillo, the frog.

Letha stopped at once. "Hello, Alice. Would you like to come for a drive? We're going out to Butchart Gardens, and we'd enjoy having you along."

Alice agreed eagerly, happy for any sort of action. When Dillow appeared at the front door to see us out, Letha told him that Mrs. Arles had said Kirk might drive us this morning in her car. So would Dillow please let the chauffeur know.

Everything was happening too quickly for me, but I wasn't sure that was the direction I'd expected. There had been something Letha wanted to try with Alice, and that plan seemed to be getting lost in this talk about Kirk McKaye. I didn't care any more about how suspicious he might be, or whether he continued in Mrs. Arles's employ. Alice was my one concern, and there was so little time left.

As it happened, Kirk was waiting in the front driveway, already in uniform and polishing the Mercedes to an even finer gleam. Dillow went to speak to him, while Letha hurried to her car to take out a large tapestry bag.

Kirk opened the car door for us, looking directly at me—a look that seemed to challenge, and left me even more unsettled. Since he'd had Dillow put that journal page of Edward's into Mrs. Arles's hands, I knew he was in opposition to everything I wanted. It struck me that he looked somewhat different this morning, and I saw that he had trimmed his drooping mustache, so that it no longer reminded me quite so much of a pirate. I could see his mouth a little better, and I didn't like the sly grin he wore.

This time Alice sat happily between Letha and me in the car, the frog mitt on one hand, letting it make faces at her. She was clearly intrigued with Letha's gypsy aspects, and now and then glanced at her beads and color admiringly.

Letha caught my eye over her head and her look seemed to say, *Don't worry. I haven't forgotten.* She spoke to Kirk as he turned the car down the driveway.

"I'd like to make a stop before we go out to Butchart Gardens. We'll go first to my son's apartment. Have you ever been there, Alice? It's a beautiful, quiet spot that will be just right for something I want to do."

She gave directions to Kirk and then spoke again to Alice. "I hope you'll help me."

"Sure," Alice said. "Doing what?"

"It's a sort of magic thing. If it succeeds, you might be able to remember more about when you were little. That would be interesting, wouldn't it?"

Alice wriggled between us. "I don't want to remember! Sometimes I dream, and Ma has to come into my room and hold me. She gets scared when I dream—and Farley gets mad."

"Do you remember the dreams?" Letha asked.

"Only that there's a bad feeling. If you do a spell, will that come back?"

"It might," Letha admitted. "But if it does I think it would be for the last time. Then you wouldn't have the bad dreams any more. That's worth trying for, isn't it?"

Alice listened to her doubtfully, and so did I—not at all sure how much of this I accepted, or wanted to accept. But I had to try something.

---

# 10

I always lost my sense of direction when we drove through the outskirts of Victoria. Streets wound, and water cut in unexpectedly as the road crossed bridges and curled around inlets. The view often took in glimpses of the sea, with puffs of green islands floating on the surface. Whenever the clouds thinned, the long ranges of mountains on the mainland of the United States and Canada were visible.

I was beginning to discover that people in British Columbia thought in terms of north and south, rather than east and west. Ottawa was far away and hardly considered, while California and even Hawaii seemed close at hand

Joel's apartment was only a short drive. He lived in a two-floor stretch of condominium that overlooked an inlet at the back. Redwood siding and a gallery, with long boxes of geraniums, offered a pleasant contrast to higher apartment buildings nearby.

When Kirk had parked the car and opened the door for us, I was out first, and Alice followed. Letha sat for a moment talking to Kirk.

"I've been thinking about something," she told him. "I would like you to come inside with us, if you will."

"Of course, madam," Kirk said, sounding like Dillow.

She let him help her from the car and then led the way to redwood stairs that mounted to the second level. Doors ran along the stretch of gallery, and she had her key ready when she came to Joel's apartment.

The door opened into beige-carpeted quiet, and when it had closed behind us, I felt an immediate sense of peace and seclusion. Down the long living room, two picture windows met in a right angle—a V that extended out over greenery at the back. Alice ran directly to look down upon a narrow strip of lawn above the water.

"What a funny-looking tree!" she cried. "All its bark is coming off."

Letha joined her at the windows. "That's an arbutus. It grows along the U.S. Pacific coast, but only in a few areas of British Columbia. You can tell it by its reddish, peeling bark with green underneath, and by those glossy evergreen leaves."

"It's such a twisted tree," Alice said. "Like out of a fairy-tale book. Could I have a piece of that bark?"

"Later we'll get you some," Letha promised. "Right now we have something to arrange, and you are going to help me."

She pulled drapery folds across the two windows, dimming the room. Two chairs of light-colored wood, their seats covered with a leafy green print, were set in the triangle made by the windows. Letha sat down in one, crossing her knees so that the lavender skirt flowed into graceful folds, sphinx heads shimmering in silver thread. She fingered her strands of beads thoughtfully, considering the room. I noticed that another chain hung among the amethyst and amber—fine silver links, with a small crystal as a pendant. Somewhere I'd read about the magnetic power of natural crystals, and now Letha seemed lost in some private reverie as she fingered the pendant.

Kirk remained standing near the door, watchful, and perhaps for once uncertain of his role, but I took the opportunity to wander about the room so I could see where Joel Radburn lived. I liked the subdued colors of pale green and beige he had chosen, with only an occasional flash of color in a cushion or painting. He hadn't allowed his mother's taste for the exotic to influence the way he lived. I glanced at the title of a book on the coffee table and recognized a current spy novel—what the scientist read for relaxation.

Two of the paintings on the wall were of coastal scenes—a range of snowy mountains, with Mount Baker standing clear against a blue sky. The second painting was of a dense forest of hemlock and Norway pine, with a rustic lodge in the foreground.

Joel's desk drew me. Letha was there, smiling in a silver frame. Not an open smile, but enigmatic, like the woman. On the desk lay a wooden paper knife, carved at one end with the profile of a Northwest Indian. Beside it stood one of Uncle Tim's small totem poles, topped again by a thunderbird—except that Uncle Tim had added a whimsical touch. The bird face resembled Corinthea Arles—its nose more beaked than hers, its mouth without expression. The old man had a gift for these miniature portraits that were sometimes caricatures.

Letha had finished her silent communication, and she left her chair. "Kirk, will you move the coffee table for me, please? I'd like to free space in the middle of the floor. That's where we're going to set up the crystals."

She opened her carpetbag and brought out various articles, one by one. First, a floor pad covered in pale green silk that she unrolled for Alice to lie upon. Next came several plump, amber-colored candles set in crystal bowls which she indicated to me.

"Jenny, will you set these on the end tables around the room? The scent will help purify the air when they're lighted."

I didn't look at Kirk, lest I catch some hint of mockery in his eyes, and I placed the candles carefully. I no longer thought of this as a performance, or of Letha's dress as strange or inappropriate. This was my last chance, and I

155

meant to go along with whatever she wanted. Though I did wonder if Joel knew what his mother was up to here today.

"Joel told me to go ahead and try whatever I liked," Letha said, and I started. I didn't really believe in ESP to this extent. She simply interpreted intuitively.

Now Letha spread the crystals in an oval on the floor. "Please lie down in the center, Alice," she directed when she'd finished.

Uncertainly, Alice obeyed, stretching out on the pad and staring at the ceiling. Not for a moment had she let Amarillo go, and Letha didn't object when Alice placed the frog so that its green legs sprawled across her body.

Letha moved Alice's hands so they rested on a crystal in the oval on each side. "Try to feel the energy," she said softly.

She put a crystal at Alice's feet and another large, perfect crystal at her head, so its tip pointed toward the child.

"These form an energy mandala," Letha explained. "Natural crystals are often used for healing, but this morning these are for a different purpose. Perhaps healing for Alice is important as well, since we do want her to be rid of bad dreams."

When all was in place, Letha sat at Alice's head and took the large crystal in her cupped palms, her legs crossed in the lotus position under her full skirt. She closed her eyes and tilted her head back slightly. I sensed that she might be praying, asking for help.

After a moment she opened her eyes and looked directly at Kirk. "None of this will be effective if there is hostility in the room."

"Shall I go back to the car, madam?" Kirk asked.

"No, I want you here. I'm not sure why, but your presence is needed. You have some connection with Edward Arles, I think."

How did she know that? I glanced at Kirk and saw that she had startled him.

"Sit over there, please," she told him, gesturing toward the sofa. Then she rose and went to sit beside him. "Give me your right hand."

Fascinated, Alice rolled over to watch.

When he didn't immediately offer his hand, Letha reached for it and held it between her two palms. Again she closed her eyes and remained very still.

Alice whispered to me, "What's she doing?" I touched my fingers to my lips.

After a moment Letha opened her eyes and nodded at Kirk. "Yes—there is *so* much anger inside you. But it doesn't belong in this room. No one here wishes you any harm. Can you let it all flow away for a little while? It is damaging to *you*."

"I don't know how," Kirk said, his voice lower than before, the mockery gone.

"What *you* want will never mend the past," Letha told him.

"For me it might, Mrs. Radburn. I'd better return to the car and let you get on with whatever you want to do here."

She spoke firmly. "No—you are instructed to stay. Not only by me. Something could happen in this room that will change whatever may be driving you. Keep your mind open for a little while. Nothing can ever come through steel doors or a closed mind."

She released his hand and motioned for him to stay where he was. For once, Kirk seemed unexpectedly subdued, as though he might be feeling a reluctant respect. Alice lay on her back again, and when Letha found matches in her bag she lighted the candles one by one, all the way around the room. The small flames brought the room to a soft yellow glow and caused rainbows to sparkle in the crystals. The faint scent of sandalwood rose from heated wax, with an added sweetness—water lily, perhaps?

The room seemed tranquil now, and I sensed that this was

157

the atmosphere Letha intended to induce. I could even feel my own tensions relaxing, falling away, as I watched.

Now she took the big crystal in her hands again and spoke softly to Alice. "Close your eyes. Breathe deeply, slowly. You are safe here—nothing can hurt you. There are only good feelings in this room."

Alice lay stretched with the green frog sprawled across her chest, so that Amarillo's front legs seemed to embrace her. Letha knelt at Alice's head, touching the girl's forehead with light fingers, then resting her hands on Alice's shoulders.

"All I want is for you to relax and be very calm and quiet— let whatever wants to come, come. You can even go to sleep if you like. No bad dreams will touch you now." Her fingers moved along the child's eyebrows, rising upward to the temples, pressing gently, then returning to her shoulders. "Try to remember something, from when you were little. Something pleasant—anything at all."

Alice's eyes flew open. "I don't want to think about the jungle!"

"No—think about something that made you happy. Something you had fun with when you were little. Go back to that time and let it happen again. When it does, tell me about it and we'll talk."

For so lively a little girl, Alice lay surprisingly still. The frog lifted gently on her chest as she breathed, its limp green forelegs reaching around her almost lovingly. Perhaps the frog remembered, I thought ruefully.

I had chosen a chair in a corner away from this "magic" circle where I could watch whatever happened, yet be removed from it, lest my own anxiety convey itself to Letha. Or to Alice. Once, when I glanced at Kirk, I found him staring at me, and I knew that he understood what was involved for me in all this—even though what he might hope for was different.

Now I tried to focus wholly upon Alice, lying so still, with the crystals around her almost vibrating in candlelight and their own energy. There *were* no inanimate objects, really. Even a table was a mass of invisible movement as its atoms collided. The room seemed utterly quiet, now insulated from outside sound, and Alice breathed more deeply—long, regular breaths that made a faint whisper in the stillness.

I could remember how Debbie had felt in my arms, quick to wriggle away, yet loving to be held—loving me. All my doubts and questions were fading away. Alice was surely *my* child, and I began to pray that she would be brought back to me. I didn't know what candles and crystals and Letha's communing presence meant, but something—some power —seemed to touch me. Some *presence.* Perhaps some spiritual essence that spoke the truth.

Alice moved slightly and made a sound like a whisper. At once Letha placed a quieting hand on her shoulder.

"It's all right, Alice dear. Nothing can hurt you. Have you found what you'd like to talk about yet?"

Alice put both hands on her chest, clasping the frog. But she had nothing to say, and lay still again. All the hope and love and certainty that had risen in me began to subside as moments passed and nothing happened. Letha's eyes were closed now too, as though she might be listening to her own "voices," and she began to sway slightly. I didn't look at Kirk again, but he too was quiet, watching all that happened.

Suddenly Alice herself broke the spell. She sat up, flinging out one hand, so that she knocked a crystal out of the circle.

"I don't want to do this any more!" she cried. Tears began to roll down her face and her hands clasped each other, fumbling. Letha raised a warning finger, lest I move to comfort her. "Wait," she whispered.

Alice's attention was fixed on her own two hands. She folded her right hand into a fist with the thumb sticking out, and stared at it as though it were telling her something. Then hesitantly, still uncertain, she covered the fist with her other hand, except for the extended thumb. I held my

159

breath when she began to move the thumb up and down. This was an Ameslan sign, and it wasn't one I'd shown her recently.

"What is that?" I asked softly. "Tell me what you're doing."

Her tears were still flowing as she stared at her hands. "My turtle died! Mommy, I forgot to feed it and Shelly died!"

Shelly! She *had* remembered. Her emotion was true and real and it had its source in her baby years. She had loved to make that sign for her grandparents, and "Shelly" had died just as she said. Yet I knew the cry of "Mommy," which had come from her heart, didn't mean me—now. She was calling out to the long-ago mother her deepest feelings remembered.

A great clear light had flooded through me, banishing darkness and doubt. I said a small fervent prayer of thanks to whatever power had touched this room. I wanted to rush to Alice and hold her tightly, kiss away her tears, knowing she was Debbie. But I also knew that I mustn't confuse and frighten her at this moment when she'd reached back into her own memory and feelings.

In the end it was Letha who held her and soothed her tears. "It's all right, Alice. You did very well. It's over now, so I'll pick up my crystals and you can blow out the candles. In a little while we'll make our trip to Butchart Gardens."

Alice seemed a little dazed, with no full understanding of what had happened, but she crawled about willingly on hands and knees, helping Letha.

Kirk came over to me. "You're satisfied now, aren't you?"

We spoke softly, and Alice wasn't listening. "Yes, I'm satisfied. That was a turtle sign she used to make for her deaf grandparents when she was little. And the name she gave her turtle was Shelly. There isn't any way she could remember this unless she was really Debbie. Now the Corwins will have to give her up."

"Be careful," Kirk warned. "They aren't going to admit to

160

kidnapping, and I don't know if what just happened will hold up in a law court."

"But you and Letha are witnesses. And my parents will support this too."

"Take it easy. Don't move too soon. They'll find lawyers to prove you wrong. They'll say you planted the name and the sign in Alice's mind. This could go on in the courts for years. And in the meantime the Corwins have custody."

My state of euphoria began to fade. "They haven't any money for lawyers—those two."

"Maybe not. But Mrs. Arles has plenty."

"Surely she won't—she can't—"

"She can, once she's made up her mind that Alice is her great-granddaughter. Dillow's told me that. I don't think anything less than strong *proof* will make her change."

"Not since you put that page of Edward's journal in her hands," I said bitterly.

"I know, Jenny. I wish now that I'd waited until I saw what happened here today. Perhaps that's why Mrs. Radburn wanted me here, but don't give up. There are other ways to be rid of the Corwins. That's what I'm working on. I owe Edward that much."

I didn't want to think about what he might mean. I was afraid to trust him. The important thing that I must recognize concerned the delicate matter of Alice herself. There was no reason for her to turn to me as her mother, just because I made claims. There was her attachment to Peony to be considered, and I didn't know how deep her emotions might run.

Letha spoke to Kirk. "I think Alice needs some fresh air and activity now. Will you take her outside, please. Mrs. Thorne and I will be along in a few moments."

"Yes, madam," Kirk said. "Come on, Alice. We'll go get a piece of that arbutus bark you wanted."

First Alice brought the frog to me. "Will you tell me what his name is? What did Debbie call him?"

---

161

"She named him Amarillo," I said.

Alice repeated the name, rolling out the syllables, enjoying the sound. "Amarillo! I like that. Will you keep him for me now?"

She went happily off with Kirk, and Letha moved to the sofa to sit down, lavender skirt and silver sphinxes shimmering around her.

"Can we talk for a moment, Jenny? I heard what you and Kirk were saying just now. No—don't worry. Alice wasn't listening. She was in her own world, busy blowing out candles. But I think Kirk is right about not moving too fast. I've watched him too and I understand a little better. I still think he's a pretty uncertain fuse, and I don't know what the future holds. He makes me anxious."

"I thought knowing the future was your thing."

She smiled. "I don't go around reading minds and predicting as a regular thing, Jenny. When it comes, it comes. But I don't think he will hurt you or Alice. You're satisfied about the child now?"

"I can't believe anything else. Not when she made the sign and said the turtle's name. Alice *is* my little girl. But what am I to do?"

"The way will open. It always does when there's a serious need. You'll see."

I shook my head. "I lost my confidence in fate a long time ago. Everyone goes around with unanswered needs and questions—and *nothing* happens."

"You don't know that, any more than I do. Sometimes reasons aren't evident until years have passed. And you must admit that something *has* happened for you, here in Victoria. Perhaps it was intended that you should come. Just be a little patient until we see what develops. Don't say anything to Mrs. Arles right away. It's better if she can come around to this on her own."

"What she's already come around to is the intention to send me home as soon as possible."

———

162

"Then we'll find a way to postpone that."

"You have so much confidence. Why are you helping me, Mrs. Radburn?"

She looked serene, fully in control. For her it didn't seem to make any difference whether others believed in her gifts, so long as *she* believed, and she answered me frankly, openly.

"First, I'm sure that you and Alice have suffered enough, and that she is your child. So she must be restored to you. But even before you came, I wanted her *not* to be Edward's daughter. It means a great deal to Joel, if Mrs. Arles's long-time will continues to stand. Edward was her only direct descendant, but Joel is related to her, and she is very much attached to him. Also, he is Lewis Radburn's son. A long time ago she believed that Lewis was her one great love. Deceiving herself, of course. She can be very good at that. In her present will Joel inherits everything."

"But should that matter to him? I thought the Radburns were well off."

"We keep up a good front but there's not nearly enough to help Joel in his important research. Corinthea has made small gifts, but he needs a great deal more. He's on the verge of success, and he's been working on something that may affect the immune system—which means helping in the fight against almost every disease. That's why I knew a way would open for him with your coming. It would be too awful if her fortune fell into the Corwins' hands through the little girl. Large sums might be wasted before they could ever reach Alice. Or it might all be tied up in a trust. Either way, Joel would lose out."

Letha began to roll up the mat on which Alice had lain, and then packed candles and crystals carefully into her carpetbag. She seemed cheerful and satisfied over the success of what she'd arranged, yet a nagging doubt had started up in me. I didn't believe that Joel's mother meant to depend entirely on "energies" from some other plane to help her

163

son. She was managing much of this herself, with the strongest of motives. Nevertheless, something *had* happened inside Alice. Not only the name that had come to her, but the turtle sign as well. This result was beyond any mortal powers Letha might have—and this I could trust.

The carpetbag was full, but Letha sat down again. "Please understand, Jenny, that what happened here this morning is important to others besides yourself. This was good energy—positive energy. Something is working against forces that are evil. But now Corinthea must be convinced, and that may be harder to do."

"What about Alice? What if she is tied to Peony as though she were her real mother?"

"In the long run, that won't matter."

"It might if Alice feels a strong love for Peony."

"As she very well may. But she is also her own person. I've seen that. She has an intelligence beyond her years, and she will adjust to whatever happens. Children do—perhaps better than adults sometimes."

That was what I feared—that Alice had already adjusted away from me to such a degree that she could never come back.

"It can never be the way it was," Letha said wisely. "Just wait a little longer. Can you manage that?"

I made no promise. All this must be played from hour to hour, and there seemed no guidelines I could follow.

"There's something I haven't told you," I said. "Around three this morning I was awakened by a whistling sound in my room. When I found an old speaking tube behind the desk, a voice warned me to leave."

"That sounds desperate. I hope it doesn't go any further than a warning."

I hoped so too. "When I went into the hall to see if anyone was there, I found Crampton asleep, sitting on a bench with her back against the wall. Apparently she'd meant to guard my room. Though I didn't know why."

"Crampton! The nurse-companion? I don't know her but I've heard Joel speak of her. Perhaps you can find out what she knows."

I could only shake my head at the thought of Crampton as an informant. She had already told me as much as she meant to.

Letha started toward the door. "We'd better go now, if we're to visit Butchart Gardens before lunch. And I think we *must* go. I have an odd feeling about that. A sort of—urgency —as though we are meant to go there. As though something is waiting for us—something that can't happen until we arrive."

"Do you really believe in such premonitions?"

"Too often they turn out to be true."

"Then perhaps we should listen and not go to the Butchart Gardens today."

"We *must* go. It's necessary to face whatever's there waiting for us."

This was beginning to be too much for me, but I asked another question. "Do you believe in thought transference?"

"ESP? Of course."

"In that case, isn't it possible that everything Alice did and said came out of my mind? What if the turtle sign and Shelly's name were so strong in my subconscious that she picked them up?"

"I don't think that happened. Do you?"

"Not really. At least, I don't want to. Will you tell me one more thing? What happened at the time when Mrs. Arles sent Edward away?"

"That was so long ago. And I only heard about it second-hand. He displeased her in some way, and she threw him out."

"Because of articles he was supposed to have pawned? That seems pretty drastic. And besides, it was Tim who pawned them."

---

165

"There was more. Edward did something else that she found unforgivable. But never mind that. Jenny, tell me what happened with the lotus pin."

She'd opened the door and we started along the upper stretch of balcony.

"Mrs. Arles recognized it," I told her, "just as you knew she would. She tried to take it away from Alice. But for once she met her match, and she ended up giving it to her."

"Good for Alice!"

"The pin upset Tim too. Because it was he who took it in the first place."

"We must go down," Letha said, and hurried ahead of me. "I can feel the urgency growing, so we mustn't wait."

I held back. "I really do need to know what happened that caused Edward to be sent away. I can't deal with what's going on in that house if I don't know as much of the truth as I can find out."

"Well, I suppose it really doesn't matter now. Edward was supposed to have made a young girl pregnant. The thing that most upset Corinthea was that the girl happened to be Dillow's daughter."

She hurried toward the stairs and I went with her. This was astonishing. I hadn't thought about Dillow as a man with a daughter, a wife. He'd never seemed to have any connections outside of Radburn House.

"Is his wife alive? What happened to the daughter?"

"His wife died years ago—before it all happened. The girl went away somewhere—presumably to have the baby. It was a hoax—just a way for that young woman to get her hooks into Edward. Perhaps that's one reason he was anxious to leave. Corinthea has talked to Joel about this, which is how I know a little of what happened. Though of course by the time the truth came out Edward was gone, and he never came back. That's all I know."

We were nearing the car, and I saw Kirk sitting on a patch

---

166

of grass with Alice kneeling beside him. Both were watching a huge raven strutting nearby.

At the mere sight of her all my long-suppressed love was ready to overflow and engulf me. I longed to touch and hold her—claim her as the daughter I knew she was. Yet I knew I had to wait, and that Letha and Kirk were right. First, Alice and I must become friends. Perhaps I'd made a small beginning there.

Letha, however, was watching the chauffeur and the child, and she stopped me before we reached the car. "Don't let Alice get too friendly with him."

I had no influence with Alice, and Kirk was still a large question mark in my mind, even though he'd seemed to come over to my side to some extent.

The raven, however, reminded me of the feather in my handbag, and when we were in the car—this time with Alice up in front by choice—I took it out and held it out to Letha.

"Why did you give me this?"

"I'm not sure. I don't always understand what I'm prompted to do. It just seemed right." She took the big black feather from me and put it to her forehead. "This is where the vestige of the third eye is, Jenny. Sometimes it sees more than the eyes we use. But nothing comes to me now. It may be a talisman—anything."

I took back the feather, thinking that I would never fully understand Letha. Corinthea Arles's world was made of bricks and mortar—real. I had no idea what Letha's plane of existence was really like, and probably never would.

She patted my hand to reassure me. "The way *will* open. Something always happens—you'll see. But first it may be rough going—even dangerous."

The dangers I feared weren't physical—only mental and emotional.

We were following the highway toward the airport now, and Kirk was driving with his usual skill. I noticed again how

167

his dark hair curled crisply beneath his cap, and knew just how springy it would feel if I touched it. Impatiently, I banished such an unwanted response. I must focus now on whatever lay ahead at Butchart Gardens.

# *11*

On the way to Butchart Gardens Letha told me a little about the couple who had created this beautiful place —Robert Pim and Jenny Foster Butchart. Their vision, and a great deal of work and imagination, had turned a quarry that had been used for Mr. Butchart's cement works into a glorious garden. Rock and rubble had to be cleared out and tons of earth brought in. Jenny Butchart knew very little about gardening to start with, but she was always a doer. She began by putting in a series of individual gardens around the residence she and her husband built near Tod Inlet. Next she turned her developing talent to the sunken garden that would fill the big quarry.

Letha warmed to her account, and I tried to listen.

"What's more, Mrs. Butchart managed it all with surprising speed. In a few years there were flower beds, newly planted trees, and winding paths, all surrounded by steep rock quarry walls. A deep part of the quarry became a lake, and later there would be a fountain. But Jenny hated those walls of bare rock, so she did something about them. She had herself lowered in a bosun's chair and she planted ivy everywhere across the walls. Today you'd hardly know the rock was there."

Alice looked around in the front seat. "Can we walk around in the gardens, Mrs. Radburn?"

"Of course. No cars are allowed inside. There are so many paths that we can't cover it all today. But this is a good time, since the summer tourist season is over, and the next crop of visitors hasn't arrived yet. It's beautiful here in winter, too."

We'd turned off the main highway onto a long avenue lined with cherry trees that would be glorious in spring bloom. When we came to parking spaces, Kirk pulled into one. Ahead rose the rambling brown building that had once been the Butchart residence.

"Benvenuto, they called it," Letha said, "which of course means Welcome."

Now we could glimpse flower beds, bright with the yellow and orange of fall. Roses were still blooming, pink and red in their own enclosure. The Sunken Garden lay beyond the house.

As we left the car, Letha spoke to Kirk. "You're on your own, so you can do whatever you like. We may stop for lunch, and we probably won't be back for a couple of hours or more."

Alice put the frog on the front seat of the Mercedes. "Can't Kirk come with us?" she asked.

Kirk answered quickly for himself. "I've brought my own lunch, and a book to read, so I'll stay here for now. But, Mrs. Radburn, do you see the car parked over there?"

We turned to look at a solitary BMW in a parking space opposite. An empty car.

"Why, that's mine!" Letha exclaimed. "How in the world—?"

"You told me to give the key to Dillow, madam, so he could move it out of the driveway," Kirk reminded her.

"But who would bring it here?"

Kirk hunched his shoulders, watching Letha curiously. She didn't seem to be getting any message at the moment.

"Well—let's go ahead. We'll find out eventually, I suppose."

If Alice was disappointed because Kirk couldn't come

with us, she forgot him quickly when she discovered the Butchart Boar. Letha, playing guide, told us that Ian Ross, Jenny and Robert's grandson, and his wife Ann-Lee had placed the boar here, dedicating it to all the children and animals who visited these gardens. "Tacca" was a copy of just such a statue in the Straw Market of Florence, Italy—a big bronze fellow with ears cocked alertly, forelegs propping him in a sitting position, and his snout dripping water into a small pool. The snout had been polished by thousands of visitors who touched it for luck. Clearly, he was amiable and invited affection, so Alice ran over to pat the shiny snout. Her enjoyment of every new experience touched me. So little effort seemed to have been made by the Corwins to stimulate all this eagerness for something new.

Letha paid the entry charge and brought us maps. Several of the individual gardens were labeled within the whole— Italian, Japanese, a rose garden, a water lily pool, among others. Before we started off we looked through a moon opening in white latticework to what had been Mrs. Butchart's private garden and its rose-surrounded pool.

The winding path we followed beyond the house curved beside a waist-high supporting wall of stone that kept the steep bank of trees above from sliding down. Most of these were dark evergreens, though we caught glimpses of autumn flame through their branches now and then. Above one bank, gnarled roots were exposed, knotted and tangled, and at once Alice clambered up among what she called the "witch trees."

I found myself watching every move she made, listening to every word. She *was* Debbie—all my uncertainty was gone. Yet I still tried to hold back the tide of affection that wanted to pour through me and reach out to her. What if she were never returned to me? How could I bear to lose her all over again?

Here and there along the paths had been set teakwood

171

benches protected by sheltering roofs. The wood had come from the decks of old sailing ships.

As we walked, Letha and I were on the lookout for whoever had come here in her car, but in this maze of gardens we might not meet the driver unless, as Letha pointed out, this was intended to happen.

Around a curve, the sunken garden burst upon us in all its form and color. We stood at a vantage spot high above the deep quarry, so that the entire tapestry spread away at our feet. By this time the rock walls were hidden, not only by ivy but by tall trees that made a green frame for all that lay within. Colors had been grouped and spaced, so there were beds of scarlet, of yellow, of pink and white, purple and blue. Low green growth separated these splashes of color, and arborvitae stood like dark sentinels, beautifully shaped and tall. Smaller trees, alive with leafy growth, softened the contours and lent their own beauty to the patterned scene. Maples seemed to glow with autumn fire, and green grass bordered the beds. A gracefully winding stone path curved along the floor of the quarry, itself an exclamation of contrasting white amid all the color and greenery.

Chrysanthemums, begonias, geraniums, roses—all had been planted with an eye for design, and a recognition that the entire panorama would be viewed from where we stood. It was like looking down upon the vast, framed painting of a garden—so astonishingly beautiful that it could hardly be real. Yet the air was sweet with the scent of living flowers and plants.

I glanced at Alice, who was holding to the rail beside me, and wondered what all this meant to her. "Tell me what you feel," I said.

She answered softly, "It *sings!*"

Delight touched me. When Debbie was little, I'd tried to stimulate her senses with sight and sound and texture. I used to tell her that "pretty" and "beautiful" were easy words to say, but there was more to be found when we let what we saw come through and speak to us in its own special way. Now *this* child was sensing the orchestra of color that lay spread below us.

"I can hear it too," I said.

She looked up at me happily. "Farley thinks I'm silly if I talk like that."

"And Peony?"

She moved away uneasily and didn't answer.

"Every year"—Letha was enjoying her role of guide— "the plantings are different. Every year tulips are brought from Holland and the whole pattern keeps changing. It's a living tapestry."

Alice came suddenly alert. "Look! Down there!"

Her quick eyes had spotted what we hadn't yet seen. Coming into view between two arborvitae that guarded each side of the curving path was Crampton, large and implacable, wheeling Mrs. Arles's chair.

"So *this* is what I felt," Letha said. "It must be serious to bring Corinthea out here in my car. We'd better go down to meet them right away."

Alice slipped her hand into mine, for once uncertain, and I squeezed it reassuringly—even though alarm was what I too felt as we started down the switchback stairs to the quarry floor.

The two below had seen us, and Crampton stopped the chair. The moment we reached them Corinthea Arles spoke sharply.

"Where have you been? We've been here for nearly an hour! I couldn't bear sitting in the car, and I thought you'd come here."

"We didn't know you were waiting for us, Corinthea," Letha said mildly. "Otherwise, we'd have hurried. We stopped off at my son's apartment first, since there was something I wanted to show Jenny and Alice."

In this natural beauty both Crampton, in her nurse's uni-

173

form, and Mrs. Arles, wrapped in a long black coat, struck a note of inappropriate darkness amidst all the color.

"What did you want to show them?" Mrs. Arles demanded suspiciously.

Alice had recovered from her moment of uncertainty. She dropped my hand and went to stand before Corinthea Arles, unintimidated now and ready to explain before Letha did.

"Mrs. Radburn made a spell," she announced. "A magic spell, but not tricks like Farley does. It was so I could remember."

"Remember what?" There was sudden tension in Corinthea's voice.

"I don't know if the spell worked or not," Alice told her, "but anyway I remembered my turtle's name. The turtle I had when I was little."

"And what was that name?"

Alice shook her head. "I'm not sure. I feel sort of mixed up about what happened."

A turtle's name was obviously not the memory Mrs. Arles feared, and she dismissed Alice's words with a flick of her hand.

"None of that matters. Something dreadful has happened at the house. I couldn't find Joel to talk to, and I had to discuss this with someone at once. Since I knew you'd be out here, I had Crampton bring me." She looked up at the nurse. "Will you take Alice for a walk now? Just show her some of the gardens. Jenny can wheel my chair, if necessary, but we'll stay right here. Come back in a little while."

Crampton and Alice stared at each other, neither one moving. Alice made up her mind first. She darted away, running toward the higher ground from which we'd just descended.

"Go after her, Crampton!" Mrs. Arles cried.

"No, Mrs. Arles," Crampton said firmly. "I'll stay right here with you. Let younger legs go chasing after the child."

"I'll follow her," I offered, and didn't wait to see how Mrs. Arles would respond to Crampton's rebellion.

By the time I reached the upper level Alice was only a flicker of long legs disappearing around a far turn. I hurried in pursuit, but by the time I reached the curve in the path she was out of sight. The branching way to my right was labeled JAPANESE GARDEN. This might appeal to Alice, and I turned off to search.

A thicket of bamboo hid the next turn in the path, and there were no strollers in sight. I'd lost the sound of her feet, but I heard new sounds of running water, where a stream flowed underground to feed a small pond. Stepping-stones led across a surface that reflected green plantings all around, and a small red torii gate on the bank cast streaks of reflected red across the water. No sign of Alice disturbed this quiet place, and the outer world seemed far away.

She could be hiding nearby, or she could have run off in almost any direction. I would search for a few moments here and then try another path.

Above me, as I followed the narrow climbing way, stood a small pavilion, its sides enclosed and brick steps leading to an open doorway. The little Japanese house might appeal to Alice, so I found my way past gracefully dwarfed bonsai trees and ran up the steps.

Inside the single small room the floor was rough stone, with wooden benches along the walls. On one of these Alice huddled, wide-eyed and hostile now, her knees drawn up beneath her chin. She looked like some small hunted animal, and I knew she might run off again at the slightest alarm. I blocked the doorway and stood listening to sounds the stream made, tumbling beneath the pavilion on its way to the pool.

Alice watched me warily, and when I said nothing she burst into words. "I won't go back with *her!* I was having fun —but she's spoiled everything!"

I sat down on the bench, not touching her. "You can come

with us, if you like. We can return to Mrs. Radburn's car, and Kirk can drive Mrs. Arles in her car."

"What if she won't let me? She only sent me away so I couldn't listen. Like always! But I don't want to go back. I like it here." Alice raised her voice above the sound of tumbling water. "Maybe I'll stay here forever!"

"You might get hungry," I suggested. "Mrs. Radburn said we could have lunch before we go home."

Alice brightened a little. "Just so we don't have to eat with old Corinthea."

"I don't think she'll join us. Suppose we find our way back to where we left Mrs. Radburn? Then I'll explain that you'll come with us."

She made no move to stand but I could almost see the wheels going round in her head as she puzzled.

"How did I know about the turtle?" She sounded hesitant, a little fearful. "How did I know its name and how it died?"

"You knew because you remembered." That was as far as I dared to go.

One thing I could do, and I gave in to my own longing and put my arm around Alice. For just a moment she resisted, and then leaned against me, needing whatever human, loving support I could offer.

"I wish I could run away from Victoria," she said.

"Away from your—mother?"

"Sometimes I think maybe I'm a changeling, and I make up stories—like maybe my real mother is a queen someplace. Or my father is rich and important—not dead like Edward. If I ran away maybe I could find them—my real mother and father."

Her words gave me a surge of unreasonable hope, though I knew by this time that what Alice said one day might be totally the opposite the next. Most children played such make-believe about who they were.

"I don't think you should run away," I said gently, "but it's time to go back to the Sunken Garden. Mrs. Arles and Mrs.

176

Radburn have probably finished talking now, and they'll be worried about you. Besides, I'm getting hungry."

Again I'd spoken the key word. Alice came with me more willingly and we found our way back to the main path. We didn't need to descend, however, because we found Letha seated alone on a low rock wall at the higher level. She waved when we came into sight, and hurried to meet us.

"Thank goodness you've come back! Crampton has taken Mrs. Arles home in her car. She was upset and feeling ill, so she wanted to go home as quickly as possible. Are you all right, Alice?"

"Sure—I'm fine. Jenny said we could have lunch here."

"We'll do that right away," Letha promised.

Satisfied, Alice wandered ahead, exploring along the way.

"Did you find out what upset Mrs. Arles?" I asked.

"Yes." Letha sounded grave. "But I can't explain till we're alone. It seems that Farley has thrown a wrench into the machinery, and he's disturbed Corinthea badly. I'll tell you as soon as I can."

We lunched in the Conservatory—a restaurant that occupied part of what had once been the main residence. It was a bright room, filled with plants, with sunlight pouring through latticework. The meal might have been pleasurably uneventful, except for a question Alice suddenly threw at me.

"Where is your little girl's father?" she asked.

I told her that he had died in an accident a long time ago—before my daughter was lost.

"So your Debbie didn't have a father either?"

"When she was little she did," I said.

Alice sighed. "I wish I could have a real, live father."

I sat in stricken silence, while Letha managed distraction with some story I didn't listen to. Perhaps Alice herself had some protective safety latch that kept her from opening doors into further confusion, for she dropped the subject as suddenly as she'd brought it up.

177

When we returned to the parking area, Kirk and the Mercedes were gone, and we drove back to Victoria in Letha's car. Alice was comfortably full of food and a little sleepy. She sat between us in the front seat and leaned drowsily against me, so that I could put my arm around her again and feel her child's warmth. I could even catch that odor of the outdoors that is familiar to any mother. When Debbie smelled like that, I used to rush her off for a bath. Now it was a good, earthy, child scent, and for a little while I could be mindlessly content.

When we reached the driveway outside Radburn House, we found Joel's empty car near the door—so he had been located and would be inside. Kirk sat on a rock near the porch, waiting for whenever he might be needed next, his expression deliberately blank. Letha pulled up beside her son's car and beckoned to Kirk as we got out.

"Is there trouble?" she asked.

"Mrs. Arles has had some sort of attack," Kirk said. "Dr. Radburn's been called and he's with her now. I'm waiting in case he wants to take her to the hospital."

"Maybe I upset her too much," Alice said.

"I don't think it was your fault," Letha assured her quickly. "She was already disturbed when she came to meet us."

"If she's my great-grandmother, why don't I feel sorry? Why don't I care?"

"It's not whether she's related to you that matters," Letha said. "She's old and lonely and sick. Maybe we all need to think about that." But she spoke as though her heart wasn't in her words, and I thought again of what Letha Radburn wanted for her son.

Alice remembered something. "We left the frog—whatever his name is—in the other car. Do you want him back, Jenny?"

"If you'd like to keep him, that's fine," I said. "I think Debbie would like you to have Amarillo."

---

178

Though I watched carefully, Alice didn't seem to react to the frog's name. She repeated it again as though she liked the sounds, but my words had separated her from Debbie. She needed that—needed her own accustomed identity, without all those confusing questions. Though she was too intelligent not to return to them.

Kirk reached into the car and pulled out the frog, handing it to her. At once she slipped her hand into the mitt, and as she went off in the direction of the rear garden, the frog seemed to be talking to her busily.

Letha said, "Please wait for me inside, Jenny. I'll join you in a minute."

Clearly, she wanted a moment alone with Kirk, and though I wondered what that was about, I climbed the steps, leaving them alone.

Dillow met me at the door, filled with disapproval. "Mrs. Arles should never have gone to the Butchart Gardens. *I* wouldn't have taken her, but she wouldn't listen to me. Crampton did what she wanted, the way she always does."

For once he sounded open in his complaints. "What happened here when they got back?" I asked.

But now he withdrew. "Dr. Radburn will talk with you when he is free, madam. Please wait in the parlor, and I'll let him know you are here."

I asked a direct question. "Tell me why you took Kirk McKaye on as chauffeur?"

His look slid away from my face, and he began to move down the hall, not intending to answer.

"What would Mrs. Arles think of what you've done?" I pressed him.

He paused in his retreat. "I believe that she would thank me," he said.

"Because of Kirk's connection with Edward Arles? Then why haven't you told her?"

His look was carefully blank as he hurried off toward the rear of the house.

179

For a few moments longer I stood in the foyer at the foot of the stairs. Light from stained glass speckled my hands as though they'd broken out with some curious disease. Certainly a sickness pervaded all of Radburn House and the people under its roof. Including me.

Back toward the library the door remained closed, and I heard no sound of voices. The house had shut itself away from me—the outside intruder. The very quiet seemed ominous, too secretive, like its residents.

I went into the parlor and sat on a velvet-covered sofa that fought my weight with its hard springs. Victorian furniture hadn't been very comfortable.

Joel found me there and sat down beside me. He, at least, always seemed sane and direct, not given to evasions and secrets. Now, however, he seemed worried.

"I'd like to know what happened, Jenny. Corinthea can hardly speak. She won't go to the hospital where she belongs, and gets excited when I suggest it. Crampton mutters and Dillow's avoiding me. What can you tell me?"

"Not much. I don't really know what happened. Mrs. Arles spoke of Farley upsetting her. Your mother should be in soon, and she spent some time with her before she became ill."

"Where did you go with my mother today? Besides Butchart Gardens?"

I told him about the visit to his apartment, and described Letha's ritual of candlelight and crystals. I told him of Alice's identification of the turtle by name. And of the way she had used the deaf sign without understanding what she'd done.

"For me this seems final proof," I finished. "I know now that she's Debbie."

Joel touched my hand. "I'm glad. This is what *you* needed. But I'm not sure it will stand up as legal proof. Are you certain you haven't mentioned the name to Alice—perhaps saying it without thinking? Or even showed her the sign—so she simply stored it away?"

These were things Kirk had suggested too.

"I don't believe that," I told him. "In fact, I've been careful up to now not to speak the name she gave her turtle, or to show her the sign."

"I'm afraid lawyers aren't going to believe in my mother's spells, and Corinthea seems to have become convinced of the opposite. Though she was still hesitating because she distrusts the Corwins."

"Why did she invite me here in the first place? When I arrived, she seemed open-minded."

"She has that strong conscience she brags about, and the resemblance to your child impressed her."

"Then why has she changed? Is it because of that page from a journal Edward is supposed to have kept? Do you know about that?"

"She showed it to me, and she believes there was a baby, and that Alice was that baby. She *wants* to believe. My mother thinks differently, as you know. How did Alice react to what happened today?"

"She's confused—puzzled. She's trying to figure things out, with not much to go on. She's smart and she knows something is wrong. I haven't dared to say very much."

Joel's look was kind and he put an arm about me, not entirely impersonal. "You've had a rough time ever since you came here, Jenny. But we'll work this out. Somehow."

Sympathy could weaken me. For just a moment I leaned into his arm, reassured because his touch didn't start up wild fantasies I couldn't deal with. But what must be done I must do myself, without any weak leaning, and I straightened a bit stiffly.

He took his arm away casually. "You're right not to say anything to Alice yet. Give this a bit more time, even though I know that's hard to do."

Time was not something I could count on.

Letha came in, looking for me, her eyes bright with something that might be anger, and I wondered what she and

Kirk had said to each other out on the driveway. He could be so easily antagonistic—and then what?

"Corinthea's had another attack, hasn't she?" she asked her son. "Is it serious?"

"I can't tell yet. She can barely talk, but I think her mind is clear, and she knows what she wants—which is *not* to be taken to the hospital. I've done what I can, and Crampton is with her."

Letha turned to me. "Have you seen the Corwins?"

"Not since we got back. Dillow mentioned that they'd gone out for a walk."

"Good—perhaps we can talk without the house listening. I had a little time with Corinthea before she began to feel ill, and she told me what had happened. Farley gave her a flat ultimatum this morning. Either she must decide that Alice is her great-granddaughter, Edward and Peony's child, and make changes in her will to take care of the Corwins for life, or else Farley will take Peony and Alice away, and Corinthea will never see her again. She thinks that Farley is bluffing, but he's pretty slick, and she believes that she hasn't much time left to play games. This is what sent her so urgently to talk with me, when she couldn't find you, Joel. This time, even though she hates to give in, I think she will. She wants Alice and is already convinced about her."

"If I could just tell her what happened today—" I broke in.

"You can't," Joel said firmly. "Not now."

"I started to tell her," Letha went on, "but she wouldn't let me. Of course she's always imperious, so she said I must find you at once, Joel."

"How far did you get in telling her?" Joel asked.

"Naturally, I told her she needn't worry about any of this, since Alice isn't Edward's child."

"No wonder she collapsed!"

Letha paid no attention. "She has chosen the most effective weapon against Farley that she could use. She's moved out of his reach and bought herself some time."

182

"If it doesn't cost her life," Joel said.

Letha looked thoughtful, and I remembered what she had told me about Corinthea's will. If Mrs. Arles should die now the will would stand in Joel's favor, and the Corwins would be left out. This didn't make me feel any better, however. As Alice might be slowly coming to realize that she was my lost Debbie, *I* must face the fact that Peony and Farley really were kidnappers. Farley, rather than giving up, could be a real threat, and there was no telling on what new path of attack his plotting might take him.

Joel went on. "Our first concern must be Corinthea. Everything else can wait. She shouldn't be left alone in Crampton's and Dillow's hands. Will you stay with her for a while, Mother? I have something on this afternoon that can't be canceled, but I'll come back here as soon as I can get away."

"Of course I'll stay. And Jenny will be here to help as well —won't you, my dear?"

They both looked at me.

"I'm not going anywhere," I said. "Though I don't think I'm a calming presence for Mrs. Arles right now."

Letha had begun to look at me rather strangely, her eyes suddenly wide and searching. It was as though she were looking, not at me, but at something beyond me and far away. The back of my neck prickled and it was all I could do not to look around. She was probably hearing her own "voices" again, and I didn't want to know what they were telling her.

"Something is stirring in this house, Jenny. Something unhealthy that must be resisted."

"Mother!" Joel broke in. "Stop that! Jenny's been upset enough for one day, so don't go spooky on us now."

Again I was thankful for his sanity.

"I can't help it when this happens," Letha reminded her son, but at least she stopped staring past me. I already knew

183

that inimical forces were alive in this house, and that Farley Corwin was to be feared.

"If you'll go in to sit with Corinthea now," Joel suggested to his mother, "Crampton can use a break."

Before either of them could leave, however, Farley came hurrying into the room. "Have you seen my wife?" he demanded.

He hadn't met Letha until now, and Joel introduced him briefly before he answered. "I thought she'd gone for a walk with you."

"She did. But we had a disagreement, and she ran off. She's easily upset these days, as you can imagine." He glanced in my direction—a look that added to my uneasiness.

"Why is your wife upset?" Joel asked.

Farley's magician's fingers flicked the air, as though he would make the question vanish. "All these hints and challenges—even accusations! Ridiculous, of course, but very upsetting. Since Mrs. Arles is ill, we must wait a little while longer. But not too long, Dr. Radburn."

For once, Joel lost his patience. "It's because of you that Mrs. Arles has suffered this second stroke, Corwin. It might be a good idea if you and your wife would just go away. There's nothing to hold you here now."

I didn't want that to happen—because they would take Alice with them. Perhaps even use her to fight the will.

Farley shrugged elaborately. "You don't know that there's nothing to hold me here. Anyway, the immediate problem is to find my wife. She goes to pieces so easily these days." He gave us a derisive bow and walked out of the room.

Letha spoke quietly. "We mustn't let him upset *us*. Go along to your appointment, Joel, and I'll sit for a while with Corinthea. When you get back, I'll call the Empress Hotel and see if my favorite room is available. Perhaps I can stay there tonight, and then if you need me I'll come at once."

"Thanks, Mother. I don't think you'll need to stay for long.

184

But if it makes you feel better to be close at hand, that's fine." He looked at me. "Just keep your courage up, Jenny. My mother's hunches usually pay off, and she's probably right about Alice."

"*I* am right about Alice," I said quietly.

Letha smiled at us both. "Of course you're right, Jenny. And I'll forgive you the word 'hunch,' Joel."

When her son had gone, she rose gracefully in her swirl of skirts and beads. "What do you plan to do now, Jenny?"

I hadn't the slightest idea. "Mark time, I suppose. Perhaps I'll go down in the garden and just sit for a while—where it's beautiful and peaceful."

"A good idea. I'll see you later."

There was a question that had, for some reason, been nagging at me, and I asked it now.

"Before I go, will you tell me one thing, Letha. You mentioned Dillow's daughter and said there was a scandal concerning Edward. What was her name?"

"Let me see." Letha considered for a moment. "Yes—I remember now. Though I never really knew her. It was Eleanor. Eleanor Dillow. Everyone used to call her Nellie."

# 12

After Letha had gone, without any notion of the way her words had affected me, I sat for a while, the stained glass aura of the room glowing darkly about me. From the way she had spoken, Letha seemed to have no idea that *Peony* must be Dillow's daughter Nellie. Letha had been out of touch with Radburn House for years, and in this case her intuition certainly hadn't been working. She'd said she hadn't known Nellie. And Joel's close connection with Mrs. Arles hadn't developed until after his father died. So neither would have recognized the adult Peony.

If Peony was Dillow's daughter, all sorts of alarming possibilities opened up. This meant that the girl who had tried so long ago to play a hoax of pregnancy with Edward had eventually married him years later in Brazil. Perhaps she'd even gone there in pursuit of him, only to fall into Farley Corwin's hands first. But she *had* found and married Edward Arles, in spite of having caused him to be disinherited by his grandmother.

Questions crowded in on me. Why had no one mentioned that Peony-Nellie was Dillow's daughter? Mrs. Arles had said nothing of this, and neither had Peony. Nor had Dillow ever indicated a relationship. In fact, I'd had the impression that he didn't like either of the Corwins. Though now I recalled that I'd seen Peony, Farley, and Dillow talking secretively on the dimly lighted driveway last night. Did he really believe that *he* was Alice's grandfather? He had been in Mrs. Arles's confidence all along, and had known from the first why I was here. No wonder he'd seemed disapproving. And Dillow had hired the new chauffeur because Kirk had known Edward Arles and had a letter from him. Perhaps he'd hoped that Kirk would be able to further Peony's claim to being Alice's mother.

There were more questions than there were answers, though it was all beginning to come together. Now I needed to talk with Kirk again as soon as I could.

I went into the hall and glanced in the direction of Mrs. Arles's room. The door was open, but everything seemed quiet, and I started toward the front door.

"Jenny!" That was Alice, calling to me softly from the stairs.

I looked up to see her on the landing, with Uncle Tim descending behind her. Alice held one of his carved totems in her hands and she ran down to show it to me.

"Look! Isn't this beautiful? Uncle Tim's been working on it for a long time, and he wants to give it to *her.*" She nodded toward the library down the hall.

"This isn't a good time," I told her. "Mrs. Arles isn't feeling well. It's very beautiful." I took the carving and smiled up at Uncle Tim.

This time the painted faces in the wood all seemed to be human, though exaggerated and formalized. Alice explained that Tim had carved likenesses of Corinthea's and his parents, as well as the face of a sister who had died when she was small. She identified each one for me. Joel's father, Lewis Radburn, was strongly portrayed—a handsome face, with strength of character in every line. Perhaps because Tim knew this would please Corinthea, and so had taken special pains?

"Maybe you could give this to Mrs. Arles," Alice said.

———

187

"Uncle Tim wants her to have it so she won't be mad at him any more and send him away."

"He needn't worry about that now," I assured her. "She's too sick to do anything."

Tim came down to our level. He couldn't have read our words, and he looked anxious. Once more, I was aware of what a big man he was, with powerful shoulders and strong, sensitive hands that could use carving tools with delicacy. Or pick up a man like Farley Corwin as though he weighed nothing. A mild man, except when pushed too far, when sleeping anger could waken in him ominously. I knew very well where the source of his anger lay. I could understand because of my own father, who could sometimes be driven to a fury that rose out of his own frustration.

I held up the small totem as I spoke to him. "This is beautiful. Interesting."

He looked pleased, though his smile was unsure and tentative. It was as though he apologized for his deafness—when it was really the people around him who made the disability a handicap through their lack of understanding.

I returned the carving to Alice. "Let's try this together. We'll go down to Mrs. Arles's room and *you* take the totem to her. Tim and I will stay back at first and see what happens." Tim watched my lips, and I hoped he understood some of what I was suggesting.

We got no farther than a few steps through the door, however. Mrs. Arles lay propped against fluffy pillows, her eyes closed, and her face as pale as the pillowcase. She looked thinner too, as though she had begun to shrink. Letha sat beside her bed, and when she saw us she touched a finger to her lips. At once Crampton came to block our way.

I attempted to explain about the totem carving Tim had made, but Crampton was too impatient to listen.

"You can't come in," she told us. "I don't think she'll want that heathen thing anyway."

Alice made her own decision. She marched straight past

188

Crampton to the bed. Letha made no effort to interfere, and I hung onto Crampton's arm when she would have gone indignantly after Alice.

"Wait!" I said softly. "Let's just see what happens."

Beside me, Uncle Tim stood watching, his face expressionless.

As Alice put the totem on the pillow beside Mrs. Arles's cheek, the old woman opened her eyes and stared at it.

"Uncle Tim made it for you," Alice said softly. "The faces are all from your own family."

Mrs. Arles closed her eyes briefly, then opened them. It was, perhaps, a sign of acceptance. She fixed her attention upon Alice and her words came with an effort.

"Thank you. Stay—awhile."

She meant only Alice, and her thanks had not been directed toward Tim. Crampton came quickly to remove the totem from the pillow and place it on a table away from the bed. But when she tried to pull Alice away, the child slipped out of her grasp and drew a chair over to the bed, sitting down with new determination.

Letha came to her aid. "Perhaps you could read aloud to Mrs. Arles for a little while," she said. "I was reading to her until she fell asleep."

She handed the book—*A Tale of Two Cities*—to Alice and indicated the place on the page. The scene was a dramatic tumbril sequence leading into Madame Defarge knitting beside the guillotine. Alice plunged in with enthusiasm and she read well. I noted this with pleasure, and wondered how she could ever have learned while she was in the Corwins' hands. Mrs. Arles closed her eyes again, but her face seemed more alive, as though she were listening and relishing being read to by the child she believed was her great-granddaughter.

I slipped my hand through the crook of Uncle Tim's arm and drew him back to the hall.

———

189

"She will look at your carving later," I told him, and he seemed to grasp my words.

I felt increasingly sad when I considered his position in this house. He had been cut off, as the deaf could so easily be. He would not be comfortable among the hearing, but he had no deaf friends either. He had been isolated, treated as though he were half-witted, and for this Corinthea Arles was to blame. It was a shame that she could still hold over him the threat of being sent to an institution unless he pleased her in every way.

"I think it will be all right," I told him, and he seemed to understand "all right." I went on, using expressive signs. "Thank you for the totem you made for me."

He nodded, eager to understand, as the deaf always were when hearing people made an effort. Much of the time the deaf person had to pick up clues that gave a sense of what was being said, so the right word choice could be made. How good Tim was at this I didn't know. He must have few contacts with the hearing world.

I remembered that Kirk had played chess with him, and I tried a question.

"Kirk?" I said. "Chauffeur." Then I remembered that this word would be hard for him to read. I changed it to "driver." "Do you like him—Edward's friend?"

He stared at me for a moment, struggling to figure out my meaning. Then he shook his head and went hurrying off upstairs to the safety of his own rooms. It might be too late to pry Tim from his shell and help him to a wider communication. By this time perhaps all he wanted was to be let alone to live in the unobtrusive way he'd worked out for himself. He was not unhappy, and to meddle, even out of good intentions, might only make everything worse.

Now, at least, I was free to look for Kirk. I wanted to settle a few matters that troubled me. He was not at the front of the house or in the garden. I went inside and walked quickly through to the back door. On the porch, Dillow sat in a rocking chair, polishing a pair of his own black shoes. He gave me a dour look and didn't trouble to rise.

I stopped in front of him. "I've just found out that Peony Corwin is also Nellie Dillow, your daughter. It seems strange that no one has mentioned the relationship since I came here."

"It's none of your business," he said, his insolence unconcealed. He'd made up his mind about me—I no longer counted.

"There's Alice," I pointed out.

This brought him reluctantly to his feet—perhaps only so he could face me on my own level. "You know by this time that she isn't your child."

"What I know is that her real name is Debbie Blake, and there isn't any more doubt about her being my daughter. This morning she remembered a name out of the past. She even remembered a deaf sign that she used with her grandparents when she was little. I'm afraid your Nellie hasn't been telling you much of the truth."

Elbert Dillow had been schooled to hide all private emotions under the facade of his position as butler. But there must have been times when the pretense slipped and the real man came through. It came through now, and I didn't like what I saw. Letha had spoken about some mysterious danger that might beset me at Radburn House. Now I saw it, for just an instant, looking out of Dillow's eyes.

I stayed long enough to ask one more question. "Have you seen Peony? Farley is looking for her, and he seemed anxious. Do you know where she is?"

He merely shrugged and went back to his shoe polishing.

I hurried down the back steps and found my way once more into the lower garden. The bench was empty and I sat down for a moment, breathing the fragrance of autumn roses. On the rise of hillside to my right was the small building Kirk had called a potting shed, where he had his quar-

her butler's daughter. So when Farley and I came here with Alice, she wouldn't let him acknowledge me. She hates it that I'm the mother of her great-grandchild."

"*Are* you?" I challenged. "Are you really?"

She managed to look surprised. "Of course I am. That story of yours doesn't mean anything. You made it all up."

"Why would I do that? Don't you remember a grocery store in Connecticut, Peony? I think you do. And I think you remember asking me where the mustard was. *Mustard!*" I could hear emotion rising in my voice, feel the way my hands had begun to shake. In a moment I'd be out of control.

It was Peony herself who stopped me. The very look in her eyes was blank and empty. I knew what had happened. The moment I had begun to speak she had tuned me out. I doubted that she'd heard a single word she didn't want to hear.

I tried to rouse her to a different reality. "What are you holding behind your back?"

Almost as though they didn't belong to her, she drew her hands around and stared at what she held. I saw the crumpled, half-torn sheets clutched in each hand—and the handwriting in ink.

"Those are from Edward's journal, aren't they?" I said.

Without answering, she ran back to the bedroom. I followed and saw what she'd done. On the floor beside a chair, where she must have been sitting, the cardboard covers of a brown notebook lay open, only a few pages remaining intact. Before I could move she snatched the book up and clasped it to her chest.

"I had to do this!" she cried. "I had to do it before Kirk could stop me. Dr. Radburn sent him out for a prescription for Mrs. Arles and he's sure to be back soon." She began to tear frantically at the few remaining pages.

I picked up some torn scraps and tried to examine them, but her destruction had been too thorough. "Why are you

---

afraid of Edward's journal? Are you afraid that what's left of the pages might prove that Alice couldn't be your child?"

Once more she shut out my words. "I'd better go. Before he catches me here. He might—hurt me. The way he destroyed Edward!"

I wanted to shake her. "What do you mean—destroyed? Was Kirk McKaye in Brazil?"

"You don't understand, do you? He *murdered* Edward—though he tried to blame Farley. He's violent and cruel! Edward was *good!*" She tore out the last page, ripped it to bits, and started out the door.

It was Kirk himself who blocked her way. He took off his uniform cap and sailed it across the room. "Well!" he said. "I never expected to come back to find two charming ladies waiting for me." Anger, barely expressed, deepened his voice. He took the notebook covers from Peony and opened them to scraps of paper left at the binding. "Nice work. Did you find what you were looking for?"

She was frightened now, and she spoke faintly. "I don't think Edward ever wrote those pages."

Kirk glanced around at the paper-strewn floor, and the silence froze into a threat that Peony must have felt. She rushed wildly out of the house as though some demon might pursue her.

Tossing the notebook covers aside, Kirk returned to the small living room and I followed him. "You came to find me, Jenny?" His fury was still being held in check, and perhaps not all of it was for Peony. I too was an intruder here.

There were only two chairs—a straight chair before a desk, and an armchair. I chose the straight chair and pulled it around so I could face him. There was no assurance left in me, but I tried to answer him.

"Yes, I came to look for you. When you weren't here, I'd have settled for Edward's journal, but Peony was ahead of me. Though I wouldn't have done what she did."

Unbuttoning his jacket and loosening his tie as though it choked him, Kirk sat down in the armchair.

"What did she tell you?" he asked grimly.

I looked up at the young man in the photograph, forever engaged in cutting down a tree that would never reach the ground. "She told me that was a picture of Edward Arles."

Kirk nodded. "It was taken when he was a greenhorn and first came to the logging camp. That was his first tree, and he was proud of bringing it down so it would fall where he intended. What else did she say?"

"That she'd always loved him, and that was the way she would remember him. She told me he was kind to her."

"She hardly showed her love in the end, plotting with Farley as she did."

I spoke softly. "She also said that *you* murdered Edward Arles."

I expected him to deny and scoff at the idea, and I felt disturbed when he turned away from me to pace the room. When he came back to stand before me, he said, "Do you believe her?"

"I don't know if anything she says is true. But I don't know *you* either."

"That's right—you don't. What if it's true—what I did to Edward?"

I didn't want to believe this. I was surprised at how fervently I didn't want to believe.

"*Were* you out there in Brazil?"

"You don't need to know all that, Jenny. It's not down your road."

I seemed to have lost my road, but I answered him quickly. "Only if it concerns Alice. Only if it might give me information about that baby who was born in Brazil. That's all I care about!" But was it? Did I also want to believe in this man against all my better judgment?

"I don't see how that can happen," he said.

———

196

"I'm thinking about the Corwins and what they were guilty of in that Brazilian jungle."

"It's not your problem," he repeated. "Stay out of it."

"I wish I knew where you really stand. I thought you believed me about Alice. What game *are* you playing?"

"It doesn't concern you. It's a game that needs to be played through to the end."

There was nothing more for me to say and I started toward the door.

"Wait, Jenny. First, tell me about Mrs. Arles. How is she?"

"Surviving. I left Alice reading Dickens to her. At least I know now that Peony was Nellie Dillow. That seems to complicate everything even more. You know that, of course."

Again he didn't answer.

"I wonder why Edward ever married her."

"I've wondered that myself." His anger had faded, and only the strange sadness was left. "Who knows why anybody does anything? I suppose born victims like Peony can be helpless and appealing. He'd been in love with her when he was young and they were growing up together. Anyway, what he wrote in those pages that Peony's torn up wouldn't do you much good."

I looked up at the pictures on the wall. "Peony said he was beautiful and fragile. Those are the words she used."

"Beautiful, I don't know. But fragile, yes. I suppose he was. But that was taken before Brazil. Years before."

Once more I moved toward the door, and Kirk grinned at me in the old way. "Next time you come to visit, let me know ahead of time. Then I can give you a better welcome."

I walked away from his mockery and out of the little house. In a curious flash I knew that in another time, in other circumstances, Kirk and I might have been drawn to each other. When I went down through the garden I paused to look back. He stood in the doorway, watching me, and that

197

strange sadness had touched him again. I turned and hurried through the garden.

The minute I reached the house I went directly to Mrs. Arles's room. Alice had gone, but Joel Radburn was there with his mother, and Crampton sat in her usual place beyond the bed.

"So there you are!" Letha cried as I walked in. "I've just asked Dillow to see if he could find you. Joel's letting me off duty now and I thought you might like to come over to the Empress Hotel with me. There's no point in your sitting around here for the rest of the day, and you really must see the old place. Tea at the Empress is a ritual in Victoria and I've made a reservation for us."

"Where is Alice?" I didn't feel social.

"Peony came to fetch her," Letha said. "Peony seemed upset about something, but you'll need to let that alone for now. Your time will come, Jenny, but not right yet. Try to be patient."

To wait helplessly, while something beyond my power to prevent took over, didn't appeal to me.

Joel seemed to understand what I was feeling. "My mother's right, Jenny. This is hard for you, but you need to relax a little and you can't do any good here."

What were we all waiting for, and why was I so anxious? No one was going to run away with Alice. Farley would simply sit out Mrs. Arles's illness, and Peony, of course, usually did as he wished.

I looked at the old woman in the bed, but if she had heard any of what we'd said, she gave no sign. Her eyes remained closed, and the life that had come into her face while Alice read to her had died away.

I stood up. "Thank you, Letha. I'd like to see the Empress Hotel."

"I do have something to suggest," she said. "Something that might be helpful, Jenny. So, if you're willing, we can leave right away."

---

"Perhaps I'll come with you," Joel decided. "I can help Mother settle into her room, and then, if I'm permitted, I can take you both to tea."

Letha looked pleased, but she glanced toward the bed. "Will it be all right—?"

"Everything's under control, Mother. Crampton will be on duty and I don't expect any great change tonight."

The nurse stood up. "Of course I'll be here, Dr. Radburn."

Then, as we reached the door, I looked back and saw that Corinthea Arles's eyes were open and their expression stopped me. The look she turned on Crampton was baleful with anger, and suddenly I wasn't all that sure about leaving.

In the hall I spoke to Joel. "What do you know about Crampton? Is she really trustworthy?"

He seemed surprised. "After all these years with Corinthea, I can hardly have any doubts about her."

"But Mrs. Arles looked so angry with her just now. Did you see?"

Dillow must have been hovering in the shadows near the stairs, and he stepped out into the mottled light of stained glass. "If I may say so, Dr. Radburn, Mrs. Thorne is quite right. Crampton has been behaving strangely lately."

Joel treated Dillow's words in his usual calm manner. "I'm sure she will take care of Mrs. Arles to the best of her ability. All patients resent their nurses some of the time."

"Perhaps I will go in there and watch awhile," Dillow said.

"Why don't you do that?" Joel agreed.

For a moment Dillow looked as though he might say something more, then changed his mind and went huffily back to the library.

"Crampton and Dillow have never liked each other," Joel commented.

Letha was watching me intently. "Never mind all that, Jenny. Just let it go for a while."

We went outside to find that the afternoon had clouded over and a drizzle was beginning. Before we reached the car, we were stopped again—this time by Farley Corwin, who came running down the steps after us.

"Mrs. Thorne!" he called.

I turned. "You've found Peony by now, I'm sure?"

"Yes! She's inside bawling her head off. She won't tell me why—only that you'd upset her. What did you do, Mrs. Thorne?"

I tried to answer him quietly. "I'm sorry if she's upset. I was talking to her about Alice, and she didn't want to listen."

"I think you're a little crazy," Corwin said rudely, and went back into the house.

"Is *he* beginning to crack up?" I wondered.

"Let's just give him enough rope." Joel drew my arm through his as we walked, but Letha shook her head.

"Rope isn't what's needed right now. I may have a better idea. Will you drive, Joel? We'll go straight to the Empress. Do sit in front, Jenny, and try to let everything unpleasant flow away from you."

I got into the front seat and attempted to obey. I didn't want to think about anything more that I couldn't deal with. I wanted to get away and try to figure out a plan of action for reaching through to Alice.

# 13

The Empress Hotel first opened its doors in 1908, and it had never ceased to be a major attraction in Victoria. Its appearance was that of a massive French château, and its high ceilings made it seem a lofty structure, though there were only six or seven floors. It held its own in dignity beside the Parliament Buildings, across the angle of the harbor, both designed by the same architect.

Inside, we walked down a wing of the great lobby to the elevators, and Joel came with us. Letha's favorite room was up under the eaves, where the steep slate roof began. When the elevator door opened at the top floor, a long tunnel-like corridor stretched ahead, and we stepped out onto an endless length of red carpet.

Light fixtures with curving bronze arms and big glass globes hung at intervals from the ceiling, dispelling shadows. There was no one in sight, and the silence up here seemed eerie. At the far end, past all those closed doors, we could see gray daylight at a window.

"Ghosts," I said softly as we followed the beckoning ruby carpet.

Letha smiled. "Of course. Up until Depression times the widows of wealthy colonial officials lived out their lives here. They had permanent suites and their own tables in the dining room. The lobby became their drawing room, and the

English custom of serving tea there began. I'm sure the spirits of those ladies still haunt the Empress. In fact, I think I saw one of them sitting in her special place in the lobby the last time I was here. There's still an aura of elegance about the hotel, and it's never been busier."

When we reached Letha's room, Joel took her key and opened the door. Pale light pressed at the windows, and I went to look out from under the peak of a gable. Opposite, across a lower section of roof, rose another steep, protruding gable that must duplicate this one.

Rain had begun to fall heavily, and rivulets streamed down slate roofs, splashing into gutters, pouring toward the earth. The color of the grass in front of the hotel seemed intensified in that silvery light. Along the Causeway far below, the steady traffic was punctuated by high red buses, and the water of the harbor looked choppy, with small boats bobbing at anchor.

I stayed at the window, not wanting to think or act—just to be still and exist.

Letha spoke behind me. "We must talk, Jenny."

I turned to look around the comfortable, rather old-fashioned room. In the days of the dowagers there'd have been no television set, and that was the one anachronism. There were chairs for the three of us, and when we were comfortable, Letha began to tell us what she had in mind.

"Your one hope, Jenny, is to get an admission of the kidnapping out of Peony. Your one chance is to get her to admit what they did."

"Do you know that she's Dillow's daughter?" I asked. "Her real name is Nellie."

They looked at each other in surprise, and I explained what Peony had told me about Mrs. Arles's refusal to admit that Edward's wife was her butler's daughter.

I told them what had happened a little while ago in Kirk's rooms, of how I'd come upon Peony tearing up the pages of

202

Edward's journal, and of what she had said about the photo-graph of Edward that Kirk had hung on his wall.

"Farley probably put her up to destroying the journal," Joel said.

"She made a very strange claim," I went on. "She told me that Kirk had murdered Edward Arles."

Even Letha looked startled. "Now there's an interesting turn! What did she say to support that?"

"There was no time. Kirk came in and found what she'd been doing. Peony is terrified of him. She screamed that everything in the journal was lies, and ran off like a fright-ened rabbit."

"Did you tell Kirk what Peony had said?" Joel asked.

"I told him. I also told him what she'd said about the picture of Edward—that he'd been a beautiful young man and that she had loved him."

Letha closed her eyes and seemed to disappear into her own silence. Joel, however, was still curious.

"How did Kirk react to the charge she made?"

"He didn't seem impressed, but he didn't deny anything either. It was as if he didn't care one way or the other what he'd been accused of. I asked him what game he was play-ing, and he just said it had to be played through to the end."

Letha opened her eyes. "I think we must get Peony away by herself. As long as she's near Farley you'll get nothing out of her. Perhaps you and Joel can bring her to my house."

"She won't come," I said flatly.

"She may if we can use Alice as the bait."

"How can she possibly believe that she's Alice's mother?" I said. "How can she go on fooling herself like this?"

"She doesn't dare believe anything else," Letha warned. "That's the difficult thing to break through. Farley has prob-ably frightened her so badly that this delusion is all she can hold onto. If we're able to get her away from that house and into my meditation room, who knows what may happen?"

That room, with all its emotional effect, plus Letha's own

special talents—perhaps there was some hope of success in this.

Joel agreed. "It might work. *If* you can get her away."

"I'll manage." Letha's smile was both assured and a little dreamy. By this time I'd be the last to discount what she might achieve in her own way.

Joel looked at his watch. "It's nearly four. Shall we go down for tea now?"

"Yes, it's time," Letha agreed. "But I'm not coming with you. I've had a long day, and I want to nap for a little while and then have a tray sent up to me."

"No use trying to change her mind," Joel said to me, and kissed his mother's cheek. "Have a good rest. Of course I'll call you if you're needed for anything at Corinthea's."

She came with us to the door and put her hand on my arm. "Is that feather I gave you still in your bag?"

I hadn't thought about the feather for a while. "Yes, I have it with me," I said.

"Always keep it with you, my dear."

Letha let us go and we walked down the long tunnel of corridor to the elevator.

A two-story ceiling, ornate with plaster designs, covered the Empress lobby. White columns separated an area of small tea tables from the main passageway, with tall draped windows beyond, fronting the hotel.

We were led to a corner table beside a window. My sense of being enclosed in the aura of another time was pleasant, and I could listen comfortably now to Joel's quiet voice.

He had, he said, seen just such lobbies as this when he'd traveled as a boy with his parents. "You'll still find them in the Far East, as well as in India—wherever the British have left their mark. I remember the lobby of the Peninsula Hotel in Kowloon resembling this. It's across from Hong Kong Island, where there's another city called Victoria."

This sort of talk was quieting, requiring nothing of me. I wouldn't think of Radburn House.

---

204

A waitress put small menus in front of us, though we weren't supposed to choose. The cards merely listed the repast we'd be served for tea.

I listened to Joel talk about inconsequential matters and for that little while was content. He never seemed filled with angry doubts. He had chosen his way of life, and he would hold to it, whether the money he needed was available or not. Letha was the one with a driving ambition for her son.

By the time tea was served I began to feel hungry. There were small, honey crumpets, homemade scones with thick Jersey cream, finger sandwiches of cucumber, cheese and ham, tomato slices and alfalfa sprouts. Citron almond tarts and a variety of Empress cakes were a specialty. All, of course, accompanied by a large china pot of Empress Blend tea. I wished that Alice could have been with us to enjoy the experience. Sometime perhaps I could bring her here.

The first crack in my brief spell of serenity came when I looked casually around the room and saw three people coming toward a table. Alice was to have her feast after all. She walked with an eager, springy step and was followed by Uncle Tim and Kirk McKaye—now out of uniform.

Joel saw my face and turned to look but his quiet assurance remained unruffled. "Pay no attention, Jenny. I'm glad to see Uncle Tim and Alice on an outing. So—good for the new chauffeur! But you'd better forget them for now."

This was good advice, but I couldn't take it, and I found myself stealing furtive looks at the other table. Kirk had brought a yellow tablet and he began to write on it with a ball-point pen, passing the words over to Tim. The old man read, nodded, and smiled at Alice as she pounced upon the menu that listed all she meant to eat. Her face wore a bright smiling look, so she too enjoyed an interval of escape. Escape that ought to be made permanent.

Tim was talking, his voice a little too loud, and I heard the word "totem." Kirk seemed to listen gravely, and then wrote again. Alice joined in excitedly, and I caught a word or two. They were telling Kirk about the totem carving Uncle Tim had made for Mrs. Arles, and of how Crampton had taken it from her pillow.

"Come on back, Jenny," Joel said. "Stay at this table."

But I had to watch those three. Their voices had dropped, so that I had a sense of conspiracy, as though Kirk were planning something, and that made me even more uneasy. Tim seemed to be growing angry.

"Kirk is stirring him up," I said to Joel.

"You don't know that," he told me calmly.

For once, I felt irritated with Joel. I wanted to challenge his everlasting calm—something I had valued only a little while ago.

"Doesn't anything ever upset you?" I demanded. "Don't you care enough about anything to fight for it?"

The ease went out of him, as though I'd touched a chord—some lever to a disquiet I hadn't known existed in Joel Radburn.

"Yes," he told me, "I *have* been worried ever since you walked into Radburn House and began to upset Corinthea and my mother."

I stared at him blankly, and he went on, continuing to surprise me.

"We never really know, do we, Jenny? We make up our minds about other people from whatever outward indications we can pick up—and we're often far off in our judgments. Unless, of course, the person wears visible emotions on the tip of her nose for anyone to bump into. The way you do. And perhaps my mother. I doubt if I'm as easily read."

I really looked at him then. Looked past the surface of the quiet doctor who could take charge without being aggressive, to the man underneath—a man I knew even less than I did the doctor.

"You need to be more careful, Jenny." There seemed to be a cool warning in his words. "You don't really know all that's going on. Not with any of us. Though of course we're all so sure about you—and that may be wrong too. What if you're not what you seem to be either? You worry me sometimes, Jenny Thorne. Because I don't know yet what *you* may be capable of in this unhappy situation. Perhaps that's why my mother wanted me to have some time alone with you."

The food before me no longer seemed delicious, but I drank the rest of the tea thirstily.

"There's nothing I want more than to fly home," I said. "If only I could do that without knowing very well what I'd leave behind. I feel sick and frightened a lot of the time. Because of Alice. Because of what's been done to her, and may be done in the future, if I don't find a way to intervene. It seems almost as terrible to leave her with Mrs. Arles as to have her go on with the Corwins."

The chill I'd felt in Joel subsided, and he spoke more kindly. "Listen to my mother. She wants to help you get Alice back, and her ways—even though I don't always understand them—often seem to work. Just don't jump furiously into something you can't handle."

I glanced again at the other table and saw that we had been discovered. All three were looking toward Joel and me. Alice smiled and waved, but Tim seemed upset, though I didn't know what that meant. It was Kirk's expression that disturbed me most—that dark, derisive look that had grown so familiar, and that seemed to read into my behavior intentions I never meant. I managed, at least, to smile at Alice.

"Can we leave now?" I asked Joel.

"Of course." He looked around to signal our waitress.

But Alice had already slipped away from her table and was coming toward ours. She greeted Joel first and then turned to me. "Hello, Jenny. Isn't the food great?" She eyed our remaining cakes with interest.

I held out the plate to her and she helped herself to the two with frosting.

"I enjoyed hearing you read to Mrs. Arles this afternoon," I told her. "Where did you learn how to read aloud so well?"

Her shrug was vague. "I don't know."

"Who read to you? Peony? Farley?"

She shook her head, as if puzzled by her own words. "No, I'm the one who reads to Peony. I expect that's how I got all the practice. My great-grandmother liked the story. She really opened her eyes and listened."

So Mrs. Arles had stopped being Corinthea, or the old lady, and was now being accepted in the role Corinthea herself had claimed.

"She may not really be your great-grandmother, you know," Joel said quietly.

Alice's eyes widened. "What do you mean? Everybody says she's my great-grandmother!"

"Not everybody," Joel told her. "*I* don't think she is, and neither does my mother. Jenny doesn't believe it either."

"But then—who am I? Who was my father, if he wasn't Edward Arles?"

I put an arm around her. "Don't worry, Alice. In the long run I'm sure it will be all right. Just wait a little while and everything will come clear."

I frowned at Joel, feeling that he'd gone too far, too soon.

Kirk was following Alice across the room, though Uncle Tim had stayed at their table, reading words Kirk had written for him on the yellow tablet.

When he reached us, Kirk put his hands lightly on Alice's shoulders, though his attention was fixed on Joel. "Hello, Joel Radburn," he said.

This familiar greeting from Mrs. Arles's chauffeur must have startled Joel, for he looked up at Kirk in surprise. The silence between them seemed alive with some meaning I couldn't catch.

Then Joel said, "My God!"

"Exactly," Kirk agreed. "It's a can of worms, isn't it?" He turned Alice toward their table, gave Joel a small salute, and the two walked away together. He had neither looked at nor spoken to me.

"What is it?" I cried. "Tell me, Joel!"

The waitress came with our check and Joel said, "I'll take you back to the house now, Jenny. We'll talk outside."

I glanced at Kirk's table as we went past, and found him watching us with an expression that again seemed strangely sad—and that disturbed me even more. I didn't understand what had happened, and the moment we were outside I repeated my plea for an answer.

"We'll take a cab," Joel said. "My car's back at the house, and I don't want to use my mother's. I'll tell you on the way."

The rain had lessened a little by that time and in the cab Joel asked me a question.

"How much do you know about Kirk McKaye?"

"Only that he's supposed to be Edward Arles's friend, and that your mother doesn't trust him."

"By this time I'm sure she's figured out why," Joel said. "I didn't recognize him until just now when I looked at him closely—without those dark glasses he wears. I've only known one person in my life who had eyes of that strange, almost navy blue. Kirk's no friend of Edward Arles. He *is* Edward Arles."

# 14

For a few moments I couldn't speak. The fairy-tale lights of the Parliament Buildings were on early for this darkening late afternoon, and we left them behind as we rode toward Radburn House. Everything outside the cab seemed to slide past me in a blur.

"He was right," Joel said quietly. "It is a can of worms."

I began to think of the complications. Kirk—he wasn't Edward to me—was Corinthea Arles's grandson. He was Peony's real husband—while Farley Corwin wasn't. No wonder Peony was desperate.

"I don't think Farley knows," I said. "He hasn't had much to do with Kirk, who has probably stayed out of his way. This will cut Farley out of the whole picture."

"Right. Though if he still doesn't know, I don't think Peony will tell him."

"But why hasn't Kirk told his grandmother? Why didn't he go directly to her long before this?"

"You'll have to ask him that."

I didn't want to ask him anything. He had taken me in along with the others. He might even have considered that Alice was *his* daughter. He had shown a special interest in her all along.

"And then"—I went on with my disturbing list—"Elbert Dillow is Kirk's father-in-law. No wonder Dillow took him in and kept quiet about his secret. But there's still so much I don't understand."

"Perhaps you needn't try," Joel said. He covered my tightly clasped hands with one of his own, and I relaxed a little. "Just stop worrying, Jenny. Nothing can be done right away—not while Mrs. Arles is ill. So there's still time for things to shake down and find their course—whatever it is."

"And if she dies? If she dies without ever knowing that her grandson is alive?"

"There's nothing we can do. She shouldn't be told now."

If she died before she knew, I thought, then her old will would stand and her fortune would go to Joel—which was what Letha wanted. If Mrs. Arles understood that her grandson had returned, that might change everything.

"The worst thing for me," I said miserably, "is that Alice is beginning to seem farther away than ever. Farley might have been stopped, but if Kirk chooses to claim her—"

"You're thinking too far ahead, Jenny." His hand tightened around mine. "Mother still has the plan for opening Peony up. Once she can find out the truth about Alice's birth, perhaps everything will be clear sailing for you. Just remember that there are people who don't want that truth to be known. So be careful. It might be wise for you to move out of the house for a time. You could go to Oak Bay and stay with my mother."

"I don't feel I could do that," I said. "I must be here now."

The cab had turned up the driveway to Radburn House. This time no one appeared at the front door as we got out and went up the steps. Oddly, in spite of the fact that it was growing dark, no lights burned in the front hall. Only a single light was on in the library at the far end.

"I'll look in on Corinthea," Joel said. "Then I'll leave her to Crampton for a while. I need to get back to the Empress to talk with my mother about what's just happened."

Joel switched on hall lights as we walked along, but Dillow didn't appear, and neither did Peony or Farley. In the dining room the table had been set for four—which would include me—but no one was there. The house had an empty feeling about it—unnatural.

When we entered her room we found Mrs. Arles asleep, her lips puffing rhythmically. Otherwise, the room was empty. No Crampton sat beside her bed, and her absence seemed unusual.

"I'll see if I can locate someone," Joel said. "Will you stay with Corinthea until I come back?"

I sat down beside the bed. "Don't forget I'm here. I don't think I can take much more of this day."

His look seemed kind, understanding. "I know, and I won't forget."

I heard him out in the hall calling for Dillow and Crampton, though no one answered.

Only the sound of Mrs. Arles's breathing ruffled the texture of silence. Once I got up and went to a long french door, across which draperies had been drawn. When I parted them to peer out, the garden foliage below the house was lost in mist in the last glimmer of light. No lamps were on in the direction of the potting shed, so Kirk-Edward had still not returned from tea at the Empress. Another point for my list—Uncle Tim was really related to Kirk. And now I suspected that Tim had known who he was all along, and had willingly kept his secret.

I didn't know how to deal with any of this.

Joel returned in a few minutes. "I've just talked to the cook. Grace is upset because Peony and Farley decided to go out for dinner—when she was already preparing a meal. I told her that you and Alice probably won't want dinner now either—right?"

"If we get hungry later, I'll fix something," I said. "You might as well tell Grace to go home. But what about Dillow and Crampton? Where are they?"

"Grace doesn't know. She thinks it's strange that Crampton should go off without a word. Usually, she and Dillow have an early supper in the kitchen. Dillow did come in, but she said he was acting—as she said—sort of crazy. Almost as though something had frightened him. He didn't eat much, and he went off quickly on his own. I've already suggested that Grace go home. I said I'd ask you to stay until someone shows up. I'll come back myself after I've talked with Mother. I'm sure everything's all right, and we'll have the answer soon. Are you willing to stay?"

"Of course I must stay," I told him.

He thanked me and went off looking concerned, in spite of his reassurances. I couldn't settle into a vigil in this room without something to do. Perhaps this was the time to write to my parents, and I sat down at the desk and turned on the lamp above it. Pigeonholes offered stationery, and I took out a cream-colored sheet engraved with *Radburn House* at the top. There were pens in a holder, and I started my letter. I had altogether too much to tell that I couldn't explain in detail. Instead, I settled for describing Victoria and Radburn House, trying to give my parents a glimpse of the place, at least. I could write about Uncle Tim freely, and they would understand and empathize. It was necessary to tell them my belief that Alice was Debbie—since that was what they wanted to hear—but I also wrote that there were complications I couldn't explain in a letter.

As I thought about these two who were so dear to me, I choked with tears. Whatever courage I found in myself today was given to me through their nurturing. They'd helped me to stand against adversity—as *they* had done. They'd seen me through so much, and while I couldn't tell them in this letter all they wanted to know, I *could* set down how much I loved them, and how fortunate I felt to have them in my life. How grateful.

For a little while the present went away from me. But when I laid down my pen all the terrible questions that faced me surged back. What had really happened in Brazil? The journal must have been real, and it must have recorded the suspicions Edward Arles—Kirk—held against Farley. Even, perhaps, against Peony. If they had tried to kill him, he'd managed to escape. But he hadn't—as he'd told me—been able to locate where they were until recently, so years had passed while he wandered about. Bent always on revenge?

Of course Peony knew who he was, and she must be frightened half out of her wits. Yet she'd told me that she'd loved Edward, and that Kirk had "murdered" him. Perhaps, in a strange way, he had done exactly that to the young man he'd once been. The "beautiful," frail young man Peony had loved had disappeared long ago. He had hardened, toughened, changed physically and emotionally into a merciless stranger of whom she was afraid. Probably with good reason.

Time wore along and Joel didn't return. After two hours I phoned the Empress and asked for Letha's room. I was told she had checked out—which further alarmed me. Surely this hadn't been her plan when I'd seen her. I tried calling Oak Bay, but no one answered. So where was she, and where was Joel? I had a sense of being cast adrift on an island in space. Grace had gone home and it seemed that only Corinthea Arles and I were alive in this empty house. Alice and Kirk and Uncle Tim hadn't returned, as far as I knew, since there'd been no sign of any of them.

In her bed, Mrs. Arles hardly stirred, and I wondered if she ought to be turned to a new position. The bedridden shouldn't lie forever motionless.

By this time the silence had grown eerie, and I found myself listening to creakings I'd never noticed before. When the front door slammed, I jumped. Someone was coming down the hall, and I grew suddenly anxious—as though something was about to happen that I didn't want to face. The sound of steps was muffled by the carpet, but they thudded heavily, and I held my breath. When the door opened and Uncle Tim stood looking at me with a curious uneasiness, I didn't feel entirely relieved. He too had his secrets.

When I gestured to him to come in, he advanced uncertainly toward the bed. "Crampton?" he asked.

I shook my head and shrugged.

He walked to the table where the nurse had placed the small totem he'd carved for his sister, but it was no longer there, and he looked at me inquiringly.

Suddenly I realized that Mrs. Arles was awake and watching us. She seemed to know what Tim wanted.

"I told Crampton to take it away," she said, her voice foggy with the drug she'd been given. "It made me nervous."

She turned her head and seemed to fall asleep again. Tim stood looking down at her, and I sensed a heavy sorrow in him. All the anger he must have felt toward her seemed to have faded into a more generous pity than she deserved.

I stood up. "Let's see if we can turn her on her side." I illustrated with motions. He came at once to help me and together we rolled her onto her right side—so she could watch the door if she wanted to. She grumbled a little but seemed comfortable in the new position.

Uncle Tim looked at me. "Where is everybody?"

That was impossible to explain, and I just said, "Not here." Then I asked him where Alice was.

He read my lips. "She stayed with Kirk. He wanted to show her something in his rooms."

That left me with more uneasiness. If Kirk decided to tell Alice who he was, and she attached herself to the idea that he was her father—but I didn't dare think about that.

Perhaps Tim understood more of what I was feeling than anyone else. It was likely that someone had explained my situation to him—probably Kirk.

"You're tired and worried, Jenny. Go upstairs and rest. I'll stay here until somebody comes."

I was too weary to struggle with anything more, and I

215

began to feel almost fatalistic—unable to act. What would happen would happen, and it might not matter in the least what I said or did.

I thanked him with a sign he recognized and went upstairs. Again, there were no lights on, and I fumbled my way to the front bedroom and pushed the door ajar. It was dark inside, except for a patch of moonlight falling through from the porch. Apparently the night had cleared. I was sure I'd closed the porch door when I left the room earlier, though it was open now. For a moment I stood very still, listening, half expecting to hear that eerie whistle come out of the old speaking tube. There was nothing—at least nothing audible.

The moment I came into the room, however, a heavy breath of violet perfume assailed me. Not even the breeze from the porch had dispelled it. Crampton must have been here. But when I turned on a lamp and looked around, no one was there.

I took the black raven's feather from my bag and held it, wondering again about Letha's "powers"—good or bad? Perhaps this was the moment when I needed the feather— for whatever charm against evil it might possess.

Feather in hand, I went out into the clear, cool evening, free of violets and smelling of a world refreshed. Winds had swept most of the high clouds away, and as I watched, the moon emerged, big and round and pumpkin-colored. Some sort of ritual seemed required, and I held the feather up against the globe of the moon, so that its black plume shut out the light, with only slits of yellow showing through the fine comb. I smiled wryly over performing some spell for a moon goddess. I'd better get *myself* in hand first of all!

When I started back to my room my foot struck something that skittered away on the floor of the porch, and I reached down to pick up a piece of wood. It was the small totem pole Uncle Tim had looked for in Mrs. Arles's room. I could sense the carving of the small faces under my fingers. So Crampton had certainly been here, had brought the carving to my room—and then for some reason carried it out on the porch, where she'd dropped it. All very strange.

I looked around carefully. This small outdoor space was above the front end of the parlor, where bay windows jutted below. On one side I could look down upon the roof that covered the entryway to the house and see the steps beyond. The other side overlooked a small rock garden that I'd noticed when I first came.

There, however, the wooden railing had been splintered and broken through, so that an open space stood between me and the rocks beneath the porch. I held the feather tightly and went to a place where the rail was still intact and I could look down. Something white and still lay across the protrusions of granite.

I rushed into the house and down the stairs, still carrying both the feather and Uncle Tim's totem. Alice was coming in the front door and she saw my face.

"What's happened?" she cried.

"Go and fetch Kirk," I told her. "Please get him right away."

"Maybe he's still here—" She gestured. "He brought me up through the garden from his house. The back door was locked and we could see Uncle Tim inside with Corinthea, but he couldn't hear us knocking. So we came around to the front." As she explained, Alice ran down the steps and called to Kirk.

I hurried to meet him. "Something terrible has happened —around on the other side."

I wanted to hold Alice back, but she didn't mean to miss anything, so we stood together watching as Kirk climbed onto the rocks and knelt beside the sprawled figure.

"It's Crampton," he said.

Alice sniffed the air. "Smell the violets, Jenny? Cramp's been stealing my great-grandma's perfume again. I saw her once taking some up to her room, and she always uses too much."

217

I already knew that Crampton must have come through my room, but the fact that she'd fallen through the railing seemed impossible.

Kirk looked down at us from the rocks. "I'm afraid she's dead. She fell with her head against this outcropping." He stood up to stare at the broken railing overhead, its splintered sticks gleaming like white bones in the moonlight.

"That's where she fell from," I said needlessly.

The ugly fact that Crampton was dead somehow made her more real to me than she'd been when she was alive. I wondered what *her* secrets had been. Her fondness for Corinthea seemed suddenly touching and pathetic.

Alice slipped her hand into the crook of my arm and clung tightly. "I never saw anybody dead before." Her whisper indicated that excitement was mounting in her, and I felt her tremble. In a moment she would be keyed up and hyper —ready to fall apart. I put an arm about her, trying to offer a steadiness I didn't feel.

"How come Crampton was up there on the porch?" she demanded of Kirk.

"That's a good question." He looked at me. "Have you any idea, Jenny?"

I shook my head. "I've been sitting in the library with Mrs. Arles, and I didn't hear or see anything. Not until I came up to my room just now and found the broken railing."

"She's been dead for a while, I think. She might have been pushed from up there. It seems unlikely that she'd lean on the rail so heavily that she'd fall through."

Alice pounced on this. "I bet somebody *did* push her. Nobody liked old Cramp—not even Corinthea. She was too bossy!"

Kirk recognized Alice's growing state of excitement and spoke quietly. "Let's not jump to conclusions. Does anybody know where Joel is? He'd be useful now as a doctor!"

I looked up at the broken railing with the horror of growing realization. Until Kirk's words, I'd thought only of a chance fall. "He was going to the Empress to talk with his mother. She meant to spend the night there. But he hasn't come back, and when I phoned the hotel they said she'd checked out. I tried to call the house in Oak Bay too, but no one answered."

"What about Peony and Farley?"

"They went out to dinner and I haven't seen them. Grace was in the kitchen earlier, but Joel told her she could go home, since no one wanted dinner. When Joel brought me here after we'd had tea at the Empress, Mrs. Arles was alone."

"Dillow was waiting for me when I got back," Kirk said. "He and Alice and I had a visit, but Tim didn't stay. He doesn't like Dillow."

A family reunion? I wondered. Except that Alice was not Kirk's daughter—she was mine.

Alice started to climb up the rocks for a better look, but I pulled her back. For the first time she noticed the feather and Tim's totem in my hand, and her nervous excitement spilled into more words.

"Why are you holding that feather and the totem pole, Jenny?"

I tried to speak in a quieting voice. "I took the feather from my bag, and I found the totem on the porch floor up there—as though Crampton might have dropped it when she fell. Perhaps she brought it up to leave it in my room—since Mrs. Arles didn't want it."

Kirk looked uneasily at Alice, and she recognized what might be coming. "Someone always sends me away when something interesting happens!"

"This isn't television," Kirk told her. "This is really happening. 'Interesting' isn't a good word for it."

Sometimes he even sounded like a father, I thought. But *I* really was her mother, and I must help her to calm down. I started toward the steps, drawing her with me.

———

219

Kirk saw what I was about. "Let's go inside and I'll call the police and get an ambulance on the way."

As the three of us started up the steps, Dillow came rushing out the front door, having let himself in at the back with his own key.

"Why is Tim with Mrs. Arles?" he demanded. "Where is Crampton?" For the moment the butler had vanished, and he was one of the family.

"Crampton's dead!" Alice cried. "She's lying out there on the rocks in front of the house. She fell through the railing of the porch outside Jenny's room, and maybe somebody pushed her!"

For a moment I thought Dillow might faint. He clung to the rail beside the steps, his color ashy in the moonlight.

Kirk said, "I'm going inside to phone. Get yourself a drink, Dillow."

I wanted to ask Dillow where he'd been this evening before he went to Kirk's room to wait, but he looked too awful.

The tight clasp of Alice's fingers told me that the real world was beginning to come fearfully through to her.

In the parlor Kirk sat beside the phone, while Dillow went to get the suggested drink. Kirk was still phoning when Farley and Peony walked into the room. Alice let go of me and rushed toward Peony, who backed away from her assault. She never liked to be mussed or hugged.

"Crampton's dead!" Alice cried. "She fell off the porch upstairs outside Jenny's room and hit her head!"

Peony gasped and leaned into Farley's arm. His usual stage presence was intact, however, and he looked as suave and unshaken as ever, though his first words were defensive.

"My wife and I have been away from the house for several hours. We've been out to dinner. It's all right, Peony—the dead woman had nothing to do with us."

Dillow came back into the room, weaving a little, as

though on rubber legs, and sat down with his glass of Scotch in hand. He'd heard Farley's last words.

"Maybe this has something to do with all of us. It could have been anyone who pushed her over, couldn't it?"

"Pushed her?" Peony's voice rose to a screech.

"Why do *you* think it wasn't an accident?" Kirk asked Dillow.

"Because she's been asking for trouble." He sounded angry now, and more sure of himself.

"You might explain that when the police come," Kirk said, and Dillow subsided.

At Dillow's words, Peony began to cry helplessly, and Alice put both arms around her.

"You'd better go upstairs," Farley said to Peony. "And take Alice with you." Then to me, "My wife is easily upset, and—"

"*Your* wife?" Kirk asked quietly.

Peony rushed out of the room, pulling Alice with her, but Farley remained unshaken.

"She will be, of course. As soon as she divorces you. After all, you've come to life pretty suddenly. Naturally, Alice will stay with her mother."

Kirk let that go, and turned toward the door at the sound of a car braking in front of the house. However, it wasn't the police but Joel Radburn who walked into the parlor, looking surprised at the tableau we must have presented.

"I'm glad you're here, Joel," Kirk said. "Come outside and have a look at Crampton. She's had a fall—fatal."

Dillow and I watched as the two men, who had once been boyhood friends, went off together.

"It's strange, isn't it," I said to Dillow, "—the way everything has changed, so nobody has to keep up a pretense any more."

Dillow took another long swallow that finished his drink. "I think that goes for you too, Mrs. Thorne."

———

221

"You mean that you can accept the fact that Alice is my daughter?"

Of course he would accept nothing of the kind. "That, if I may say so, is ridiculous."

We could hear the ambulance coming from far off, its siren wailing—or sometimes yelping at intersections. It had just pulled up to the house when Uncle Tim came running down the hall and burst into the parlor, excited, his words rushing out.

"She's—she's awake! She's talking! She wants Crampton. Right now!"

Both the totem and the raven's feather were still in my hand. Tim saw the carving and pounced, snatching it from me.

"That belongs to my s-s-sister!" he cried.

"I know." I nodded. Dillow had started toward the door and I stopped him. "Let me go and see her. You're upset now, and she won't like the smell of liquor."

The old habit of taking orders was still natural to him, and he didn't oppose me.

I found Mrs. Arles sitting up on the side of her bed, reaching for her dressing gown. I ran to hand it to her before she toppled off.

"You're feeling better," I said, hearing the false note in my voice.

She took the paisley silk gown and tried to slip her arms into it, then gave up. "Why am I so weak? Where is everyone? I want to see Crampton at once!"

# 15

I helped to ease Mrs. Arles back against her pillows. "Crampton can't come right now. Is there anything I can do?"

"Why was Tim here? I don't want him in my room! I sent him to find Crampton."

"Your brother came to sit with you so I could get away for a little while. When Joel brought me back from a visit with Letha Radburn, he couldn't find either Crampton or Dillow."

"I don't want Dillow! I want Crampton!"

She was getting excited, and I wasn't the right one to tell her. "Someone will come soon, I'm sure."

"There were sirens a little while ago. They sounded very close. What has happened? What are you keeping from me?"

I tried a partial truth. "Crampton's had a fall and she's hurt. Joel is outside now, to see that she's taken to a hospital. I'm sure—"

She interrupted me. "Crampton was with me this afternoon. She sat right there in her usual place and told me lies. She read something to me and told me lies!"

"Please don't get excited," I said. "Joel will be here in a few minutes, and I know he'll want you to keep calm."

"I don't care what he wants! I'm through with a whole

lifetime of not getting excited. I am an old woman and I don't care about all those vanities I had when I was young. I care about changing my will so that what I have can be left to my grandson's daughter, Alice Arles. Crampton was trying to undermine everything I want."

Since there was no stopping her, I asked a question. "In what way was she trying to change your mind?"

"She tried to tell me that Alice couldn't be Edward's daughter. She had something she was reading to me—something that didn't make any sense."

"What did it say?" I asked softly.

"I—I don't remember. I don't want to remember. It was just more lies. I must talk to Crampton right away. I want to tell her that everything she said was false."

Joel stood in the doorway listening. I didn't know how long he'd been there, but now he came in and went at once to take Mrs. Arles's wrist.

"Be good," he told her, "or I'll have to give you something to help you sleep."

I glanced at my watch, remembering that what seemed a long time ago I had been very tired and had gone up to my room—to rest. It was only eight o'clock of this long, crowded day.

"Never mind any more pills!" Mrs. Arles cried. "Tell me at once, Joel—what has happened to Crampton?"

I moved away from the bed as Joel pulled up a chair. "I've explained that Crampton may be badly hurt from a fall," I told him.

He didn't try to spare her. "Crampton managed somehow to fall from the porch outside Jenny's room. She must have been killed instantly by striking her head against a rock. Jenny found her because the porch railing was broken through, and she saw Crampton lying on the rocks below. We don't know yet when or how it happened. I think she's been dead for some time."

Mrs. Arles's eyes were so big in her thin face that they

seemed its entire focus. She appeared to have stopped breathing, and Joel put a hand on her shoulder and shook her gently.

"Don't do that, Corinthea. If you start going to pieces I'll have to send you to the hospital."

That brought her to life at once. "I won't go!" she told him passionately.

"All right, then. Tomorrow I'll bring in a team of new nurses. Crampton was never all that expert anyway, though she was usually dependable. For tonight—if you'll behave—there are enough people in the house to take turns sitting with you. And after I phone my mother I'll stay for a while."

Mrs. Arles looked suddenly alarmed. "I don't think Crampton fell off that porch by accident. And I don't want to be left alone with any of you!"

"All right—I'll see to it that there are two people in the room all the time, until I can get some new nursing help."

Her outburst had tired her, and she closed her eyes, giving in. Joel nodded to me and I walked to the door with him.

"Why did Corinthea say she didn't think it was an accident?" I asked him.

"I don't know. She seems afraid of something, but perhaps that's due to her weakened state. She's not used to being completely helpless."

"And why did your mother check out of the hotel?" I went on. "I tried to phone her, and she was gone."

"She changed her mind suddenly. She said the vibes were bad. So I took her out for something to eat, and then drove her back to Oak Bay. I should have phoned you. I'm glad now that she's not around to be involved in what's happening here. The police have come, and since you found Crampton, they'll want to talk with you. I said I'd send you in."

I glanced at the woman in the bed. Her eyes were still closed. "I'll come back later," I told her.

225

She opened them at once. "You're a liar too, Jenny. Just go away!"

I looked at Joel, wondering what had brought on all this suspicion, but he only shook his head, and I went out to talk to the police.

The next hours and days were hard for all of us to get through. Police questioning was courteous and thorough, but it didn't bring out very much that we didn't already know. The young policeman who first came gave way to a detective. But there were no clear answers for anyone.

In a strange way, all those at Radburn House seemed to fall back into the roles they'd played before Crampton's death. Only now there was a difference. I had the feeling that, while much of what they'd done in the past had been role-playing, they were no longer as easy with their parts as they'd been when I'd first arrived. No one suggested to the police that Crampton might have been pushed. There appeared to be nothing to back up such a theory except Kirk's first suspicion.

Corinthea Arles accepted the new nurses who took turns caring for her, and this released the rest of us, except when we chose to visit her. Whether we visited or not, however, seemed a matter of indifference to Mrs. Arles.

Once Joel said to me, "It's as though she's waiting for something. I wonder what it is?"

"Probably for her plans to be settled as far as Alice is concerned," I told him.

Dillow made an effort to retain his butler's duties and manner, though now there was something uncomfortable about his performance. He was still solicitous toward Mrs. Arles, but when he was forced to wait on his daughter and her husband in the dining room, some of the facade cracked and fissures showed. I avoided eating with those two when I could. Whenever I was there in the room with them I was aware of how sharply Dillow and Farley watched each other.

Peony seemed afraid of both of them. Only Alice was herself and I think she grew bored playing nursemaid to the jittery Peony.

Kirk still made no attempt to identify himself to his grandmother, though, except for Alice, she was the only one who didn't know who her chauffeur was. I thought she ought to be told, but Kirk insisted on silence. He said it wasn't time yet—as though he too were waiting for something.

We were all cautious and careful at this time, fearful of opening up the charge of murder in Crampton's death. The police had decided that it was an accident and no inquest was held. I didn't want to see Farley frightened into kidnapping Alice all over again, and I had the feeling that any sudden alarm might send him flying. He seemed no nearer than before to imposing what he wished on Mrs. Arles. She had a convenient way of slipping in and out of reality whenever she pleased, and that was something he couldn't fight.

The one piece of information I clung to was what Mrs. Arles had said when she'd told me that Crampton was full of "lies." I wanted to know what the nurse had been reading to her. Nothing significant turned up in Crampton's meager possessions. I offered—to Joel—to go through everything and sort out what was worth sending to some charity. The police had examined everything first, and they'd come up with little information about her.

As I handled Crampton's few things, she became more real to me. Once she had been young, and she must have had friends and family. There was a marriage certificate, and only a few years later divorce papers. There were no photographs of her husband, no letters. In fact, she seemed to have destroyed any correspondence she might have had from anyone, and Dillow said no mail ever came for her any more. The only relative found was a distant cousin, who wasn't interested in Rosemary Crampton. For me, her first name, Rosemary, seemed the oddest item of all to surface about her. The name seemed to belong to a delicate, feminine woman, who would surely lead a romantic and interesting life. One could understand why she preferred to be called Crampton.

I said nothing to the police about the totem carving I'd found on the porch, which had probably taken Crampton to my room in the first place. I didn't want to drag Uncle Tim into this and chance his additional bruising at the hands of a tactless interrogator. So, since it had no significant bearing, I let it go.

When I went through her room, nothing turned up that she might have read to Mrs. Arles, and I started to develop a private theory of my own. If Crampton had come on something or other that might prove Alice was not Edward's daughter, then that item would have been dangerous for her to have. What if she had brought it to my room to show me— only to have someone else catch her there when she perhaps went out on the porch for a breath of air? What if she had been killed in order to retrieve whatever this "proof" might have been? A theory there was no possible way of proving.

Once I tried to talk to Joel about this idea, but he was busy with his own work now and seemed remote and preoccupied. He merely advised me to say nothing about so nebulous a theory. I did remind him that his mother had promised to help me get a confession out of Peony, but he said Letha was busy right now, and he turned away from any further involvement.

Only those moments when I managed to be alone with Alice brought me any pleasure. And even that was bittersweet. I felt that she liked me, was even growing fond of me, but her first concern right now was Peony and the way Farley treated her. That was as it had to be, in the light of what Alice believed.

Farley and Peony wouldn't allow her out of the house with me, but when I could manage it we did small things together. Once we watched a movie on television and I discovered that Alice liked Clint Eastwood. Sometimes we borrowed books from Uncle Tim and read to each other. Tim was teaching her to play chess and I enjoyed seeing them together.

Alice still didn't know who Kirk was. No one was likely to tell her, and I still hesitated, waiting for the "right" moment.

During that time a letter came from my parents, but I couldn't answer their questions. I didn't even know what "truth" I could tell them.

The present state of affairs might go on for as long as Mrs. Arles was ill, and that was driving me a little wild. Either she would get well and do whatever she wanted to do—or this could stretch on and on, even ending in her death. I didn't want Alice by default. I wanted to prove she was mine and see those who had taken her exposed.

One late afternoon, when I was sitting alone on the bench in the lower garden, Kirk showed up suddenly in front of me. I'd been so lost in my own unhappy thoughts that his appearance startled me.

"You need to get away," he said abruptly. "You're looking worse all the time, Jenny. Losing weight, aren't you?"

I hadn't been near a scale. I hadn't been watching a mirror. "I don't really care," I said.

"That's what's wrong. The only thing you care about is something you can't change. Not right now. So you're being self-destructive, and that is no good. You need something to try for."

"There's nothing I *can* try for. You've said that. What are *you* trying for?"

"A lot of bits and pieces that are beginning to fall into place. When I'm sure, I'll know exactly what to do."

I didn't like the sound of that. Somewhere along the way, Edward Arles, who must have been a likable though rather aimless young man, had turned into one whose whole direction was vengeance. A man I'd better stay away from.

"Will you come out to dinner with me tonight?" he asked, still abrupt.

---

229

My reaction—the sudden lifting of my spirits—disconcerted me. "I'd like that," I told him, and closed all the doors on good sense.

"That's fine. Suppose you change from those jeans, and tell Grace you'll be out for dinner tonight. I'll meet you here in an hour, if that's all right with you. It's early, but I have a stop to make first before everything closes."

For once he was consulting me—just a little.

I went up to my room and looked through the few clothes I'd brought with me. There was one dress I'd packed in case of need but hadn't worn before—an apple-green wool jersey. The cowl neck was flattering, and I added my own black velvet belt with a gold dragon's-head clasp. Just as I was putting on filigree earrings, Alice came to my door. When I invited her in she looked at me with flattering approval.

"I wish I could be beautiful and really dress up. I don't mean in all that fancy stuff my mother likes on me."

"I think you're already beautiful," I said.

She made a face. "I know I'm beautiful inside—isn't that what people always say when you're plain? Only I'm *not* beautiful inside. I know that."

"Give yourself time, Alice. Growing up isn't easy, but things do have a way of straightening out." I wasn't sure I believed my own words, but she looked more hopeful.

"Where are you going?" she asked.

"Kirk has invited me to dinner. I don't know where we'll go."

"I wish I could go out to dinner."

"We'll do that," I said, "another time."

"Okay." She sat down in her favorite chair to watch as I put on black sling-back pumps. She'd come to talk to me about something, and I looked at her encouragingly.

Finally she took a deep breath and plunged. "I've just found out something, Jenny. I've got a real grandfather. Of course I'd rather it was somebody else—but I suppose Dillow's better than nobody. Did you know all the time?"

"No. Only recently. Who told you?"

"Farley. He said the reason I wasn't told before was because my great-grandmother didn't want to accept Peony in the beginning. I guess she's a snob. And she didn't want Dillow to be related to her by marriage. It's all sort of mixed up, I guess."

"How did Farley happen to tell you?"

"It's funny—he's been kind of friendly lately. Not so mean. He says he'd like me to help him put on a magic show for the old lady. He thinks something needs to be done to wake her up. Peony doesn't want to help, so Farley said I could. I've watched lots of times, and sometimes he's let me come onstage to hand him handkerchiefs or take away a cage of birds. Of course he hasn't any birds or rabbits now—not around here. But he'll use other things. I've still got a costume I had for those times, though it's a little tight now. It's red, with spangles and a short skirt."

"I expect you looked fine. But a magic show might upset Mrs. Arles. I'd better talk to Joel about this."

Alice shrugged and returned to her earlier topic. "Dillow isn't anybody I'd pick for a grandfather. He's too stiff and proper. Only lately he's jittery about something."

I wanted to tell her that she had a wonderful *real* grandfather who would remind her of Uncle Tim as he might have been. But this was still not the right time—not until she could be legitimately separated from Peony and Farley. I picked up on something else, however.

"Why do you think Dillow is jittery?"

"I'm not sure. Maybe he thinks he'll get killed the way Crampton was."

"What do you mean by that, Alice?"

"Oh, he's always looking behind him, and around corners. He walks fast in the halls—as though somebody might jump out at him. Once I did, and he practically fell apart. He had

---

231

to sit down at the foot of the stairs and mop his face. I didn't know he was my grandfather then, but *he* knew, and he was never nice to me. So I'm glad I scared him."

I managed to answer her quietly. "We're all jittery after what happened to Crampton. I wish you could get away from this house for a while."

"Maybe I will. Farley said if things get too bad we might go on a trip somewhere. Though I don't know if I want to go with *him.*"

"What does Peony think about that?"

"She's not thinking about anything right now. She even acts scared of Dillow. But she always does what Farley says, so maybe we will go away."

These were things I must talk to Kirk about—not Joel. Now Joel seemed distant and preoccupied. I couldn't imagine what Farley could possibly intend by setting up a magic show for Corinthea Arles, who would be anything but pleased. If Kirk had any sort of plan, he might need to put it into action soon, and I only hoped it wouldn't be violent.

"It's too bad old Cramp caused so much trouble by going out on that porch," Alice said.

I had a feeling that she quoted Farley more than usual these days, and she had never really sensed the human loss in Crampton's death. There was still time before I needed to meet Kirk, and I had an idea.

"I want to show you something up on the third floor," I told her, and she came with me willingly up the stairs. Instead of turning back to Tim's rooms, however, I drew her toward the single small room at the front that Crampton had occupied when she wasn't on duty.

"Do you know whose room this was?" I asked.

"Sure. It was Cramp's room. The police locked it up for a while."

"It's all right for us to go in now. Joel asked me to look through her things, though there wasn't much here. And that's rather sad."

I showed her a few photographs, the limp, drab clothing hanging behind a curtain, and the old-fashioned hat I'd never seen Crampton wear. A hat with an unexpected green feather. Alice seemed uninterested until I drew out a cardboard box that held the few pieces of jewelry the nurse had possessed. This time something attracted her attention, and she picked up a pair of gold-filled screw-on earrings, set with imitation pearls.

"Those are pretty," she said. "But *she* wouldn't wear them. How silly they'd look on old Crampton!"

I held out another photograph, taken perhaps when Rosemary was in her twenties.

Alice rejected it at once. "That's not Cramp!"

"This is the way she looked when she was young. Maybe not exactly pretty, but happy-looking—hopeful. I expect she had all the dreams everyone else has."

Alice studied the picture thoughtfully. "She looks so different. So how could it happen—?"

"Some people don't manage to work out their lives the way they want. Though perhaps we shouldn't say that about her. She was fond of Mrs. Arles, and it must have given her satisfaction to look after her."

"I wouldn't want to live just for someone else," Alice said.

"I wouldn't either. It has to go both ways for people like us. Giving and taking. But we can only work out *our* lives and let others deal with theirs."

"To get pushed off a porch?" Alice asked.

"We still don't really know that's what happened. The police think it was an accident."

"Kirk doesn't think so. And that's why Dillow is scared. He won't even go near a high place."

"You have a very big imagination, Alice. And that's good. But it's not good to let it run wild."

She dropped the earring back in the box and poked a finger in among the other things, finding a gold wedding ring.

———

"We don't know about people, do we?" she said. "Dr. Joel told me that once."

As he had told me.

"With Crampton, I'm afraid we didn't even try to know. But then—maybe she didn't want us to. She wasn't real for me until I came in here and checked through what she left behind."

Alice nodded solemnly, and I knew she would have something new to think about when it came to Crampton.

I put the box of jewelry back in a drawer. "Will you tell me if Farley decides to take you on a trip?" I asked her.

"Sure. Maybe you could fix it so I needn't go. He's always grumpy when we travel. I like to see new places, but"—her eyes didn't meet mine—"in some ways I like it here." She was still afraid of Farley.

"I like it here because of you," I told her gently.

She'd had little practice in accepting affection, and she backed quickly away from that. We went downstairs together, and she ran off alone, as if relieved to escape from me. I needed to be more careful.

When I went down to the garden, Kirk was waiting for me.

# 16

Kirk too had dressed up a bit for the evening. He looked different in gray slacks and jacket and a blue pullover sweater. The most surprising thing was that he'd shaved off the mustache that had always hidden his mouth—a rather wide, straight mouth, with a quirk of humor at the corner, as though he read me very well. The change in him made me feel oddly self-conscious. All the things I'd been so eager to talk with him about fluttered into a silence I didn't know how to break.

We walked out to where he'd left his car and got in.

"We'll stop first at the Provincial Museum before we go to dinner," he said as we started downhill toward the center of town. "It's a great museum, so I don't think you'll mind waiting for me a little while."

"I don't mind," I said.

He explained as he drove. "I'm applying for a job with the museum and apparently my qualifications interest them."

That surprised me. "What *do* you do? I mean when you're not working in a logging camp, or running off to a South American jungle, or playing chauffeur in disguise?"

His smile, at least, was familiar. "Maybe I got off to a slow start. I had to try a lot of things. But I've always had Indian friends, and I've been interested in their history and culture for a long time. I've free-lanced a bit for several museums when I've moved around, but my main interest has always been British Columbia and what's happened and is happening to the Indians here. I'd like to write a book when I can get to it."

Here were layers beneath layers, I thought—discovery would be interesting, and I began to feel more comfortable with him than ever in the past.

"You'd write about the local Indians?" I asked.

"Yes, but not a sociological study. I've been collecting stories about what is happening to Indian families, and especially to young people today. A lot of the old culture has been lost, and the kids turn to other ways—as they do everywhere. Only a few, like the totem-pole carvers, try to preserve what's old and fine and traditional. But what do these boys and girls want today, and how hard is it for them to accomplish their ambitions? When we look back at the white man's coming, it's not a pretty picture anywhere."

"Will the job you're looking for help with this?"

"I hope so. It would be field work, and it would also help me to eat while I write the book."

I thought of Mrs. Arles's wealth and how much it could aid him. "Your grandmother—" I began.

"I don't want anything from my grandmother," he said quickly. "I don't care what she does with her money, so long as it doesn't fall into Farley Corwin's hands. Especially not through Alice. He's a would-be murderer, and I haven't any doubt that he's your kidnapper as well."

It was wonderful to have him so outspokenly on my side, yet the depth of his anger against Farley worried me. It could so easily explode into violence—and I didn't want that for Kirk. Not for the man I was discovering him to be.

I drew him away from dark thoughts about Farley. "I've been sitting beside Mrs. Arles's bed on and off lately, and I can only feel sorry for her. She's terribly alone. I don't think there's been anyone except Joel, and of course Crampton, to care about her. I keep wondering what it might do for her if you walked into her room and told her who you are."

"It would probably kill her on the spot."

"Or give her something to live for? She's snatching at Alice now, but I wonder if she really believes that Alice is your daughter? If you don't let her know who you are, and she dies—won't you always wonder if you shouldn't have given her, and yourself, a chance?"

Kirk's hands tightened on the wheel. "When I was a kid, living with my mother and father, there were a lot of good things in my life. Hugging and laughter—affection. Then I lost all that and came to live with *her*. I suppose a sort of drying up started inside me. It's a wonder my father turned out to be as loving a man as he was. I remember the way he'd kiss her on the cheek and hug her with both arms when we visited. Like hugging a poker. I didn't want to hug her at all. But you know what he said to me once? That she was *shy*. I'm not much like my father, though maybe Edward was a little like him—once."

"So why do you have to be like her—unforgiving?"

He looked at his watch. "It's getting late. I've just time to make my appointment before the museum closes. We'll talk later."

We left the car and walked along briskly. The magical quality of Victoria at dusk never failed to touch me—the panorama of lighted buildings, the familiar blue light standards with their bright globes and hanging flower baskets, and the Inner Harbor rimmed with still more lights that flung colored reflections across the water. The sky was pink where the sun had fallen into the Pacific, leaving a rosy stain on the water and a darkening continent behind.

We crossed the wide courtyard of the museum, with its colonnades and sheltered walks, and a sense of Indian design everywhere.

"Sometime we'll come back and I'll really take you

———

237

through." He spoke easily, as though there were a future for me here in Victoria.

In the entrance foyer the great carved Indian figure of a beckoning man served as what Kirk called a Greeter Pole. Such figures were used to welcome people coming to a potlatch—a great gathering that might be held for celebration or mourning and might involve spirit dances or other rituals. However, it was what lay beyond the Greeter that caught me up in its illusion.

A lighted curtain of "rain," as high as though it streamed from the heavens, and almost as wide as the huge room I could glimpse beyond, glistened and shimmered as it fell. Through the rain curtain, as if moving on its own waters, a canoe of Nootka Indians appeared, the harpooner in the prow striking a whale. Boat and men were slightly larger than life size, so that the scene was dramatic in its impact.

Kirk led me beyond the rain curtain to where we could stand before the magnificent wood sculpture. The boat itself had been hewn from a single cedar log. Each of the crew of six paddlers had been carved individually, all dominated by the standing figure with the harpoon. Part of a huge black whale showed close to the boat as it rose from choppy waves. On either side of the long hall gray, weathered totem poles watched as if from land. Art had caught one dynamic moment of life and frozen it forever. At the far end another rain curtain added to the splendid illusion.

For a moment Kirk stood beside me, not wanting to break the spell. Then he touched my arm.

"I have to go. Wander where you like, and I'll meet you near the door in about half an hour."

I left the main hall, exploring idly, since I'd have no time now to digest what I saw. Dioramas of the long-ago north woods were so real that I could almost step out upon the forest floor, where deer were walking. I found rooms upstairs filled with displays of Indian implements of all kinds—

carved whistles, stone clubs and tools, bark beaters, bows and arrows.

I wandered through the street of a gold-rush town, and in another section stopped before the life-size front of an Indian community house.

The half hour passed too quickly, and I went back to the whaling scene and the rain curtains, arriving a few minutes ahead of Kirk. He seemed elated, so his interview must have gone well, though he didn't talk about it.

"Now for dinner," he said. "I hope you like Greek food."

I liked it, and the Millos restaurant was only a few blocks away, so we walked.

There were crowds at every crossing now, and the two-decker buses were filled to the doors. Yet people seemed friendlier and more courteous at rush hour than I found at home in the eastern United States.

The restaurant opened off a side street and we stepped into spacious rooms with a sense of air and light. The floors were bare with wide planks; the tables and chairs built four-square and sturdy. Plants grew everywhere—in ledges along the walls, and hanging in baskets and pots from the ceiling. A waiter led us to a table with a white cloth and white napkins, and lit a candle under glass.

Greek windows with four large panes were spaced along the street wall, each with a Greek key and edging of that special blue one associated with the Greek isles.

I ordered a casserole of shrimp, tomato, and feta cheese, accompanied by pita bread and a Greek salad. By this time I would have liked to relax and enjoy this meal in Kirk's company, but too much crowded between us and needed to be cleared away before we could be entirely comfortable with each other.

He was watching me now, his look intense. "I thought you needed to escape for a little while, but maybe that isn't possible for either of us. Not yet. I know some of what's worrying you. Do you want to talk about it?"

239

"I'd like to ask some questions that no one else can answer. Will you let me?"

"Go ahead and we'll see."

That wasn't too reassuring. "All right—what really happened in Brazil? Why did you choose to come here and masquerade after all these years? Oh, I know about how you learned only recently that Farley and Peony were here, claiming the child was your daughter. But there's still more, isn't there?"

"There's the question of why I ever married Nellie Dillow."

I nodded and broke off a bit of pita, not looking at him.

"Then let's begin with that. I've told you a little. She was pretty, very young, and appealing—helpless. I fell for her originally when I was pretty young myself. She needed someone to look after her, and at that age this went to my head. I suppose we were in love, as far as kids can be at a time when the sexual attraction is stronger than anything else. Nature knows what she's about. I didn't think much ahead of my own nose and immediate impulses, and I hadn't any close attachments."

He paused, considering, before he went on.

"Or at least that's the way Edward Arles was in those days. It's funny, but I've separated myself so far from Edward that this isn't a masquerade any more. It's the way I am today—someone else who's not very much like Edward. Maybe I'm no more admirable than he was, but at least I'm finding a focus."

Thinking of Farley, I was afraid to ask what he'd focused on.

"Anyway, Nellie wanted to marry me—no matter what. And I suspect that her father urged her on. All that old servitor bit is the facade for a very bitter man. Underneath, he really hates my grandmother. His loyalty act was to keep him near her until the big chance came—through his daughter. He endures Farley for now, but he's looking for a way to keep Alice here and get rid of the magician. I suppose I'm part of that plan. Only I think Farley's likely to fight back for his own greedy reasons. Dillow has convinced himself that Alice is my daughter—*his* granddaughter—and he's never wanted you here at all."

"He doesn't even like Alice."

"That's not what drives him. He doesn't like anyone, including Nellie. But Alice could be his ticket to a better life, and put him on an equal footing with a woman he's spent most of his life resenting. Of course that's why he took me on as chauffeur and kept still about who I am. So I can be the instrument to rid him of Farley Corwin."

"And will you be?" I asked.

"Let's get back to early days, when we were still in Victoria. Nellie accused me of being the father of a child she'd never conceived. Not then. My grandmother heard her story from Dillow and blew up at me. She didn't give me a chance for denial. She was already furious because I'd been trying to help Uncle Tim. She never cared about what I might think or feel—and maybe I never cared about what she thought or felt either. We were locked away from each other, and still are."

"So you went off to the logging camp and toughened up?"

He smiled. "I told you Kirk McKaye took over and started Edward's growing up. I picked the name out of a novel whose hero I admired, and I decided to be like him. I worked at it physically, so that by the time the opportunity to go on Karsten's expedition came along in a few years, I signed up. I was still in touch with friends in Victoria, and word got back to Nellie where I was going. I don't think *she* developed the idea of coming after me—she'd never have had that much enterprise on her own. Dillow pushed her into it and gave her the money. She told me that later. So she came out to Brazil to see what she could manage. For a victim, she can have some pretty fixed ideas—and I was one of them. Out there, stranded and helpless, Nellie ran into

---

Farley Corwin and he took her over. By chance. If there is any such thing as chance. Sometimes I wonder. He became the main focus behind the whole plot—having an eye on my grandmother's money."

"But weren't you on to the Dillows by the time she found you in Brazil?"

"You'd think I would have been, if I'd had any sense. But I hadn't come through the real mill yet. When Nellie turned up, apparently alone and frightened, and wanting me the way no one else ever had—well, all my old feeling for her came back. By that time it even seemed like a lark to marry her and throw another arrow at my grandmother. I didn't know Farley was lurking in the background, or that she'd been performing with him as an assistant named Peony. He's a chronic loser who never gives up, because he always thinks it will be better next time. He has a wild imagination that guides him into elaborate plots. Of course he wanted Nellie to be pregnant from the beginning—with my child. She told him about the coming baby before she told me. So he decided to get rid of me—and I gave him the chance he was looking for."

Kirk was scarcely eating now, and all the anger he must have held in check for so long had begun to surface. It showed in his eyes, his mouth, in the tight lines of his jaw. I wished I could reach out my hand to draw him back from the grim memories he was recreating, but I knew he had to go on.

"Farley tried to kill me," he said. "I'm as sure of that as I am of anything, though there's no way to prove it. Except, perhaps, through Nellie, who must know the truth. Though truth is something from which she's cultivated an ability to hide. I'd begun to see the horrible mistake I'd made in marriage—how stupid I'd been. So my feeble solution was to run away again. I quit the expedition, though Karsten was pleased with my work. Since I'd caught a fever, it gave me an excuse. I didn't know about the baby then, and I don't know if it would have made any difference.

"Somehow—and I'm convinced of this—Farley managed to damage the boat that was to take me, along with another man who was to help navigate the river. About twenty-four hours later the boat foundered. I got away and swam for shore. I was pretty sick from fever and nearly drowned. Natives found me and nursed me back to life with herbs and local concoctions. My companion wasn't as lucky. I didn't know what happened to him until much later. He'd picked up some identity stuff of mine, and when what was left of him was found they thought it was me. When I recovered, months later, and got back to the nearest town, I learned about this. So I had the opportunity to wipe out Edward Arles, whom I didn't like much anyway, and developed the character I'd adopted in the logging camp."

Kirk's voice held steady now, so that his telling was almost matter-of-fact. But I knew better. If Farley were ever at his mercy, I was afraid of what might happen. There was a festering in Kirk McKaye that could become ugly. My own feelings were a mixture of anxiety for Kirk and a new sense of tenderness. I understood better now the events that had formed him.

"I suppose we all grow into different people over the years," I said. "Grow or deteriorate. When I look back from where I am now, I seem to have lived several different lifetimes, even though each one leads into the next. Tough experiences have turned you into someone stronger than Edward Arles. Can't you leave it at that? Can't you let go of Edward's need for revenge?"

His smile had the familiar wry twist. "Sure—I'll buy that. But there's still something that needs to be done in the life I'm living right now."

"In spite of consequences that might be worse than anything that's gone before?"

He scowled at me and began to pick at his salad.

---

243

"Believe me," I said, "I *know* what it feels like to want to punish someone. Sometimes I long with every bit of me to strike out at Farley. *And* at Peony. I want to *hurt* them. But I have to think what will bring Alice back to me and help *her.* I have to try for some wiser solution."

"I suppose I don't care any more. If I can't set this one score straight, nothing that happens afterward matters. And it's nearly time."

"But you went to the museum this afternoon. You took a new step."

"I gave a hostage to fate—that's all."

"It might help if you could think of Alice too—even if she isn't your daughter."

"The last thing I want is to have Alice get the idea that I'm her father. Not because I wouldn't like her as a daughter—I think she's come through a bad time with more resilience than many kids would. Perhaps because you gave her a good start to begin with. It's because I'm sure now that she's your daughter that I've been holding off on confronting Farley. I'd like to get the truth out of Nellie-Peony since that would help you. Right now she ducks when she sees me. After that foray she made to destroy the rest of my journal, she's run at the sight of me. She can bend with every wind, and flow away like water, and she's never learned to face anything."

"There's more to it than that," I said. "She's convinced herself that Alice is *her* child, and that's pretty hard to break down."

"Farley knows better. So that may be where the answer lies."

"Perhaps Dillow knows too. Alice has told me that he has the jitters these days, and he's behaving strangely."

"He has a reason you may not know. He doesn't want it to come out that he was the one who found Crampton first—not you. I didn't realize this until he told me a couple of days ago. He came to my rooms to see me the day it happened, and I wasn't there. When he went back to the house he found her and he was scared. Everyone knew about his feud with Crampton, and he was afraid to be involved—perhaps blamed."

"Why didn't *he* think it was an accident?"

"I don't know. He won't say any more."

Talking had, at least, released some of Kirk's tension. We were silent for a little while, and then he spoke more quietly.

"Tell me what's happening at the house. Has anything more developed?"

I told him what Mrs. Arles had said concerning the lies she claimed Crampton had told her. And about the "entertainment" Farley was planning. To "wake up" Mrs. Arles.

"Peony won't help him, so he's enlisted Alice, who loves the idea of performing."

"I don't like the sound of that."

"I don't like the sound of anything that's happening. Even Joel isn't any help now. Or Letha."

"Letha came as a surprise to me," Kirk said. "Joel and I only knew each other as kids, so he didn't make the connection. But she started to wonder about me right away."

"She was suspicious of you, and she still is."

"She was right, Jenny."

As the waiter brought us coffee and baklava, Kirk seemed lost again in his own disturbing thoughts. Neither of us could take more than a few mouthfuls of the honeyed sweetness.

Ever since we'd arrived, recorded Greek music had been playing in the background. Some of the tunes were familiar themes from movies, some more authentic. From now on whenever I heard the finger-snapping music from *Zorba* I would be here in Victoria, sitting at this table at Millos with Kirk. By then, *this* time would be past, and perhaps terrible happenings that were still in the future would have also become the past. Leaving what sorrows behind them? But while it was still *now* I must try once more for sanity.

"Can't you just take the museum job and go on for yourself?" I asked him again. "Isn't it time to leave Brazil and Edward behind you?"

"If I'm not in jail in the next few days, that's the course I'd like to take. But not yet. Forgiveness and forgetting are not what I owe Farley Corwin. I'm sorry for what Nellie has become, but that's a choice she made for herself. She has a talent for choosing the wrong road."

"But isn't that the point? *You* still have time to choose something better."

His look challenged me, and I sighed.

"I'm sorry, Kirk. I can't tell you what to do. And I suppose if *I* could punish Farley for taking Debbie, I would do it and never hold back. So who am I to talk? I'm beginning to think that the only thing I can do is to kidnap my own child."

His eyes held mine. "More than anything else, Jenny, I'd like to help you get what you want—and deserve. Returning Alice to you is one way I can even matters with Farley. I wish you and I could have met under different circumstances. I wish I could tell you how I've come to feel about you in this little while. How much I—admire you."

"Tell me!" I said.

"Not yet—maybe never. I want good things for you. You've endured enough. But not you or anyone else can stop what's going to happen, though maybe when it's over you'll have Debbie again."

"I don't want her that way! Debbie is gone. I have to accept that. None of the years I've missed with her can ever be brought back. I've come to love Alice as she is, and I want her with me. But not at some terrible cost to you. I care about what happens to you, Kirk. Please understand that."

He was already signaling the waiter for the check. "Don't take one more step in that direction, Jenny," he warned.

I knew what he meant. If he had to, he would be cruel—he would hurt me. He would do it because he thought he was helping me if he kept me outside of his life. He had turned into a man with walls around him, and there was no way to change his mind.

As we left the restaurant I could hear the familiar notes of "Never on Sunday" following us. A strange song to be the epitaph of something that might have been.

When we reached the house, Kirk left me quickly, and I went inside. When I looked into Mrs. Arles's room one of the new nurses was on duty, and the woman nodded at me reassuringly. Her charge lay with her eyes closed, breathing evenly.

No one was around when I went up to my room, but I often sensed that my comings and goings were watched, and someone was probably aware of me now. I went into my room and locked the door, remembering that other time, so recently, when the scent of violets had been strong and I'd gone out on the porch to get away from it. The porch door was closed now and I had no desire to go outside, even though the railing had been repaired and there was no danger.

When it came, that eerie whistle—out of another century —startled me. This time I knew what it was, and I reached behind the desk and put the cup to my ear. The voice whispered at once.

"Go away, Jenny! Go away while there's still time!"

The idea was neither new nor original. I left the cup hanging and ran down the stairs to the first floor. There I went straight toward the kitchen behind the dining room. An old-fashioned butler's pantry intervened, and Peony sat on a high stool, perched with her knees crossed, her legs in jeans, and a frilly blouse tucked in at the waist. On the wall above I saw the board that held the means of communication with several rooms.

She smiled at me—a kitten smile with malice in it. Yet I felt an uncertainty in her as well, and an edginess.

"I knew you'd come," she said. "Pop told me about fooling

247

you that other time. But this time I thought you'd come investigating. I wanted to talk to you—not upstairs or near Mrs. Arles's room."

I sat down on a wooden chair and stared at her, waiting.

"I know where you went tonight. I know who took you out to dinner. So I'll say just one thing—stay away from my husband!"

"Which husband?" I asked. "You seem to have two."

"Not really. Edward Arles is my husband. Marrying Farley was wrong. I'd never have done it if I'd known Edward was still alive. I sleep away from Farley now—in Alice's room, where I can keep her safe."

An odd thing to say considering the past. But then, she'd had experience with kidnapping.

"I thought Farley was planning a divorce for you and Kirk?"

She wriggled on the stool. "I've about had it when it comes to what Farley plans. Edward will stick by me now. He has to. That is, if Farley doesn't kill him before he kills Farley."

She laughed as though what she'd said was funny, and I suspected that she cared as little about Edward as she did about Farley. What she wanted was someone to lean on, someone to protect and take care of her—and Corinthea Arles's grandson must seem again the most likely candidate.

I wondered how disastrous her collapse would be if reality ever got through to her. At present she simply shut out whatever she didn't want to hear. She could make up protective lies or simply close her mind altogether—a skill for which she'd developed a strange facility.

Probably Farley was uneasy and apprehensive himself by this time. Both because of Kirk and because he couldn't be sure that Peony wouldn't pull down his house of cards. Of course, if I'd known exactly what Farley was up to by this time, and that his goal had changed, I might have been even more frightened about what lay ahead.

---

Right now there was nothing more I wanted to say to Peony. Nothing that could possibly matter. "Just leave the speaking tube alone after this," I told her, and walked out of the pantry.

I didn't go upstairs, however, but sat down in the living room to use the phone.

When I'd dialed, Letha herself answered. "I've been waiting for you to call, Jenny."

"And I've been waiting for *you*," I said, feeling exasperated. "You were going to help me do something about Peony."

"Yes—the time has come. All the portents are right—except one. I've already talked to Peony by phone and she's agreed to let Joel bring her out here tomorrow afternoon. Of course you will come too—though she doesn't know that yet."

"Neither did I," I said dryly. "How did you get her to agree?"

"I told her there were some important things about Alice that she needs to know, so that made her curious. She's rather like a child and it isn't hard to influence her."

"What do you mean about one portent not being right?"

"It's never possible to be sure of everything. When you return to your room, perhaps you can ask for help. Go out on the porch and look at the moon. Joel will come for you and Peony around four tomorrow. He can't get away earlier. Good night, Jenny."

She rang off before I could respond. While I had no belief in her portents, I was ready to ask for help. Out there where the night sky was so big, perhaps I could reach toward the infinite.

Upstairs again, I went outside at once. The air was cool and the moon had turned gibbous—that strange, rather creepy name for the humpbacked moon. However, as I stood looking up at the sky, I saw nothing else remarkable. The moon shed its luminous yellow on the driveway below the house, and shone on the rock garden where Crampton had died. I avoided touching the railing.

As I stood there the wind sharpened, cutting through my clothes. A wispy shred separated itself from the mass of clouds as I watched, and drifted across the face of the moon —a cloud like a black feather. A cloud like an omen? Or a promise?

This was the moment to ask for help—to feel myself in touch with something vast and powerful, yet *reachable*. I didn't need symbols or portents. Once, long ago, I'd known how to pray, and simple words came into my mind—asking for what was best for Alice, asking for guidance for me; asking as well for protection for Kirk and a quieting of the violence I had sensed in him.

The feather on the moon had shredded away into the sky by the time I went inside. Like my fears? How Letha had known I had no idea, but she had understood my need, and I felt more hopeful than I had in years. Tomorrow would surely bring some sort of solution—it was very close now— and I must hold to thoughts that were hopeful and positive.

# *17*

I slept late the next morning and was glad to get up after everyone else, hoping to miss them at breakfast. However, when I went downstairs I found Farley Corwin alone at the dining-room table, and this morning he put on no mock gallantry. If he noticed my arrival at all, he didn't look at me or speak—lost in his own dark pondering. My feeling of hopefulness still lingered, and I didn't want to sit at the table with Farley and have it dispelled.

I helped myself from the sideboard and carried my plate back to Mrs. Arles's room. There was altogether too much time to be spent before four o'clock this afternoon, when the real testing would begin, so perhaps I could spell one of the nurses while I ate my breakfast.

Instead, however, the nurse named Amy met me at the door in a state of agitation.

"You'd better not go in there, Mrs. Thorne. She's awake and being very difficult. She told me to get out and stay out until I was wanted. I've tried to call Dr. Radburn but I can't reach him. The child is in there with her now—Alice."

I no longer felt hungry, and I attempted to reassure the nurse. "I'd better go in and see what's happening." I left my breakfast tray on a hall table and opened the door to the library without knocking.

Mrs. Arles sat propped against a pile of pillows, and Alice, looking grubby in worn jeans and wrinkled shirt, sat on the far side of the bed in Crampton's place. Except that Alice sat closer than Crampton ever had, her arms folded on the quilt and her eyes fixed on Mrs. Arles's face.

Alice heard me and looked around. "Come in and listen," she invited.

Mrs. Arles nodded at me. "Yes, Jenny, come and sit down. And don't bother with silly questions about how I'm feeling. Alice, do you want to tell Mrs. Thorne what I've been talking to you about?"

Alice jumped up excitedly. "I *am* a changeling!" she announced. "Mrs. Arles isn't really my great-grandmother, and her grandson Edward isn't my father. How do you like that?"

"And who is your mother?" I asked softly.

"Mrs. Arles says it's not Peony. So Dillow doesn't have to be my grandfather—and that's good. But I don't want to leave Peony. Sometimes she needs me, and I don't know if she can get along without me. Maybe I can have two mothers?"

The dilemma was mine to work out, and it wouldn't be easy. To Alice, Peony was the only mother she knew, and she would never see her as a kidnapper. I sat down limply on the other side of the bed.

Alice ran on, her excitement growing. "I wonder who I really am? Maybe I'm a king's daughter—like in the stories. There are always changelings and they turn out to be princesses."

"You're too old for fairy tales, Alice," Mrs. Arles said firmly. "You have a real mother, and you need to understand that."

Apparently she hadn't told Alice I was that mother.

"It will be fun finding out who she is," Alice said happily. "I hope I'll like her as much as I do Peony."

I must have made a slight sound, for the woman in the bed spoke more sharply.

"Be careful, Jenny."

I subsided breathlessly and she went on. "Crampton told me about this. I didn't believe her. She read a newspaper clipping to me, and I was so angry that I must have had another stroke. I've been lying here thinking, and listening. To all of you. People around me talk as though I wasn't conscious. Even Joel does that. Crampton is dead because of what she knew. But when I bring up her name everybody scuttles off to some other subject. They think I'm made of glass. I miss Crampton. She was the only honest friend I had and I wish I'd appreciated her more. But I'm not going to shatter because she's gone. There's too much that must be done."

Both Alice and Corinthea Arles were a lot tougher than anyone gave them credit for.

Alice watched me, almost shyly, "I've always thought I was somebody else. I really do love Peony, but I had the feeling there was someone a long time ago . . . So when I remembered those things—about the turtle—it seemed as though I had to be somebody different. You told me, Jenny, that your little girl was kidnapped. So do you suppose . . . ?"

"Naturally she supposes," Mrs. Arles said, making up her mind. "Jenny is your real mother, Alice. That's why she came here—to find you."

Alice and I looked at each other solemnly, and neither of us moved toward the other. I wanted to run around the bed, open my arms, and hold her, but Alice's natural dignity held me off. She must be ready too. A phrase my father often used when I was young came back to me: "Not too fast, honey. Take a little time." I'd had to take so much time, and now I was impatient.

"I have to think about this some more," Alice said. "I have to go and find Peony."

I spoke to her before she reached the door. The ice was breaking up inside me, but I still had to hold back the logjam. I was much more used to the fact that Alice was my daughter than she was used to my being her mother.

"There's one problem," I told her. "I haven't any proof that could be used to convince a judge that you are my Debbie."

She paused at the door, thinking about that. "I guess I'm not really your Debbie. I'm somebody else now, and I suppose you are too. But maybe I can talk to my"—she faltered over the word—"to Peony about this. Thanks for telling me, Mrs. Arles."

The old woman nodded. "Sometimes I wish you really were Edward's daughter. You are rather an admirable child, a strange sort of child, but interesting. I've never been much interested in children before. Not even my own."

When Alice had gone, Mrs. Arles closed her eyes and appeared to sleep. There was nothing else I could talk about now. Too much still hung uneasily in the balance. And some of it lay in Alice's very young hands. But there was one question I had to ask.

"Tell me what was in the clipping Crampton showed you. Would it give me the proof I need?"

She didn't open her eyes. "How do I know? You have to find it first."

"Can't you just tell me?"

Her face took on its old blank lines and I knew she'd gone away from me. Whoever had killed Crampton probably held the clipping, and Mrs. Arles would say nothing more now. It was astonishing enough that she had told Alice the truth.

During the rest of the day, before I left for Oak Bay, I saw Alice only twice. We ran into each other in the hall the first time, and she answered my question before I asked it.

"Peony doesn't believe me," she said, and scooted away in a hurry.

The second time, when she passed me on the stairs, I saw her new excitement.

"There's going to be a wonderful surprise," she told me. "I can't explain about it yet, but you'll find out later. I have to go talk to Uncle Tim now."

Clearly, she had thrown off something that was too heavy for her to deal with—the problem of Peony and her own identity.

That day I didn't see Kirk at all, though he was never far away in my thoughts. When I'd first come here, there were so many disparate threads leading in various directions. Now they seemed to be weaving together, connecting—leading toward some event I was afraid to think about.

Peony kept to her room most of the day, and Farley seemed preoccupied and unaware of much outside himself. The very fact that I had become so unimportant to him seemed ominous.

When the endless hours finally passed, Dillow came into the parlor where I sat reading a book. He announced suspiciously that Dr. Radburn had called for me, and I went out to Joel's car.

Peony sat stiffly in the front seat, looking sullen. A bright red streak marked her cheek, so that I wondered if Farley had struck her. Neither of us spoke and she gave me no more than a resentful glance as I got into the back seat by myself.

Joel, aware of our tension, chatted idly as he drove, and seemed to expect no response from either of us.

Peony spoke to him just once. "Why are we going to see your mother? She said it was something about Alice. So why is *she* coming?"—with a nod toward me in the back seat.

"Mother wants to show you something that concerns Alice," Joel said calmly. "I'm sure you'll be interested."

"I don't know if I really want to go." Peony looked out the window and I hoped she wouldn't jump out of the car at the first opportunity. However, her curiosity was greater than her fear.

Joel offered no explanation of my presence, and she didn't ask again.

———

255

Iris met us at the door, and once more we were ushered into the presence. The stage was set, with lights soft, and Indian music a faint suggestion in the background. Letha, once more enthroned in her Indian chair with its peacock swirl above her head, wore art-deco garments that as usual drifted around her.

Peony recognized a performance when she saw one, and she was immediately ready to back away. Letha, however, spoke in her low, compelling voice and Peony approached her slowly, hesitantly, as though she couldn't help herself.

"Come in, my dear. I'm happy to see you," Letha held up an arresting finger. "Listen, all of you. This is my new beach recording."

The sitar music died away, and a new, stronger sound filled the room—like surf rolling in on a beach. Peony continued toward her as if hypnotized—just as Alice had done that other time. I came a few steps into the room, while Joel stayed back unobtrusively.

The recording was seductive. These were sounds one might hear at any shore—waves rolling in, their rush rising in volume until they broke across rocks and sand, then receded out to sea. All the roar and whisper were interspersed with the chirp of crickets and the wild crying of gulls— sounds that were soothing and repetitive, echoing the ebb and flow of the ocean on an empty beach.

The effect was strangely visual—in fact, it spoke to all my senses. I could see wet rocks where waves tossed rainbow thunder into the air. I could see sandpipers hopping along where white, curling surf touched their feet. I could almost feel the wind on my face and taste and smell the salt air, sense the wind's fingers rippling sea grass far up the beach. As my senses were possessed, my mind and spirit quieted.

What Peony might feel I didn't know, but she drifted slowly toward Letha, as though some psychic wind pushed her along. Letha held out a hand that shone with emeralds. Today there were no jingling bracelets.

"Come and sit by me," she said.

Peony made no effort to resist, and I felt again Letha's strange power. Once Peony had been captured, held immobile for the moment, Letha spoke to me. "Did you see the moon last night, Jenny?"

"There was a cloud across it," I said uneasily.

"Did it remind you of anything?"

"It looked like a feather. You must have put the idea into my head."

Her smile was gentle in the dim light, and she turned again to Peony, whose hair seemed brassy even in the hooded lights of the room.

"Listen to the sounds of the sea," Letha told her softly. "Let yourself walk along that peaceful beach, with the waves curling at your feet. Feel the touch of the sea wind on your face. Let everything else go."

Peony began to relax visibly, tension flowing away, her hands in her lap released from their clenching. When she felt that Peony was ready, Letha spoke in a voice that beguiled, instilling no fear.

"Now you can remember Brazil," she said.

The recorded sounds whispered into silence, leaving only the quiet room and Letha's voice.

"Go back to when you were Nellie Arles. Can you tell me about that time?"

Peony seemed entranced, obedient, her fears submerged for the moment.

"I remember. I didn't like it there. The heat and that awful jungle! I wished I hadn't come. But Farley—" She broke off, stopped by the sound of his name.

"You can talk about him. You are safe here. What did Farley want you to do?"

Peony answered dully. "He wanted me to have a baby—Edward's baby. Farley was wicked, greedy. But I didn't care, because that was what I wanted too."

"And you did have a baby?"

257

Peony was smiling now, transported to a happier time. "Yes! Only Edward never knew the baby. I wish he could have. He'd have loved Alice."

"What happened to the baby, Nellie? Tell us what happened."

"She was so darling. But she was sick a lot and I knew I had to take her back to where there were better doctors. By that time Edward was lost, and Farley had brought me back from the jungle. When word came that what was left of Edward had been found, I was alone and frightened, and there wasn't anything to do but marry Farley. He always wanted me, you know. He needed somebody who was afraid of him, somebody he could use." Her voice sounded strangely distant and matter-of-fact.

"Tell me about the baby, Nellie. What happened to her?"

"She died. There was nothing we could do to save her. Farley was furious. He needed Edward's baby to take home to Corinthea Arles."

"So a substitute was made?" Letha's voice hardly intruded —only suggested gently.

This time Peony hesitated. "That was a long time after. First we tried to have our own baby—but that didn't happen."

"Tell me how you found Alice, Peony." Again Letha's quiet insistence.

"We just kept looking wherever we were. By that time we needed a girl who was three years old and who looked a little like Edward. When it happened—suddenly one day in a grocery store—Farley said that was the child and we would watch for our chance. When the mother left the cart I did what I was supposed to do. Though I felt sorry for her. She was nice to me, and the little girl was sweet. I loved her right away. But she wasn't a good child and she cried a lot—so Farley hated her. Only I never let him hurt her. I *never* have let him hurt Edward's child."

---

She had gone all the way through the real story and into the fantasy again.

Letha's smoky voice merely led and suggested. "You know, don't you, Peony, that Alice isn't Edward's child? You've just told us that the baby died. Far away in Brazil. Alice is Jenny's daughter. She is the little girl you and Farley took with you that day in Connecticut."

This time, however, Letha had pressed too far. Peony's defenses were still stronger than Letha's power of persuasion. She had told the truth up to a certain point. But when it came to admitting that the present Alice was not her daughter she pulled away, startling us, and ran frantically toward the door. Joel moved quickly to hold her until she quieted, and then led her outside, back to the car.

I stared at Letha, shaken and uncertain. "She'll deny everything she said."

"We did far better than I ever hoped. Joel will drive you both back to Victoria. Tomorrow I'll talk to a lawyer friend and see what can be done."

Why didn't I feel relieved, elated, reassured? Why did I feel that it was already too late?

"Sit down, Jenny," Letha said, motioning to a chair nearby. "We need to talk a little. And it's best to give Joel some time alone with Peony."

The chair she indicated was not unoccupied. I had to move a small brass Hindu god who seemed to be using it. As I set the figure aside I looked inquiringly at Letha, and she smiled.

"Oh, him? For good luck, Jenny. I always try to touch several bases, just to make sure."

I must have looked uncomfortable, for she held out her hand with its emeralds.

"I'm not being irreverent. All these objects that mortals use are only symbols. Perhaps to guide us, perhaps to warn and remind."

"Like a raven's feather?"

259

"Yes. And you *did* see the shadow on the moon. Questions aren't much use in the face of mystery. But there's always help if we can open ourselves."

I hoped she was right. Last night, for a little while, I'd been sure.

"Corinthea must not be allowed to turn everything over to Farley and Peony," Letha said. "We had to stop that—as well as free Alice for you."

"Alice knows. Crampton told Mrs. Arles something that made her change her mind."

"What does Alice think?"

"I don't know yet. I don't think she's accepted it fully, and she's concerned about Peony—almost as though Peony were the child. I don't know what's going to happen."

"We only have pinhole vision, Jenny. We can't see the larger picture until we're able to look back. Maybe not even then. But we need to wait and trust—while still acting to do all we can." Letha stirred restlessly. "I think you must go back now. Go back quickly!"

An uneasiness had possessed me too. Even though we had Peony with us—as a sort of hostage—Mrs. Arles was alone with Dillow and a nurse. And Farley Corwin was alone with Alice.

We hurried out the front door, and when we reached the car Letha decided to come with us, gauzy draperies and all. "I may be needed," she said.

Joel sat behind the wheel while Peony lay back limply.

As I got into the back seat Iris came hurrying from the house and rushed over to Letha. There had been a call from Mr. Dillow, and he wanted them to know that something very bad was happening that he couldn't be responsible for —and we should all come at once.

This was like a repeat of the time when Tim had dealt with Farley on his own terms. Only I suspected that this might be far more serious.

"Take the shortcut," Letha told Joel, and flung a trailing

scarf around her neck as she got into the car. Joel switched on the headlights and we started for Radburn House.

Letha and I said little on the way. Alarming pictures were running through my mind—pictures that were probably worse than what was really happening.

As we reached the lights of Victoria, Peony stirred, and Joel put out a quieting hand, so that she subsided.

The upper floors at Radburn House were dark, but all the lights were on below, and Dillow waited for us at his usual post near the door, his anxiety clear.

# 18

Dillow spoke urgently to Joel. "Please come back to the library, Dr. Radburn. You must stop what's happening —if it's not too late."

Joel helped Peony from the car, and we hurried into the house. "Take care of your daughter," Joel said to Dillow. "But first tell us what's going on."

"It's Farley Corwin." Dillow seemed ready to fly out of control. "He's doing magic tricks for Mrs. Arles, and she's very upset. I tried to stop him, but I couldn't!"

This didn't sound as serious as I'd feared.

"I'll go in and see how she is," Joel said. "It's probably not upsetting her all that much."

But Dillow had pulled the cork on all his own suppressions. "He's dangerous—vicious! He's the one who pushed Crampton off the porch and now he's—"

Joel shook him by the shoulder. "Get yourself in hand." He ran down the hall and Letha and I followed him. Peony came suddenly to life and rushed past us down the hall. She had caught the word "magic," and it was like a stimulant.

"Alice!" she cried. "Oh—I've got to stop this! I know what he'll do!"

Dillow tried to pull her back, and she pushed him roughly away, strong now, for so seemingly helpless a woman. "Farley didn't kill Crampton—that's a lie!" She pushed past us through the door of the library, and we all stopped behind her, arrested by what was happening in the room.

Corinthea Arles and the young nurse, Amy, were obviously a captive and stunned audience. Mrs. Arles sat up in bed and her yellow robe gave a jaundiced cast to her unlined parchment skin. Her gray hair straggled to her shoulders, unkempt—without Crampton—as I'd never seen it before. At the moment she stared in complete outrage at the performance beyond the foot of her bed.

Farley Corwin had dressed in his full magician's regalia— shabby black evening clothes, a swirling black cape with a frayed crimson lining, and as the final touch a battered top hat tilted rakishly on his head. Alice, as his assistant, seemed a little too excited. Her smile, brightly theatric, complemented her flaring red skirt, which was alight with spangles, and her halter top, outlined in tarnished gold braid.

The two performers were taking bows as if to applause. Farley front and center, as befitted the star, and his young assistant a few steps behind.

He saw us and made a flourish in our direction with his silver-tipped wand. Alice bowed again and her eyes darted toward me. I sensed that, while she was enjoying this on one level, on another she was tense and uncertain.

"Do come in," Farley invited grandly. "I'm sorry you've missed most of the performance. Though it wasn't up to my standards, since I'm out of rabbits and doves. But it did seem a good time for Mrs. Arles to be entertained and brought out of her—uh—depression."

His words were rewarded by the same fixed stare of outrage from Mrs. Arles—a look to which he was either insensitive or indifferent. She seemed to have lost the power of speech, and Joel went to her quickly.

Farley addressed the three of us who still stood in the doorway. "At least you're in time for the grand finale," he told us, and waved his wand toward a large tin chest whose

263

chipped surface had once been painted with crescents and stars in red and yellow and green.

Peony said, "Oh, my God!" and ran away from us down the hall toward the rear of the house.

If Farley heard her he paid no attention but waved us into chairs already set around as if for the missing audience. I glanced at Letha, but for once she seemed unable to call upon any counter magic. We both sat down helplessly. Joel stayed beside Mrs. Arles, her wrist in his hand. Only Dillow stood fixed in the doorway, looking as ashy pale as he had the night Crampton died.

There was nothing to do now but watch Farley's performance through to the end. Alice still seemed tense, but in no immediate danger, and I tried to relax my own tension. What Dillow had said about Farley as well as Peony's denial, tugged at my mind, but I couldn't puzzle over that now.

Mrs. Arles surprised us by speaking hoarsely. "Watch Alice," she said.

Farley heard her and nodded. "Exactly, madam. It is Alice you must watch."

With another flourish he handed over his wand to Alice, and this time she was less graceful, nearly dropping it before she set it aside on a table. With a running patter that meant nothing, Farley pushed the big tin chest close to a French door. Apparently the moss-green draperies were to serve for concealment in this rather obvious performance.

"In you get," he told Alice, and raised the mounded lid of the chest.

She hesitated, uncertain now, and I couldn't be still. "You don't have to!" I called out to her.

But Farley's hand was on her shoulder, and she seemed not to hear me as she let him push her down out of sight. I watched helplessly, aware that Alice was no longer performing, yet telling myself that nothing could happen.

Farley lowered the lid and sat upon it, addressing us. "Ordinarily my assistant would tie the chest with ropes and someone from the audience would come up to examine them. But tonight we'll have to dispense with such finesse."

He flung off the cape, latched the chest, and covered it with the rippling folds of his cape. Then he stepped between the long draperies, holding them apart with arms held high. "Lights, please, Dillow," he called. Dillow didn't move and the lights stayed on. Farley shrugged eloquently, as though this were part of the act, and reached up and pulled the heavy draperies together, covering himself and leaving the bulge of the chest conspicuous beneath green velvet.

Nothing further seemed to happen, and a rapping began inside the chest. Joel said, "This is where Alice should appear from behind the curtain and open the chest to reveal the magician inside. Only there seems to be a hitch."

Mrs. Arles startled us by speaking again. "It's too late, Farley. You're a fool!"

Letha was the first to move. She ran across the room to fling the draperies aside and snatched away the cloak that had covered it. Quickly, she unlatched the chest.

"Come out of there!" she ordered.

The lid was pushed up and Farley stepped out, smiling. He reached inside for his top hat and patted it onto his head. "Thank you, madam. What has happened to my assistant? She was supposed to let me out."

Dillow spoke from the doorway, no longer excited, but only resigned, as though he had at last submitted to fate. "Mrs. Arles is right. You're too late, Farley. Nellie has taken her away."

From somewhere in the direction of the lower drive we heard a car accelerate.

"Stay with Corinthea, Mother," Joel said. "I'll go after them."

I started to follow him but Letha stopped me. "He can move faster without you. Now we must wait. And perhaps Farley will tell us what he really intended."

Dillow walked to a table where there were glasses and a

bottle. It was only sherry but he poured himself a generous portion and drank it down as though it were whiskey. Mrs. Arles watched ominously but said nothing.

"All right, Farley," Letha said, "suppose you begin."

He had started listlessly to pick up his paraphernalia but now he surrendered to the command in her voice.

"She's crazy, you know." He spoke with a curious sadness, and I knew whom he meant. "*I* meant to take Alice away. I have plane tickets in my pocket right now, and we'd both have slipped off while everyone was looking elsewhere. There was one more trick that would have gotten both Alice and me away. She thought it would be fun to fool everyone. I didn't figure on Peony getting back in time."

"Why would you take her away?" Mrs. Arles demanded.

"Because you'd do anything to get her back. Wouldn't you?"

"Why should I? I know now that she's not my great-granddaughter. She is Mrs. Thorne's child."

Farley looked completely stunned. Apparently no one had told him what Mrs. Arles had explained to Alice. He took off his top hat, wrapped himself in his cape, and leaned morosely against the empty chest. Who knew what he was thinking, or even what plans he might still be cooking up?

Letha spoke to me reassuringly. "They can't get off the island, you know. Joel will find them and bring them back."

But Letha's talent as a prophet had failed her and Joel didn't bring either one of them back. He had lost the trail and no one could even guess where they were by this time. Joel had already talked to the police, and ways off the island would be watched.

"They'll be found—don't worry," he told her, but I sensed the lack of conviction in his voice.

"She hasn't enough money to go far," Farley said gloomily.

I wondered where Kirk was and wished for his help. Anything was better than to sit here doing nothing, and I slipped out of the room to go in search of him.

Dillow was in the hall and now he was drinking whiskey straight. Farley came after me, looking almost as gray as Dillow. I had the feeling that he didn't much care what happened next.

"They'd better find her quickly," he told me. "Peony will never give Alice up."

I took the glass out of Dillow's hands. "Stop that! It won't help if you get drunk. Mrs. Arles may need you. Even your daughter may need you when they find her." He looked at me so blankly that I shook him by the arm, as Joel had done earlier. "What did you mean—what you said about Farley? And what did Peony mean?"

All at once there was a listening quiet in Farley Corwin— an intensity of listening, as though something did matter to him, after all.

"Dillow says that *you* killed Mrs. Crampton," I told him.

For a moment the two men looked at each other with a disliking that was almost tangible. Then Farley said, "He's as crazy as his daughter."

"Why did Crampton have to die?" I persisted.

This time Farley gave up. "She'd found the proof you wanted. Proof you could use to claim Alice. She was taking it to you that night. I suppose she would have left it in your room. But Dillow—"

Dillow took a step toward him and Farley threw out his hands. "It's no use hitting me. It's too late. Everything is too late. Excuse me—I feel very ill. I must go to my room and lie down."

Dillow watched him go. "Crampton had to be stopped," he said.

But I knew now that it wasn't either Dillow or Farley who had killed Crampton.

"It *was* Peony, wasn't it? She took whatever might have enabled me to claim my daughter."

———

267

"I didn't realize, Mrs. Thorne." His voice sounded hollow, empty. "When you came here I didn't know. I really believed that the little girl they brought to Mrs. Arles was my granddaughter."

Now no one's guilt or innocence mattered. Only Alice mattered, and she was being kidnapped all over again. I ran down the hall to let myself out by the back door. The night was dark, but mushroom lights burned in the garden, so the steps were visible as I ran down. Another light standard burned in the lower garden, and I could see lights ahead in the potting shed. I ran toward it, stumbling over rising ground, and pounded on the door.

Kirk came to open it, took one look at my face, and pulled me inside. A chess game was in progress in his small living room, and Uncle Tim looked up from the board and smiled at me.

I had no time now to include him in what I must pour out to Kirk. I told the main points breathlessly—that Alice had been kidnapped by Peony, and they had both disappeared.

"Better catch your breath," Kirk said. "We have to think about this sensibly—figure out where she'd go."

Perhaps he could guess, but I couldn't.

Kirk sat me down on the sofa because I was shaking so, and Tim came to sit beside me. "Tell me," he said.

It was a little like talking to my mother. I faced him directly and formed my words without the exaggeration one was tempted to use with a deaf person. I also used a few graphic gestures to help him understand what I was saying.

"Peony has taken Alice," I said. "We don't know where. I am frightened."

"Maybe I know where," he told me.

Kirk came to the old man quickly. "Tell us where," he urged.

"They were talking today," Tim went on, "Peony and Alice. Alice wanted to see the Butchart Gardens at night. Very beautiful. So Peony said she would take her there tonight—after the magic show. I didn't catch all their words, but I watched what Peony was saying. She never pays any attention to me because she thinks I'm dumb. Maybe she thinks I'm blind too."

I felt a rush of affection for Tim. I knew very well how stupid people could be about the deaf.

Kirk was already pulling me to my feet. "Thanks, Uncle Tim. We'll go out there and try to find them. *If* that's where they've gone." And then to me, "It might have been a bribe to get Alice to go with her."

We ran to where Kirk had left his car and got in. As we drove down the hill he tried to reassure me. "Uncle Tim undoubtedly got it right, and there's a good chance we may still find them there."

It was past the rush hour and traffic had lessened on the highway toward the airport. Kirk broke a few speed limits whenever the road was clear. There was no time for anything except to find Alice as quickly as possible.

When we reached the Butchart Gardens I jumped out of the car before Kirk had turned off the motor, and we ran together down the lighted avenue that led to the house.

"She'll probably take her to the Sunken Garden first," Kirk said. "That's the most beautiful part at night." The evening crowds were thinning, and only a few people were about. Lights embedded in the rock walls pointed the way, glowing in the surrounding darkness. On the bank above, trees were solid black, except where distant lights shone through. When we reached the spot where we could look down upon what had once been a quarry, we paused to search for anything that moved in the scene far below.

Concealed lights had been used magically to bring flower beds and trees to shining, multicolored life, glowing with red and yellow and green. Shadows had been used as well, so that a mysterious chiaroscuro blended all together. How Alice would love this. It would speak to her imagination, and Peony had known that.

269

The air up here was cool and windy, but the depths of the quarry would be more sheltered. Nothing moved down there, however—not even tall lighted trees. No human figures stirred on the white path.

"We have to search," Kirk said, and took my hand as we went down the switchback stairs. At least I wasn't alone in my struggle.

When we'd gone only a little way down, Kirk tightened his grip on my hand and we stopped. Just below us a man had appeared on the path, and I saw that it was Farley Corwin. He still wore his evening clothes and cape. He must have known where Peony would come.

Kirk held me back. "Wait. Don't rush into anything. Maybe you'd better stay here and let me go ahead."

Not for anything would I do that. Beneath my fears for Alice another apprehension was rising. Farley had been Kirk's enemy from the start. Now he was alone and no match for the man Edward Arles had become—a man who was already angry, and who would be merciless. Kirk dropped my hand and started down. I went after him. Ahead of me Farley had reached the turn in the path where it curved between cypress trees, and at that moment Peony and Alice came into sight.

The quarry had turned into a great circular stage filled with light and shadow, while overhead the sky was bright with moon and stars. The moment we reached the path, Kirk began to run, and I rushed after him. Farley had met the other two, and Alice stood close to Peony, her excitement quieting, her joy gone at the sight of him.

Kirk slowed, and kept me from running toward them. We could hear them talking now.

"Let the child go," Farley said. "The game's over, Peony. We've lost and we don't need her any more. I have plane tickets for two and you can leave with me tomorrow. They'll be watching for the girl. Without her we can get away."

None of the three had seen us, and we approached quietly.

Peony thrust Alice behind her and faced Farley. "No! I'll never go with you again. You tried to kill Edward, and you made me go after Crampton. I must have been crazy when I pushed her. I'm not afraid of you any more. Nothing matters except Alice. We belong together, no matter what. If you touch either of us I'll kill you too!"

Farley towered over her, but in that wild moment she was the stronger of the two, and he stepped back a pace.

"We have to get away," he repeated desperately. "The police will be searching and—"

"Then *you* run."

"Alice isn't your child. You have to face that. Let her go."

Alice saw us first, and she tried to break away from Peony, who grasped her firmly. Farley, suddenly aware of us, stood his ground for a moment. Then he ran off along the path that led deeper into the quarry, toward the lake and fountain at the far end. Kirk had only one purpose now, and he went after him.

Peony watched them disappear around the curve. "I hope Edward kills him! Then I'll be free of him forever, and Edward and I—we can have Alice to ourselves the way it should be."

She was no more dealing with reality than Farley had. He'd bound them together all this while with a wicked illusion, and now, somehow, I had to break through to Peony herself.

"Stop it!" I told Peony. "Alice doesn't belong to you. Farley's right, and the masquerade is over."

Alice looked desperately from one to the other of us, and when Peony tightened her grasp she twisted and fought until she broke free. She wanted neither of us, and she cut off through shrubbery and disappeared into the circling darkness. Peony and I were left to face each other in a strangely locked silence.

271

I broke it first, trying to speak more gently, so as not to alarm her even more. "There's nothing you can do, Peony. You've been used all along. But now you're free and you can tell the truth. All of it."

Her face reflected the yellow-white of nearby lights, and her eyes were bright and wild. I had the feeling that she too might break away and run before I could get from her what I must have.

"Will you give me what you took from Crampton?" I asked. "Will you let me see it?"

I knew by her face that she would never do this willingly. She held her handbag tightly to her body and began to back away. I had no choice and I wrested it from her and for a moment I thought she might struggle to get it back—attack me like the wild thing she seemed. But instead she stood frozen, staring at me, waiting.

I opened the bag, not knowing what to look for. Inside was a jumble of cosmetics, tissues, comb, a billfold, a bottle of pills—and a small, rather worn envelope. I took it out and dropped the bag. Peony didn't move.

The clipping in the envelope was a single yellowed column torn from an English-language newspaper in Brazil. I read down the print quickly.

"Listen to me," I told Peony. "Listen to what this says."

She didn't move, but I could sense that she was about to use her old trick of removing herself from whatever was happening so that no words of truth could reach her.

"No!" I cried. "Don't do that. You *will* listen!"

There had always been someone to tell Nellie-Peony what to do, and though she continued to stare at me, some of the wildness died away.

I read the words aloud. The clipping told of Nellie Arles, who had been married to Edward Arles, who had lost his life on the Karsten expedition. Mrs. Arles had borne his child in a local hospital. The baby had lived for only a few months before it died of fever. A little girl named Alice Arles. This was her obituary.

"It was your one tie to your real baby—who died so long ago," I said gently. "Even while you pretended that Debbie was your little girl, you kept this clipping."

"It was all I had," she said helplessly. "Crampton never believed that Alice was Edward's child, and she kept poking at me and picking through our things, every chance she got. And she found that. But I got it back from her, didn't I? Farley said I had to get it back. So I followed her up to your room, and I saw where she put it on your dressing table. Then, when she went out on the porch, I went out there too. She knew and she had to be stopped."

There was a bleakness in her—as though she could feel nothing.

"So now it really is over," I told her. "It has to end now."

The wildness returned in an instant. "Alice is mine!" She snatched up her handbag where it lay on the walk, and dashed off into the surrounding darkness, as Alice had done. I could hear her thrashing off through shrubbery, quickly lost in masses of light and shadow. Whatever lay ahead of Peony, she would take Alice with her if she could find her— and I was afraid.

For a moment I stood listening fearfully. Now there were no sounds at all. No sounds of Kirk and Farley fighting, or of Peony running. Few people were about. Whatever had happened by now between Kirk and Farley, I dared not think about it. Alice must be kept from Peony, and *I* might know where to look.

I ran back along the walk and climbed to the top. It was harder to find my way at night when everything looked different. I couldn't be sure of branching paths but somehow I managed to find the sign for the Japanese garden, where the little pavilion would be. I found the pavilion easily and saw that its windows were alight. Steps leading up to the door caught the reflected glow from door and windows and I could see my way.

Alice was there. She sat on a bench, as she had that other time, her knees drawn up, her head hidden in her arms—as though she was trying to make herself invisible. She must have heard me come up the steps, but she didn't move, and I knew she was afraid to see who had come for her.

"It's all right," I said softly. "It really will be all right now."

She raised her head and I saw that the old bravado was gone and she was no longer sure of anything—least of all of me.

I sat down beside her, not touching her, and told her all that I remembered. How she had been taken—how grievously I'd missed her and searched for her. And how, all these years later, a telephone call had come from Mrs. Arles, bringing me to Victoria.

Alice huddled into herself as I talked, and when I put my arm around her she offered no resistance.

"I have something," I said. "Something Peony has kept for years. Let me read it to you."

Alice nodded and wrapped her arms more tightly around herself, as if she feared snatching hands all over again. I took out the clipping and read it aloud for the second time, ending with the line about the baby being a little girl named Alice Arles.

She pulled away from me. "I'm not her! I'm not *that* Alice! I'm not dead!"

"Of course you aren't. You are Debbie Blake. You have been all along. That baby was Edward's and Peony's, and she didn't live very long."

"Peony does love me," Alice said anxiously. "Sometimes she can be mean—but she loves me."

"Of course. And I know you love her. You don't have to feel that way about me yet. That may take a little while. But I think we've begun to be friends."

274

She moved back from emotion, distrusting it. "Let's go find out what's happening."

We found our way to the main building and the moment we came out in front we saw the police—and the ambulance. Kirk was there—alive, unhurt, and for an instant thanksgiving rose in me. But Farley Corwin was there too— lying on a stretcher, his eyes closed in his bloodied face. His cape was gone, and his clothes torn—in a brutal beating?

Kirk stood talking to a police officer, and I knew in a flash what might lie ahead for him. A charge of assault at the very least, no matter what Farley had done. Perhaps a murder charge if he died.

Kirk saw us and came toward us quickly, all the anger gone out of him—perhaps because it had been satisfied?

"You've found Alice," he said in relief. "Where is Nellie?"

I shook my head. "She ran off." I could think only of what Kirk had done. Farley would never have stood a chance against his anger. One of the ambulance men was setting Farley's leg in a splint, and he moaned—so at least he was still alive.

Kirk was watching me. "I didn't do that. I didn't lay a finger on him. Though I meant to do plenty. When I got close to him and he was trapped, he tried to get away by climbing the wall of the quarry. He got almost to the top, when the vines he was holding pulled free, and he fell clear to the rocks on the bottom, scraping himself all the way. When I'd made sure he was still alive I went for help, and they brought him out."

"Thank God!" I said fervently. "I was afraid you—"

"Providence, Jenny," he said softly. "I don't think I'd have damaged him as badly as he's damaged himself. He wasn't worth killing. You were right, and there are other things I want to do with my life. But about Nellie—" He looked around. "I'll let someone know so they can search for her. Then I'll take you and Alice back to the house."

The relief I felt was so enormous that it left me weak. Alice

275

noticed my state and touched my arm. "It's all right," she said. "I guess Farley won't die."

She didn't seem to mind when I gave her a quick hug.

"You love him a lot, don't you?" she said. "I mean Kirk."

"Perhaps I do, but I'd rather you didn't say anything about that. Alice, there's something you still don't know. Kirk is really Edward Arles. It's a long story, and I'll tell you another time."

Kirk rejoined us and we started together toward where he'd left his car, Alice watching him in bewilderment.

"I've just told her that you're Edward Arles," I said.

"Does it make any difference?" he asked Alice.

"But you're not my father—not really."

"No, and I'm sorry about that because I'd have liked to be."

She seemed satisfied with that, and when we reached the car she sat between us in the front seat, more relaxed and willing to lean against me—a little sleepy now.

# 19

When we reached Radburn House, Joel and Letha were waiting in the library. Mrs. Arles was wide awake, having refused sleeping pills. By this time, however, Alice was falling asleep on her feet.

I took her upstairs and, when she was in her pajamas, I held her in my arms for a moment.

She looked up at me drowsily. "What am I supposed to call you? I don't want to go on saying Jenny. And it can't be Ma."

"Whatever you like," I said.

She snuggled against me. "Maybe I'll call you Mom."

I was happy to be called by any name she wanted to use, and I dared a little of the kissing and hugging I'd longed for. She didn't seem to mind. By the time I pulled up the covers —that familiar rite—and turned out the lights, she was sound asleep and smiling.

I returned to the library, to find that Mrs. Arles had taken charge in her old way. Apparently she'd accepted Kirk as spokesman without question, and he had been giving her a full account of all that had happened. I sat down quietly and listened.

"You know who I am, don't you?" he asked when he'd finished.

Corinthea Arles allowed her expression to break into something like a smile. "Of course. I knew who you were from the first time I saw you. But I had to know what game you were playing—you and Dillow. So I played along. Why do you suppose I gave you that elephant-headed god to return to Letha?"

I wasn't sure how much of this was bluff. Certainly she would never admit that she'd been fooled.

"Now that you've come home, Edward," she began confidently, but he stopped her at once.

"No, Grandmother. Edward Arles is gone for good and you can never bring him back."

"Perhaps I'd rather have you," she said slyly.

He grinned, comfortable in baiting her, as she would always bait him.

"I've been thinking about changing my will," she said, and glanced at Joel. "But now I don't think I shall."

"Of course you shouldn't," Kirk told her. "Joel's research is what counts. I've got a new job coming up that will take care of me. Of course half of whatever your parents left you still goes to Tim. And you'll need to take care of that."

This was something she must have deliberately forgotten long ago, and she scowled.

"Don't worry," he said. "Tim will move in with me."

"What about Jenny?" She fixed me with her challenging look.

"That's not going to be settled in this room," he told her. "In the meantime, there's still Nellie—when they find her. There's also Farley and a lot of unpleasantness to go through. Kidnapping charges, among other things."

As he talked I thought of Peony, lost somewhere out in the night—frightened and alone and running. In spite of everything, I felt a strange pity for her. Because *I* knew what it was like to lose a child.

Letha spoke for the first time, reading me with her usual skill. "Whatever happens to Peony is *her* karma. She'll probably need to come back for a few lifetimes before she's learned what needs to be learned."

"Ridiculous!" Mrs. Arles said, but she didn't sound quite as certain as usual.

Letha regarded her calmly. "Peony will be found in three days. By that time it will be too late for this life."

She was almost right. Peony was found in four days, and it was thought that she'd gone off Turkey Head Breakwater at the Oak Bay marina where the currents were powerful. She had managed in the only way she could. Karma—destiny?

So Farley was left to stand trial alone, though for kidnapping, not murder. And that was his karma, for now.

If Dillow mourned his daughter he showed it very little, though he had been trying to protect her in his own way. In the next few days he asked Mrs. Arles to let him retire—something she was happy to do. She would be up and around soon, she said, and could take charge of hiring her own employees.

After Joel and Letha left that evening, Kirk and I walked down through the garden. It was too chilly to sit on the bench, so we went on to his rooms in the potting shed. Now he walked with his arm about me and I leaned into its strength and warmth.

I only needed to *be*—to let this new feeling of contentment flow through me. Or perhaps it was joy, laced with something more—a lovely anticipation. I'd almost forgotten how that could feel.

In the small living room, where the young Edward Arles still felled a tree in the picture over the mantel, Kirk busied himself lighting a fire, while I made a pot of coffee. Then he pulled the couch around to face the hearth, and we sat warming our hands with coffee mugs, watching the firelight play on each other's faces. The picture was lost in shadow and Kirk looked up at it.

"Tomorrow I'll take that down. I don't need a reminder any more of old lives, and old debts to pay off."

I was glad he could let go of the painful past.

"How do you feel, Jenny?"

"Happy," I told him. "Relaxed and happy."

"What will you do now?"

279

I sipped hot coffee before I answered. "I haven't had time to plan. I want to take Alice home to my parents, of course."

"And after that you'll come back to Victoria." It was a statement, not a question.

I tried to see his face in the flickering light. "I want to come back."

"I mean come back to me, Jenny. I won't let you get away from me now."

I didn't want to get away from him—ever.

He went on hesitantly—he who was always so sure. "I know we got off on the wrong foot in the beginning. I know I wasn't fair to you. But then I watched you struggle against high odds, never giving up. I like courage and honesty—all those things you are. Besides being a lot more. So, against anything I intended to have happen, I fell in love with you, Jenny."

He took the coffee mug out of my hands and pulled me up from the couch. "I've wanted to do this for a long while," he said, and kissed me. His lips weren't hard and demanding, but far gentler than I ever thought he could be.

There was no more time for words, though little edges of thought flicked through my mind. I would bring my parents out here with me. My mother was always ready for adventure and she would allay any fears my father might have about change. He would love Victoria's gardens, and my mother would find ways to help Uncle Tim. Most of all, I thought of how ready Alice would be to accept Kirk as a father.

All this came in a flash—and then I was aware only of my own longing and need rising to meet Kirk's. We had both lost so much over the years, and old wounds cut deep. But now there was healing for us in this small, warm room, with Kirk's cheek against my hair.

Somehow, during the long, long journey I'd made since a telephone call had brought me to Victoria, my feather had reached the moon.